HIS

By

JULES RAE

BLURB

"Wash out," "flopped," "may never recover," "disaster," and "failure" dominated the headlines and airwaves, painting a bleak picture of Luka Kuznetsov's future in the sport after his injury.

Luka, haunted by doubts, clings to an unorthodox pre-game ritual - sex before every game - with his newfound Doctor. But what starts as a contract relationship quickly evolves into a captivating and forbidden connection that neither of them saw coming.

When Ana Sheen, plagued by depression stemming from her father's gambling addiction, mounting debts, and a string of misfortunes is offered a position as part of the medic staff for a renowned hockey team, she sees it as her ticket to a better future. Little does she know that accepting the job means becoming entangled in the enigmatic world of Luka Kuznetsov, the star player with a chilling reputation both on and off the ice.

As their connection deepens, both Ana and Luka must confront their inner demons and make choices that will shape their futures.

CONTENT WARNING

This book is not your typical romance novel. Its main trope is sexual fastburn with emotional slowburn, which comes with very trauma filled characters, a hero who is possessive and a walking red flag. This book covers suicidal thoughts, non con, dub con, punishment sex, body betrayal kidnapping and violence... and found family.

Read with caution

DEDICATION

This book is dedicated to all girls who read smut like it's the morning newspaper.

CHAPTER 1

The air hung thick with the stench of alcohol and despair, a daily reminder that this was Ana's reality- an endless, bitter cycle of broken days.

Beer bottles and lottery tickets were scattered across the floor like a haphazard mosaic around her drunken father.

Those familiar dark thoughts crept up again as she filled another trash bag, the litany of ways she could end her suffering for good. A fistful of the pills from the medicine cabinet or maybe a rope tied to one of the ceiling fan blades. She contemplated whether the rope would hold up or snap, causing her to fall with a snapping thud.

What a terrible way to die- not the hanging, but the fall.

Who would mourn for her if she died? Certainly not her father. Despite hoping, he loved her somewhere beneath the tangle of his addiction.

Her brother would miss her. He was only thirteen. She couldn't leave him; even with their shattered family, it remained her responsibility to protect him. Someone had to hold on to the wreckage of their sad excuse for a life, much as she yearned at times to let it go. She stayed- existing, not living, and warding off the darkness as best she could.

"Shit. It's morning." Her father's voice tore into her thoughts. "Why didn't you wake me? I can't be late. Have you seen my lucky socks?"

"Err... no."

"I got some money and I know if I have those socks, I'll win big," he muttered to himself, annoyed as he looked back at her. "What are you doing today? Just being lazy at home?" he hissed.

"I was thinking of looking for a job today." Her words came out like a stutter.

"What about that waitress job? At least that brought in some cash."

She no longer felt comfortable serving drinks to middle-aged men, who never kept their hands to themselves. "I quit last week."

"Stupid. You could have studied a real profession. Be a real doctor or nurse. That way I could see the benefits of you going to college, but what do we have to show for it? Nothing but debts and more debts."

Of course, he blamed her schooling for their debts, never realizing it was his gambling that caused the problem. He conveniently forgot that Ana had paid for most of the tuition fees, including those of her brother Danny.

Besides, she was a real doctor. She just had to find a job that matched her degree as a physiotherapist, in order to alleviate their financial burden.

They probably would have been homeless too if they hadn't lived in her late grandmother's house, which was why the house screamed of old age and in dire need of renovation.

With a deep sigh, Ana set to work. She grabbed another trash bag from the kitchen and began to pick up the empty bottles, wincing at the sound of clinking glass. The task was a familiar one - she had done it so many times before that it became almost automatic.

"I paid to feed you, clothe you and what do I get?" He bent down and fished out a small pair of socks from the bottom of his laundry basket. One of which had a large hole in the sole where his big toe poked through. "Bunch of college debts and a nuisance, that's all you are. I was going to be a professional soccer player. I had the scholarship too, then your mother tells me she is pregnant. Puff. There goes my dream and now I have just you. At least having Danny was a choice."

Ana's hands tightened into fists as her father spoke. His words acted like arrows aimed straight at the center of her heart.

He never failed to remind her, she was worthless and bad luck—maybe he was right, because the more often you hear something, the more likely it is to come true. Her father stumbled out of the house. From his expression, he could very well be gone for days or weeks. Silently, she prayed for the latter.

A text message appeared on her phone screen. She squinted at it, not quite believing what she was reading. She read it again–this time out loud–and a wave of hope filled her.

Congratulations, you are hired.

This was a job she had applied for months ago. They wanted her. If her memory served her right, she bombed the interview. She had stuttered and forgotten most of her answers.

Great. This was a sign that her luck was turning around. She checked the time for the interview, two hours from now. Christ. It was on the other side of town and, considering, she didn't have enough cash to spare for a taxi. It was wise to leave earlier.

She sped through the cleaning, got dressed, and was out the door.

•.¸♡ . ♡¸.•

Checking the address one more time, she glanced at the building.

It was a training center for the most popular hockey team. The Crestmont Giants.

The building loomed ahead, its glass windows reflecting the bright sunlight on a dazzling display. From the outside, it appeared almost fierce with its sleek modern design and heavy metal doors.

She moved further through the hallway, passing through the gym area until she found an ice rink. It was filled with fluorescent lights flickering above the ice, casting a pale blue glow over the entire space. There was a group of players practicing their shots, sending pucks flying into the net with precision and power.

The rink was bustling with activity, but one player caught her attention immediately. He was tall and big, with an intense expression on his face as he skated back and forth with incredible speed and agility.

Ana watched as the player 24 received a pass and fired a shot. His movements were mesmerizing but intimidating.

She was captivated by his skill and athleticism, though a shiver of fear ran down her spine at the thought of working closely with someone like him.

Suddenly, the coach's voice cut through the air, loud and urgent. "Hey, take it easy."

The player didn't seem to hear him at first, so focused on his practice session, causing the coach to yell out again, even louder this time. "I said calm down, Kuznetsov, dammit!"

This time, the player slowed down his movements, taking a few deep breaths to steady himself.

"Kuznetsov." She mouthed the name. Even though she was not really a big fan of hockey, she knew who Luka Kuznetsov was. His face and name has been everywhere since recently. Didn't he suffer from an injury?

He skated over to the boards where the coach was standing, his chest heaving with exertion, the cool air caused his breath to form a misty cloud around his face. Dressed in the Crestmont Giant blue jersey, adorned with the recognizable 'G' logo on his jersey.

Luka Kuznetsov removed his helmet, revealing a sweaty mess of hair. He was talking to the coach when his gaze lifted up to her, his eyes blazing with a fierce intensity that was almost frightening.

The coach turned around following the player's gaze.

"I'm here for an interview. I got a text." Ana reached for her phone.

Before she said another word, the powdered-haired man came forward. "Coach Thompson. You must be Ana sheen. Do you have your Credentials here?"

They walked ahead, leaving the ice rink as she handed him the papers from her purse. "Err... this is my first job since I graduated last year and I know you would like to have someone with experience, but I assure you—"

"You got the job. I'm not in the position to look for another." He shifted in his stand, pulling on his trousers as he added, "We might do a trial but just make sure you do a good job."

"Hey you," he called out, shoving his helmet at one of the gym staff.

"Her name is Ana." The couch snapped, before turning to her, "right?"

She nodded.

"Whatever. Let's see what you got."

For a second, she was cut off guard. What did he want from her? An obvious look on the coach reminded her.

"Oh right. Do you have any special needs, any joint pains perhaps?" her voice was soft and hesitant, as she stumbled over her words.

He said nothing but continued his walk ahead, pushing through a blue door to a private room.

•.¸♡ . ♡¸.•

The office was a bright, airy space with white walls and large windows letting in plenty of natural light. The floor was made of a soft, padded material that's easy on the feet. The room was furnished with a comfortable massage table covered with a clean white sheet, a few chairs, and a desk with a computer on it. She took a break from admiring what could be her office to find Luka undressing.

He peeled off his shirt, the sinewy ridges of his muscles flexed. She struggled to keep her eyes from wandering over him but couldn't help but marvel at how toned, chiseled, and strikingly handsome he was.

"Is this okay for you?"

Ana jolted back to reality and swallowed hard. "No problem. Whatever you feel comfortable with." Her gaze dropped down to her fidgeting hands.

She silently prayed that he hadn't noticed her ogling him like a love-struck schoolgirl.

Ana tried to ignore the heat that spread through her body as she began the therapy session. She slipped on a pair of gloves. Despite her obvious nervousness, Ana tried her best to appear confident and professional, or this could be the last day she ever worked here. She straightened her back, stood by the cot.

"Do you have a particular concern?"

"Just give me a little of everything."

He collapsed onto the treatment table, winced as Ana began to massage his sore muscles.

"Wow, do you grate cheese on this thing?" She said, feeling his abs in an attempt to lighten the mood.

Luka's face remained stern and unsmiling, his brow was furrowed. There was no sign he thought her joke was funny.

She muttered an apology, clearing her throat. "Sorry. I say stupid jokes when I'm nervous"

He groaned as she dug into the knots in his shoulders. She was determined to pass this interview or test or whatever it was, but every time their eyes met, she felt a warmth spreading through her body that she couldn't ignore.

Ana tried to focus her attention on the sound of the blades on the ice, with its reverberations bouncing off the walls, periodically interrupted by shouts from Luka's teammates.

It was hard with Luka's eyes fixed on her actions. She couldn't focus with his watchful stare.

Ana took a deep breath and began to massage Luka's shoulder, trying her best to apply the right amount of pressure. However, her hands were shaking with nerves, and she ended up pressing too hard into the inflamed area.

"What the fuck are you doing? That hurts!" Luka snapped, pulling away from her touch with a wince.

"I-I'm sorry, I didn't mean to," Ana stammered, her cheeks flushing with embarrassment. She tried to adjust her technique, but Luka's shoulder was already aggravated from her earlier mistake.

"Is everything okay over there?" the head coach pushed himself into the room.

Luka shot Ana a scathing glare before turning to address the coach. "No, everything is not okay. This new physio doesn't know what she's doing. She's just making my injury worse," he said, his voice dripping with contempt.

He picked up his gears and clothes, walking out of the office, not bothering with the rest of her words.

Ana felt her heart plummet into her stomach. A lump formed in her throat as she fought back tears, knowing that this disastrous first impression had likely ruined her chances of succeeding in this job.

"I-I'm so sorry, I'll leave," Ana whispered shakily, quickly gathering her things and hurrying out of the training room, her confidence thoroughly shattered by the embarrassing incident.

Ana rushed to the bathroom, holding back tears. She had fumbled the interview badly and feared losing her chance at this job. The job, desperately needed to keep a roof over her head and food on the table, felt like it was slipping through her grasp. Panic, a cold, clammy hand, tightened around her throat.

She prided herself on her independence, on always paving her own way. But right now, that independence felt like a flimsy shield against the crushing weight of potential failure. Tears spilled over, tracing hot tracks down her cheeks as she splashed water on her face, trying to wash away the sting of disappointment and the fear clawing at her insides.

Just as she was starting to regain some semblance of composure, the bathroom door creaked open. Luka, his tall frame filling the doorway, blocked the exit. His usual carefree demeanor was replaced by a concerned frown that sent a jolt through her. He didn't speak at first, just watched her with an intensity that made her skin prickle.

Finally, he spoke, his voice surprisingly soft, almost a whisper. "How badly do you need this job?"

Ana hesitated, her heart pounding so forcefully she could feel it reverberating in her throat. She gave a small, reluctant nod, suddenly acutely aware of how vulnerable she was alone with the imposing athlete.

"No, I need to hear you say it," Luka pressed, taking a deliberate step forward, crowding her space. "How much does this job mean to you?"

A shiver ran treacherously down Ana's spine as her widened eyes met his piercing stare. In that moment, the lines between desperation and a dangerous gamble blurred. "I...I will do anything," Without another word he turned and left.

A heavy feeling of dread settled in Ana's stomach. She wondered what Luka Kuznetsov might demand in exchange for giving her the job, and what unethical or degrading things she might have to do to get it.

CHAPTER 2

Ana laid on her bed, her thoughts racing through the day. She had a brief moment of hope where she thought things were finally turning around, only to be followed by an unfortunate blunder. If she was honest, Luka Kuznetsov scared her, but his chiseled jawline, piercing blue eyes and muscular build would make any woman feel weak in the knees.

Ana was not any woman. She was going to be his doctor, and Luka would be her patient. That was if they called her back.

She forced herself upright, remembering her priorities. She needed this job and dared not let anything get in the way. One thing still confused her: Why did he suddenly change his mind?

Her phone suddenly started buzzing, informing her of an incoming call. She noticed it was from Danny's school principal before she had a chance to contemplate further.

"Mrs Harper, sorry I missed your call. I had a very busy day today." Ana spoke first.

"I know it's a bit late now, but I wouldn't have called if it wasn't urgent."

"How is Danny? Is he alright?"

"He is still having trouble making friends, but I wanted to talk to you about the school fees. You know, the payment was due last month, and we haven't received it yet."

A bitterness rose in her throat as she thought of how far behind she was with the fees, how little she had to live on this month. "I'm sorry, Mrs Harper. I've been struggling financially lately. I lost my job a few weeks ago." She quickly added, "but I just got another one today so that won't be a problem." She winced, because she was not certain about her employment status even though the coach had said he would get back to her.

"My hands are tied. We can't keep doing this, miss Ana you have till next week."

"Thank you and goodnight." Ana hung up and fell back into the mattress.

Drowsiness weighed heavily on her eyelids as the sound of her breathing filled the silence.

The blaring light from the phone illuminated the darkness of the room. Another incoming call. She reached over and picked it up to see an unknown number displayed across the screen.

Her thumb grazed the smooth surface, answering it on the third ring.

"Hello?" she said, waiting for a response.

"My opinion matters a lot in the new hires of staff. They are to be most efficient and professional in matters of the team."

The chilly voice came from the other end of the line, causing her to involuntarily shudder. She could barely make out what the man said. It wasn't just because of his thick Russian accent, but because she was still groggy from sleep.

"Yes." Was all she uttered, then almost instantly realized who the caller was. "Mr. Kuznetsov, I'm sorry about happened today-

"You have another chance." He cut her short.

"Huh?"

"I'm sending you my address."

"Oh, you mean right now."

"Why? are you fucking busy?" His tone came out sharp and she couldn't tell if he was angry or it was the accent.

"No. No." She scurried out of the bed, silently thanking herself that had not yet undressed.

He hung up and a minute later, her phone buzzed one more time as a text came through.

•.¸♡ . ♡¸.•

She left to follow the directions to a penthouse apartment in the heart of the city.

It was nearly freezing outside, but the buildings were a haven of warmth. She entered the elevator and pressed the button for the top floor. A sense of anticipation built inside her. She had no idea what to expect, but thankfully she had her bag with her. It was filled with every essential thing a physiotherapist might need when called unexpectedly at 11pm at night.

The elevator doors opened and Ana stepped out into his home. The walls were painted a deep red, and the floor was covered in a plush carpet. The space was filled with sleek, modern furniture and tasteful works of art, and she noticed the twinkling lights of the city skyline through the floor-to-ceiling windows.

"Ana? Come with me."

She flinched. Her hand turned white from gripping the strap of the medic bag too tightly.

Luka stood with a glass of some amber liquid, still in his robe, revealing his chest.

Ana followed him into the bedroom, trying not to stare at the surrounding mess.

It was clearly obvious what happened here. There were traces of it. A condom wrapper lying on the floor, a tube of lube was squeezed flat, clothes littered and a half-empty bottle of whiskey was perched precariously on an end table.

She couldn't imagine he did all this the night before his game. She tried to focus on what she was called here for and ignore the sour stench of sweat and sex. It didn't matter what her patients did in their private time. She was here to do a job.

"This place is a mess, but just come on in."

"It's okay. I will set up now." She straightened a part of the bed and prepared her oils while Luka leaned against the mirror, his hands crossed against his chest.

Luka's gaze never left her as she moved around the room, setting up things on the table. His eyes roamed from her slender neck, her hair was fixed into a bun, his gaze dropped to her jeans that hugged her ass perfectly. He bit his lips as his mind conjured the inviting image of himself slamming into her ass.

"Lie down, sir," she said, finally turning to him.

He didn't. Instead he covered the gap between them in two long strides and leaned down to her.

"I brought some oil, so maybe they could help you sleep tonight." She said, the words came out like a stutter.

She was still nervous around him. He knew he had that effect on people and obviously enjoyed that.

"Aren't you a bit curious why I called you here this late?"

The question caught Ana off guard. She blinked, her mind scrambling as she tried to make sense of what had just been asked. "I am guessing you have a game tomorrow and you need to be in shape."

His eyes narrowed as he stared at her. Contemplating. There was something off about her. He couldn't place a finger on it. He didn't have time to be picky right now. She would have to work for now. Besides, if she revealed his secret, he would destroy her. That part was certain.

"There are many players who have their... pre-game ritual, something they do before they go for a big match, something that makes them feel lucky if you do say so."

"Ah. My father has some lucky socks." She paused. "It doesn't work though."

Luka parted his mouth for a moment, then nodded. "Hmm... Well, mine is different. I need to have sex before I play. It doesn't matter who the person is, as long as it's mind-blowing good sex."

She blinked, a million things running through her mind as she waited for him to continue.

"The team has an upcoming game tomorrow. A lot is riding on it... a lot is riding on me. You see where I'm going with this?"

"Not sure if I say I do." Ana took a step back now. "I.. I... I just came to give your treatment, help with your pain and..."

He advanced on her with a feral gaze, closing the distance between them as she shrank away in fear. Her feet knocked against the bed, falling onto the soft mattress.

In the next second, her body was pinned beneath him. Luka's face held an icy mask of determination as he leaned down, planting his elbow on either side of her body to take the weight off of her fragile frame.

"This is crazy, don't you think so?" She said with a nervous chuckle.

She pushed herself from underneath him because he allowed her to.

Luka looked irritated as he sat up on the bed.

"I'm sorry, Mr Kuznetsov. I don't mean your pre game ritual is crazy, but me? Trust me I can't.. I am the most unlucky person I know. I am so unlucky. I'm sure black cats cross the streets when they see me."

He cocked an eyebrow at her. Now she was saying nonsense just to get out of his proposal. He had assumed she would jump at the chance, considering his fame and wealth. Maybe she was the type that wanted the chase. Fuck. He didn't have time for that now, he would just find another person.

"Don't you have... girls for this kind of thing?"

"I found out she was selling stories to the press so I had to chase her out. I guess you don't need the money, fine." He stood up. "Leave. What I need is sex. A good fuck, not some massage treatment."

A brief silence filled the room.

"Am I still hired? You know, for the team physiotherapist job?"

Luka looked over his shoulder and said nothing. He flopped himself onto a chair at the corner and picked up his glass one more time. "You were not going to be the team physiotherapist, but mine."

Okay. That was news to her and now it meant her employment was tied to Luka's strange proposal.

She squeezed her eyes, and couldn't imagine she was back to the same position again. Surviving instead of living. "How much?" she silently cursed herself for asking.

"Five thousand dollars." Luka said. "For tonight."

She could use the extra money to pay for Danny's tuition, he would not have to come back home, come back to live with their father. It would be enough to repair the house that was slowly falling apart or move to a better apartment. God the money would be like a magic wand that could make her problem disappear.

If she rejected his offer, Luka might make her lose the job and she would be left with nothing. If she agreed, she would be five thousand dollars richer.

"You will actually give me the money?" she asked again, wanting to be certain.

"I don't joke with things like this."

"Just tonight?" her voice broke, she fought the tears that gathered in her eyes. Her mind slowly made peace with the fact she was going to have sex in exchange for money. How low could she go?

"Just tonight." He had risen up and walked up to Ana who had her head lowered, staring at the marble floor.

Luka grinned, the corner of his lips lifting as he watched Ana fiddling with her finger, slowly coming to terms with it.

CHAPTER 3

"Go ahead." She said, squeezing her eyes shut and opening her hand wide.

Beaded patterns of sweat snaked down like festive holiday lights, sparking from Ana's dark skin,

He composed himself. He wasn't sure what she thought was going to happen, but he wasn't going to approach this like a wild animal. Even though most of his past encounters had strangely used those exact words to describe him.

"Have you been with a man before?"

"Huh?" she opened her eyes one right after the other.

He groaned, "I don't like repeating myself. I asked if you are a fucking virgin?"

She cleared her throat. "Does it matter?"

He snickered. This girl didn't know what she got herself into. He was not like any of her supposed boyfriends, who would shower her with kisses and whisper sweet nothing in her ear. For starters, he hated kissing. The mere idea of sharing saliva with someone gave him the ick. It might be counterintuitive, especially since he was considering his new doctor as a toy. The basis was that kissing required emotions and intimacy–something he was not interested in. For him, tonight was transactional.

She must have done this before, and he wouldn't be taken in by her faux innocence. They all began the same way—acting pure—until they spotted an opportunity to make money.

"You are right. It doesn't matter. I guess there is no need for me to go easy on you."

She swallowed.

"Strip." He commanded, his tone firm and authoritative.

Her eyes widened at the bluntness, and her mouth hung open.

"I am not going to fuck you while you are wearing clothes, am I?"

She reached up and began to unbutton her blouse, her fingers trembling as she tugged at the fabric. Luka watched her, growing more impatient as the seconds ticked.

He set his glass down. "Fuck this," he growled, pushing her hands away and ripping her shirt open. Buttons flew through the air like shrapnel from a bomb blast.

His eyes lingered on her naked body. Perky breasts that sit right on her bra.

His cock jerked at the thought of burying his face in them.

That image was strange. He wasn't a boob man and least of all, someone he was literally paying for.

Luka's hand moved over her waist and in just an instant, he threw her onto the bed.

"Wait... wait. Wait. Please." She struggled against him as he climbed onto her. "I changed my mind." She whimpered, terror palpable in her words.

"I can't—I can't do this."

"Jesus fucking Christ." He pushed himself from her and scowled. "Will you stop being so dramatic?"

He snatched a bottle of whiskey from the bedside table and paced over to the window. His body was taut as a bowstring, with barely leashed rage.

"I don't have time for this. If this is too much for you, Get the fuck out of my house."

Ana sat small and silent on the edge of the bed, hands folded primly in her lap. He was right. They made a deal. She had agreed. It was ridiculous, but she was desperate.

One night, she recited in her head. Five thousand dollars was a lot of money for one night.

At that moment, Ana made a decision. She refused to let her body deceive her mind into enjoying this experience. It was strictly contractual, and there was nothing obliging her to give herself over entirely to him.

This way, once it was over, she could at least pretend it never happened. And she would believe it. It may be a little crazy, but that's all she got right now.

She stood up and slipped off her bra from her body and slowly got out of her panties. Her gaze remained fixed on him, letting him know her decision was made. His steps faltered when he turned to her.

She bared herself for him.

He took her in. He didn't blink, didn't stop. His eyes slowly traced the curve of her hips, the roundness of her ass, the roundness of her breasts.

"Get on the bed, ass in the air."

She awkwardly did as she was told. Luka positioned himself up behind her and got himself ready to thrust inside. She glanced at his cock one more time.

He tore a condom and slipped it on a hardened cock.

She flinched. "Wait. I-i d-don't think it will fit."

He gripped her hips and leaned against her shoulder. "Relax, it will fit."

Her hands tightened around the bedspread, as she braced herself, her body tensed.

"Goddamnit, would you relax? I am not even halfway in yet."

The lack of lube made her tightness nearly unbearable for him. He hissed as he pulled out, reaching for a lube.

"I've never done this–"

"Take it up your ass? I'm sure you haven't," Luka taunts her. He spread open her cheeks and pressed a finger inside her.

She gasped, burying her face in the pillow at the sting. His finger felt good, but then he added another finger in. It was mild but different, and her body tensed a bit as she tried to adjust to the feeling. He slowly added another finger in. She tried to control her breathing.

He withdrew his fingers, and she felt an aching emptiness inside of her.

"You will get used to it."

Luka gripped her hip, holding her in place, his cock ready to thrust inside her.

"Spread your legs wider."

She did.

His body was hot and hard, and he was pressing into her.

Ana let out a sharp cry when he thrust his full length into her ass. She stiffened at the feeling. It burned, but as he started to move. He slammed into her at a rate that would leave her sore for days.

She held a stifled scream as he penetrated her, stretching her beyond belief. He growled, shoving her head down into the soft pillow as his cock jack-hammered into her, almost mindlessly.

She couldn't take it, the way his shaft dragged against her now throbbing clit every time he thrust into her. Ana appeared calmed and collected, her face expressionless, like a peaceful and subdued porcelain doll as she took the aggressiveness, trapped under his strong body.

Like that encouraged him, he rammed into her ass cheeks, making a clapping sound as he fucked her, hard and fast. It was too much. The discomfort had all but melted away after a few minutes. The pleasure overwhelmed the pain and her body started to move with him.

Her pussy was drenched, aching to be touched and her brain was absolutely mush. Still, she was determined not to give in, not to let herself climb.

Whatever happened, she was not going to let her body willed her brain to enjoy such an assault.

"I'm going to cum." He had said it like he was giving her permission to back out when he knew he clearly had the power here.

She bit down on her bottom lip and held on. The little energy in her body drained out, and she laid limp under him while he fucked her hard, chasing his own high.

Not long after, Luka came with several low, rough grunts in her ear. His fingers dug into her skin. She was sure would leave a mark.

It was over. He slumped onto the bed beside her.

All she could focus on was the soreness between her thighs. As much as she wanted to get up and shower, her legs were throbbing just lying there, let alone walking.

"We are done, right?" she said softly.

"What? That was just round one. We have the rest of the night.

CHAPTER 4

Luka woke up to the sound of birds chirping outside, feeling the aftereffects of the night before. He got out of bed quietly, glanced at the woman beside him. Ana was still fast asleep. He walked into the bathroom and turned on the shower, letting the hot water wash away the remnants of the night's activities.

Luka padded out of the steamy bathroom, a white towel wrapped around his waist. His footsteps echoed off the tile floor as he headed to the kitchen.

Luka stood in his kitchen, blender whirring as he prepared a protein shake. He knew he shouldn't check his phone, but curiosity gnawed at him like an insatiable hunger. He reached for the device, eager to discover what the media anticipated from the upcoming match.

However, he braced himself for the all-too-familiar reports filled with doubts and skepticism, undermining his confidence.

As he scrolled through the news headlines, each one seemed to cast a shadow of uncertainty over his return to the ice. The media reports, like venomous whispers in the back of his mind, chipped away at his confidence. *"Luka's Comeback: A Long Shot at Redemption,"* one headline screamed, the words stabbing at his resolve. Another read,

"Can Luka Ever Regain His Position as the one Top Player in the NHL?"

He scrolled further. *"Career in Peril: The Defining Match for Luka Kuznetsov,"* one article proclaimed, its words like a sledgehammer to his spirit. Another headline declared, *"Luka's Return: A Disastrous Flop or an Inspiring Triumph?"*

The weight of those headlines bore down on Luka's shoulders, threatening to extinguish the flickering flame of hope within him. It felt as if the world had already written his comeback story, painting it with hues of disappointment and failure.

He set his phone aside, took a deep breath and willed his thoughts to focus on the day ahead.

He stilled. His mind shifted to the woman in his bed.

Ana ought to be awake by now. He had left an envelope on the nightstand, not wanting to deal with the awkward morning-after talk. He despised that moment more than anything else. That's one of the reasons he preferred being single: he could have as much sex as he wanted and still enjoy a peaceful morning like this one.

Last night... Last night... He pushed aside the thoughts when he failed to find a word to describe it. It didn't matter what last night was — a casual hookup and nothing more. He did what he had to do and she... Well, he couldn't tell if she had enjoyed it or not.

Luka Kuznetsov was used to his previous partners exaggerating their moans. He hated that. The terrible acting. He knew they wanted to boost his ego, but Ana.... She laid there; her face having the same pained expression.

Had he not been good? Why did that bother him now? Why was he concerned about his performance? It shouldn't matter. They had agreed this was a transaction. He got the sex, and she... got the money.

Luka willed his thoughts to turn to the day ahead. He took a long breath and prepared himself for the upcoming match.. This was his first game post surgery and everyone was going to be watching. An injury like his had caused many to end their career, and he could not see that for himself.

If he weren't playing hockey, what would he do? He didn't want to be like his brother, confined behind a desk while their dad pulled the strings. The doctors had done their best. Everything seemed alright at least physically.

The team was squaring off against the Boston Bears, and he had a feeling that it would be an amazing match. He just knew it.

Irritation suddenly rose in him. Would she not get her ass up and leave?

He marched into the bedroom, expecting to call her out, and surprisingly, found the room empty. She must have gone while he was in the bathroom.

He grinned to himself. He liked her. She understood their agreement. No strings attached.

It was better this way.

•.¸♡ . ♡¸.•

The crowd buzzed with a mix of anticipation, and unease as Luka Kuznetsov got on the ice. Everything about his grace and power was predatory. He was famous for his savage outbursts and the opponent's left shattered in his wake.

The score was tied, tensions rising as the clock ticked towards ruin. Caleb glided the puck to Luka, and with serpentine speed he wove through their defense, barring his path. Their defenses crumbled before his advance. A deft flick of his wrist had sent the puck rocketing into the net with crushing force, and the goalie could only stare in disbelief at being so thoroughly outmatched.

The crowd erupted, caught between dread at his prowess and awe at the spectacle of his dominance.

The buzzer sang his victory.

Luka was mobbed by his teammates, but even in the chaos, he could hear the fans chanting his name. It had been his best game yet, and everyone in the stadium knew it. Luka basked in the moment, knowing that he earned every bit of the adulation that was being thrown his way.

•.¸♡ . ♡¸.•

The locker room was a blur of activity as the hockey players stripped off their gear, music blared, teammates shouted and laughter echoed off the walls as the team basked in their victory.

Luka Kuznetsov, in particular, was the center of attention, the other players clapping him on the back and shouting their praise.

"Did you see them? Those Boston bears didn't know what hit them." One of them hollered.

"The beast is back, boys!" Caleb, the team captain, slapped his shoulder loudly, shaking his head in awe.

Luka's performance on the ice had been the stuff of legends - unstoppable, merciless, fueled by something only known to him. He had scored 5 goals and 2 assists and not to mention the winning goal.

The coach pushed through the crowd of players with a bemused smile, coming to stand before Luka.

"Whatever - or whoever - lit that fire in you tonight, I hope we see more of the same. That was a master class out there. What the hell got into you?"

Luka shrugged, the picture of indifference. But behind his nonchalance lurked something sharper in his gaze, hints of the primal thing that had driven him to dominate so completely.

"Just felt like winning." The sly half-smile accompanied his words, meant to warn against prodding too deeply into the source of his outburst. Seemed he had found exactly what he was looking for. No whores were able to do it for him.

With a chuckle and shake of his head, he clapped Luka on the shoulder and moved away to congratulate other players. Despite their exhaustion, there was a sense of camaraderie in the air, a feeling of shared triumph. The players joked and bantered with each other, swapping stories from the game and reliving their best moments. They had played a great game, and they knew it - and they owed much of their success to the skill and talent of their star player, Luka.

Before he left for his home, Luka typed a message for his coach. "Hire the doctor. I want the doctor as my physiotherapist."

•.¸♡ . ♡¸.•

Days had passed since their win against Boston. Despite the upcoming game against the relatively weak New York Titans, Luka's team was forced to endure a morning practice by the coach– just one thing, he couldn't concentrate.

Luka paced the sidelines, his gaze glued to the phone clutched in his hand. His teammates skated by on the ice, their voices muffled through his haze of frustration. He had been attempting to reach Ana for over a day - 10 calls the night before to tell her about his decision to hire her, and the 20 calls that followed to ask why she hadn't picked up. Now, climbing to 30 missed calls. This time to tell her he was considering firing her. All went unanswered.

Annoyance rose in his chest and his frustration had reached his peak. Luka's face contorted with emotion, a mix of redness from both the cold air and his internal rage. Where was she? He dialed her number again, willing the phone to pick up. His fingers clenched around it so tightly that his knuckles were turning white, but still there was no answer.

"Hey Kuznetsov."

"Fucking damn it." He ran a hand through his hair, the familiar motion bringing no comfort.

His teammates gave him a wide berth, wary of the anger roiling off him in waves. "What crawled up his ass and died." One of them asked.

"Who fucking knows. He must be in one of his moods again."

He heard of their words, but their words mattered little in his decision as he set out of the ice rink with a determination that radiated through his every movement.

The heavy pads of his gear creaked, his shoulders hunched and brow furrowed with an intensity that showed he could not be bothered for small talks when he entered into the locker room.

With practiced ease, he began to remove his gear, starting with his helmet and gloves. The pads and armor followed, layer by layer, until he was left in just his jersey and compression shorts. Even without the added bulk of his equipment, Luka still looked like a force to be reckoned with, his broad shoulders and powerful arms testaments to years of hard work and training.

He didn't break stride as he approached the gym area where many of the players usually warmed up, the coach was sitting with a clipboard in hand. Luka towered over his short frame, his imposing figure seeming to fill the space between them.

"Shouldn't you be on the ice?"

"The doctor... where is she?"

"I don't know. I sent her the contract a couple days ago, and she didn't respond." He shrugged like it couldn't be a bother to him.

Luka seethed with rage as he stared into the phone one more time.

Pavel approached, a teasing grin on his face. "Maybe she got a better offer, huh?" He shoved Luka on the back, oblivious to the threat in simmering silence.

In an instant Luka grabbed him by the jersey, pulling him onto his toes. "Maybe I'll knock that smile off your face. Pound it through your teeth into the back of your skull," Luka growled, eyes burning with barely restrained violence.

"What the heck! Kuznetsov."

"It was a joke. Geez."

He shoved Pavel away with disgust. His heavy breaths echoed through the silent gym, no one daring to meet his eye.

"I have to go." He stormed out of the facility, too fired up to focus on his practice.

CHAPTER 5

Ana sat on the edge of her bed, clutching the thin sheets to her chest. Tears slid down her cheeks as she looked at the books she had collected over the years, their promises of a happily ever after feeling out of reach.

Her phone vibrated for the 10th time, all through she ignored them all. Shame filled her chest as she didn't have the mental strength to pick any calls or even talk to anyone. She recalled the mix of desire and roughness with which Luka had explored her body, leaving invisible bruises that would last days.

Her gaze fell to the stack of money on her bedside table and remembered her brother. Fortunately, Today was a visiting day.

Despite the temptation to mope in her sorrows, Ana gathered her strength and stood to face the only thing that kept her going before the dark clouds of depression crept in.

•.¸♡ . ♡¸.•

She peered out the window of the taxi as it drove the winding road that led to her brother's boarding school, surrounded by lush greenery that seemed to stretch on for miles. They reached the top of the hill, and she was greeted by the sight of a grand, ivy-covered building that looked like it had been plucked straight out of a Gothic novel.

She made her way towards the main building, walked down the long corridor, her heels clicking on the polished floor. The familiar ache of missing Danny swelled in her chest. It had been over a month since her last visit; her demanding job, allowing little free time.

The school was abuzz with the commotion of visiting day. Parents chatted with teachers while children raced up and down the corridors, their excited voices bouncing off the walls.

She drank in the warmth and joy of families reunited, however temporarily.

A pang of longing struck her as she observed a young boy showing his mother an art project, the father looking on proudly. Ana quickened her steps, the reminders of what she couldn't provide Danny too painful to bear. She finally stopped in front of a wooden door, gathering herself.

She squared her shoulders, loosened her features, slipped on a wide grin as she threw open the door.

Danny was sitting at his desk, poring over a pile of textbooks, but he looked up when he heard her enter.

His face lit up as he greeted her with a smile.

"What are you doing here alone?"

His principal voice echoed concern in her head. "Danny is quiet and likes to remain by himself."

"It's a bit chaotic out there." His smile faded. "Dad didn't come with you. I thought he might by now."

"I'm sorry," Ana said, "but I'm here." She moved around behind the wheelchair, placing her hands on the handles located at the back of the wheelchair. She pushed her brother through the hallway. Many other parents were also visiting their children.

“Let’s go to the Art class, I painted some stuff, I want to show you.”

Ana was pleased to see the school has implemented accessible pathways throughout the premises, allowing Ana to maneuver the wheelchair with ease.

The school was expensive but from her extensive research it had been the best in dealing with special cases like her brother.

As she stepped into the classroom, she was greeted by a gallery of artwork that spans the entire spectrum of creativity. The walls were filled with an array of drawings, each one a unique representation of a child’s imagination. From delicate pencil sketches to bold and vibrant paintings, the diversity of styles and techniques was evident in every corner.

“Look at it over there.” Danny, pointing to a particularly colorful drawing, exclaimed, "Look at that one! It's beautiful. Let me tell you about it."

He began describing his art with enthusiasm, his voice brimming with passion. “This piece represents the world of dreams and imagination. I wanted to capture the fantastical elements that exist in our minds.” He continued, explaining his style and technique. “I used a combination of acrylic paints and colored pencils. The bold brushstrokes and intricate details merge to create a sense of depth and texture.”

Ana smiled as she listened to him. Guilt weighed on her heavily. She wished she could give him a better childhood. He was the main reason she had chosen to study physiotherapy. She wanted to take care of him and provide for him like she had promised, but there was so much more that needed to be done.

"I love how big and green you made the grass. It looks so fluffy!" swallowing the lump in her throat.

Danny grinned. "I wanted it to feel like your hair when you give me piggyback rides!"

Ana's heart swells with love for her little brother.

She'll always give him piggyback rides, help him however she can. She'll give him the best life possible.

"You have such a gift for color and shapes. This is a work of art."

The boy beamed. "Really? You think I could be an artist someday?"

"I know you will be. You just need time to find your style and voice." Ana responds confidently as she tug on his cheek.

"Hey, stop doing that. I'm not a kid anymore."

"Well excuse me." She teased, chuckling when the bell rang. "What's that for?" she straightened.

"Visiting hours are over." Danny said with sadness hinted in voice.

"I will visit you soon, okay?" she brushed his hair with her fingers.

They returned back to his dorm and he reached for his table.

"What's that?"

He held up a small paper bag. "They served brownies today, I got extra and I know they are your favorite, i... I just want to make sure you at least eat."

"Danny..."

"You work a lot doing a job you hate and no time to eat. There is also the fact that dad isn't helping." He stumbled on the words, "will you just take it."

Tears welled in her eyes, her lips tingle with the urge to divulge the truth, that she had finally freed herself from the confines of her waitress job but decided against it.

She didn't want him to be worried about her. "On one condition... that you would make one friend this year. Your principal is worried."

His lips twisted and he thought for a moment. "Fine. I will try."

She wrapped her hands around him.

•.¸♡ . ♡¸.•

Ana stood outside the school, her phone rang. An unsaved number displayed across her screen, but she recognized the last four digits. Luka Kuznetsov.

It was time she stopped avoiding him. She pulled up his address one more time, she was going to meet him.

CHAPTER 6

Ana's hands trembled as she rang the doorbell to Luka's penthouse. She didn't know if he would even answer, after ignoring all his calls, but she had to try.

The door flew open and there he stood. Ana's heart seized at the anger that radiated from Luka in waves. His usual composure shattered.

Luka's eyes were glacial, his jaw clenched. But at the sight of her, his rage seemed to fade into exhaustion.

"Wow, look who is here," he said flatly, moving for her to enter.

She twirled to face him. "I need to be certain. Are you hiring me as your doctor or because of your... Pregame ritual?"

Luka crossed his legs as he settled on a leather seat, his head craned up, staring at her. "Believe it or not, both."

"Why me?"

Luka let that question wallow in his brain as his eyes roamed over her flawless complexion, a canvas kissed by the sun's gentle caress, her midnight curls woven into delicate braids, tied up at the top of her head showing off her slender neck. She was pretty, he thought and she would fit just right for the part.

This playoff season was his first major game since his shoulder surgery. A lot was riding on it, from the league, the teammates who relied on him, not to mention the immense pressure he had put on himself. He was determined to show he could still play. Prove to everyone that doubted him and that included himself.

"I need someone who will take my performance to the next level and bring out the best in me. It just happens that person is you."

She tilted her head and furrowed her brows with a puzzling look.

"Did you not watch the game?" He sounded irritated.

"No." She had said it like she couldn't care less. She became a physiotherapist because of her brother, not because she saw herself in the sports industry.

"Well, we won, but I won't bore you with the details." He added, "Instead, I'm proposing a sexual arrangement that's more focused on physical intimacy than emotional attachment."

There was a brief silence.

"Then... it is going to cost you more," she said shortly after.

"Name your price?"

Her brain scrambled; she hadn't thought it would be so easy. She factored in her brother's medication expenses and tuition fees, while also striving to save money if feasible, all in her mind.

"Fifteen thousand dollars for every night."

She was confused about how he looked at her. Did she ask for too much? There was obviously no shortage of funds in this man's life, but still, she didn't think she was even worth that much and tried to focus on how the money would help her problems... if he agreed.

"ya mog by zaplatit' million."

"What does that mean?"

"Nothing. Let's make this an official agreement." Luka nodded, then rose with the words, "I believe I should initiate some changes as well."

Ana stared up at him wide-eyed, her heart racing and her mind spinning with several crazy requests he might have.

He stalked closer to her, one step at a time. "It doesn't matter if I have a game or not," he continued, "I want to have you spread on my bed, willing and ready to take every inch of my cock wherever and whenever I want."

Ana's eyes shifted like she was about to back out again, and Luka noticed.

He smiled devilishly. "Do you have a problem with that?"

"No." She said, tightening her jaw.

"Also, do you have a safe word?" he paused, then continued, "A word that would mean all of this, including the contract, will end. Do you have any?"

She shook her head.

"What's your favorite color?"

Her favorite color was beige because she related to its plain and boring nature, but as she locked eyes with the piercing blue gaze at that moment, she couldn't resist calling out. "Blue?"

"Fine. Blue. I won't stop if you say no, I take what I want. I don't care if you cum or not. I don't even care if you enjoy it.

I fuck for a purpose and right now it would seem your little pussy is my good luck charm."

She was certain that those words had never been uttered before, yet there they were, floating in the atmosphere.

"Say the word blue and it stops. Everything. Understand?" he emphasized.

She nodded.

"Use your words, girl."

She jerked, "Yes. I get it."

"Now apologize for distracting me all day at practice."

"How? I wasn't even– seriously the missed calls?" she blew out a breath, "Fine. I'm sorry for not picking up your calls." Her tone filled with a hint of sarcasm. "Happy?"

"That doesn't sound sincere enough, I think you need to learn some fucking manners and I am going to teach that to you."

"I could leave."

He smirked. "But you won't. Now the only thing I want out of your pretty lips is the words, yes sir. Please, sir and thank you, sir. Got it?" his thumb trailed along her jaw.

She nodded.

He tilted his head.

"Yes... sir."

"Good girl. Now, I want to see you put that smart mouth to good use."

Under the intensity of his gaze, an invisible force seemed to pull her down, her body instinctively sinking to her knees. Inch by inch, her face drew closer, until it hovered mere breaths away from the prominent bulge that strained against the fabric of his trousers.

He looked down at her with a hint of amusement playing at the corner of his lips. "Such an obedient girl," he commanded.

Her body buzzed at his words. She hated this, the humiliation and the cheapness of it all. She fumbled with his zipper and his thick dick sprung out. She stared at it with hooded eyes, unconsciously biting her lip.

She knew he was big but seeing him this close scared her and maybe excited her a little. He could fill her mouth if she dared to try to take him whole. Instead, she took her time, swirling her tongue around the head.

She could feel the tension thrumming through his body under her ministration and sensed each stifled gasp and choked sound drawn.

Ana's arousal grew with every sign of how thoroughly he was crumbling under her patient, seeking touch. She won't deny that she relished how the composed, self-assured, arrogant hockey player trembled and became incoherent, fueling her desire in a way that was new to her.

He must have heard her thoughts because he fisted the top of her hair, suddenly taking control and shoving himself into her mouth.

She gagged.

Luka raised an eyebrow, a smirk played over his lips though his breathing had quickened. "Take me deep." Luka let out a quiet gasp as he began thrusting his hips up into her mouth, forcing her to take him deeper.

"Such a dirty girl. Keep your teeth back." He filled her mouth, using his grip on her hair to move her at his own pace which was far from the slow torturous smooth strokes she did.

Her eyes watered, unable to breathe as he fucked her throat hard.

He came on her face. His thickness dripped down her chin.

"Yeah. I like you like this." He said with a satisfied grin.

Ana was rendered speechless. The weight of her fury threatened to consume her, yet she remained outwardly composed, as she realized that rock bottom had a basement, and it appeared she was going to be stuck there for some time.

CHAPTER 7

That evening...

Ana had pushed away any memory of her foolishness for giving in to a man who could not show her affection. Instead, she focused on the fact she could purchase food without counting every penny from her bank account.

Ana scoured aisle after aisle, as she picked out fresh produce alongside her favorite ingredients for a home-cooked meal. It had been so long since she freely went shopping like this. With a sense of fulfillment, she grabbed some painting supplies for Danny as well.

She munched on an Apple as she made her way to her neighborhood. Construction workers in hard hats scurried around like busy ants.

"Excuse me, can I help you?"

The man tipped his helmet as he turned around. "Do you live here?"

"Yes. up ahead."

"This is your final warning. You have to vacate." He said, shoving a paper in her hands.

She unwrapped the paper and took a quick scan. "Wait... I don't understand."

The man looked irritated. "The government wants to demolish this neighborhood. We sent the notice months ago. It's been on the news."

She was unaware of the news since her dad had thrown away the TV in anger after losing a bet.

"Listen, young lady, we sent out notices months ago," he repeated, "and even settled the homeowners financially."

"Every homeowner?"

He nodded and left, rejoining the others.

Ana pushed through her iron gates into the house. The house was old and definitely would benefit from remodeling. She had imagined breaking down the wall and making an open kitchen and redoing the ceiling.

What was she thinking? It was the government's now. Did her father know about the redevelopment? She should tell him, they needed to find a new place to live.

Ana chopped vegetables and stirred the sauce with skill as she cooked.

She set the table, lining up plates and silverware along the edges and waited for her father.

He would be here. She told herself. He would come and they would find a solution to their living arrangement. Every passing minute only reduced her sense of expectation as he was nowhere to be seen.

Her gaze shifted to the untouched food before her, a reflection of her dwindling appetite. The weight of worry and uncertainty burdened her thoughts, leaving little room for nourishment.

Ana wrapped her unfinished meal, placing it in the refrigerator for tomorrow's breakfast.

•.¸♡ . ♡¸.•

The sun was peeking up over the horizon when her eyes shot open, and she scrambled out of bed. Her stomach grumbled in protest as she rushed around, gathering her things. In a desperate flurry, she threw on clothes, laid her edges, and raced out of the house with no time to grab breakfast.

Ana opened the door of the hockey team's training facility and stepped inside, squinting as the morning light streamed through the expansive windows.

She was enveloped by an energetic buzz punctuated by sharp shouts of instruction and encouragement and the near-constant sound of skates on ice. Players were scattered across the frozen surface, gliding in a chaotic dance and taking turns to take practice shots at the goal.

The coach approached Ana, extending his hand.

"Welcome to the team, Ana!" he greeted warmly. "We're thrilled to have you on board. Let me show you around and introduce you to everyone."

They navigated through the maze of hallways, Ana marveled at the state-of-the-art facilities. They passed by the weight room, where players grunted and pushed their physical limits, and the spacious locker rooms, adorned with jerseys bearing the team's iconic logo.

Entering the team's medical room, Ana was greeted by a team of dedicated professionals. The coach introduced her to the staff, all of whom welcomed her. Their shared passion for supporting the players' well-being created an instant sense of camaraderie.

"You will be attending Luka, right?"

She nodded.

"Wow. That one is quite the–

The coach cleared his throat not allowing any negative remarks on their star player.

Luka was the team's most famous but notoriously hostile player. She might not be a big fan of hockey but she heard stories of his icy demeanor and challenging behavior. That didn't stop the fangirls from professing their love for the player online.

The physician forced a smile. "I'm sure you will do a good job."

"Come, let's officially introduce you to the boys."

They made their way to the ice rink, where the players were.

Ana stalled a few feet shy of the boards, willing her nerveless fingers as she watched Luka. He was crunched down, doing some warmup stretches.

His breath escaped in visible puffs, muscles rippling beneath the athletic gear as he twisted to loosen his back and legs.

What a weird way to warm up.

"Gather round." The coach announced.

She watched Luka join the others, huddled up. The atmosphere around him seemed to carry an air of intensity, his bored expression revealing little.

Her nerves threatened to overpower her, but she reminded herself of her expertise and professionalism.

She knew it would be weird sleeping with a patient or boss. Whatever he was. If anyone found out, she had everything to lose including her license. Even though he first initiated it with some weird gimmick of needing sex to play, she could see herself getting most of the heat, if things went south.

A plan. She needed a plan. She knew she would see him so often and the earlier she got used to it, the better. They would keep things professional wherever they were in public and when he needed her, she could always go to his house. That could work.

"This is Ana, she is the new physiotherapist." The couch's voice cut through her rambling thoughts.

The players knocked their sticks against the ice, cheering.

One of them hollered, "You are pretty."

The boys sounded a loud *oohhh* and jeering.

That brought an unexpected smile to her lips but when her eyes fell on Luka's blank expression, her smile flattered.

"Well, go back to practice. We don't pay you guys to sit on your butt all day."

"Here, have this." The coach passed her staff card.

She glanced down, her face broke into a wide grin and her eyes teary.

Ana Sheen. Physiotherapist of the Crestmont Giants.

"Thank you."

"No, thank you. See, Luka can be difficult but don't worry if you have any problem with him, let me know, and I'll slap him upside the head."

She chuckled, nodding.

•.¸♡ . ♡¸.•

As the day progressed, Ana immersed herself in understanding the medical history of all the players on the team and caught sight of Luka's file. That piqued her interest and she soon discovered he recently had a major surgery on his shoulder. Well, maybe that's where his superstition started.

Her stomach let out a low growl, interrupting her thoughts. She realized she hadn't eaten anything all day. Her mind flashed to the cafe she noticed when she had arrived that morning. After a quick lunch break, she walked past her office and went over to the ice rink.

They had just finished an intense practice session, and players were taking a well-deserved break. Ana observed them until she caught sight of a player massaging his shoulder with one hand, his repetitive motions indicating his discomfort.

It was Pavel, his name boldly written across his jersey.

Curiosity got the better of her, and she asked, "Is that bothering you?"

The player shrugged, loathe to admit how much the discomfort hindered his routine.

"It's kinda stiff," Pavel replied, hoping to downplay it. "But it's been bothering me for a while. Stubborn thing."

"I can help."

"I hope it's not serious, I don't want the coach to know."

"It probably isn't," Ana said, trying to appease his worries.

"This will help," she took out a tennis ball from her pocket. "Now, have a seat on that bench."

He settled onto the bench, indicating the spot with two fingers. "Right there."

She placed the tennis ball in the designated area. An involuntary grunt escaped him as she applied pressure.

"Is that right?"

"Yeah, a little higher?" he asked through gritted teeth.

The ball dug into muscle made mercilessly tender by days of abuse. Pavel squeezed his eyes shut against the urge to jerk away from the sudden pain.

"Mother of Christ," he grunted, knuckles whitening where they gripped the bench edge.

"I know it's painful, nobody will take fault in you if you scream right now,"

Her wry humor surprised a laugh from him, easing some of the tension coiled in his shoulders.

"Relax and drop your head. It takes a couple of minutes for the muscle to ease up," she advised.

Pavel obeyed, feeling the tight fibers slowly yield and come unknotted under her ministrations. The ache drained from his body along with the pent-up strain and frustration of the last few days.

"Wow," he exclaimed, lifting his head. "That's a strange sensation."

Ana released her hold on the tennis ball. "Better?"

Pavel rotated his arm in an experimental circle, amazed at the range of motion restored. His gratitude shone through as his arm came around her.

"You are the best doc." He grinned with satisfaction. "You might have magic powers in your hands."

Ana, unable to resist the charm of Pavel's theatrical antics,burst into laughter. A genuine sound that resonated in the room. Yet, as the laughter subsided, a sudden sense of unease washed over her.

Feeling an intense glare, her gaze shifted, and her eyes locked briefly with Luka's. He stood alongside the captain, seemingly disinterested in the captain's words as his focused gaze remained fixed on Ana and Pavel.

She couldn't comprehend the intensity she saw in Luka's eyes. It unnerved her, for their relationship had been one of shared intimacy of the business nature but not a committed romantic one. Ana was certain that he didn't harbor romantic feelings for her and she didn't either.

With a deep breath, she refocused her attention on her latest patient and resumed their conversation, attempting to push aside the confusion and unease that Luka's piercing gaze had stirred within her.

CHAPTER 8

The sound of skates scraping against the ice, pucks hitting the boards, and coaches shouting instructions filled the air.

She walked through the hallway, taking in the hockey players milling about, some in full gear and others in street clothes. The players chatted and laughed, their easy banter reflecting the strong bond forged through their shared love of the sport.

Ana was so lost in thought that she didn't notice Luka creeping up behind her. In a single, swift motion, he grabbed her wrist and yanked her into a nearby storage closet. Ana gasped in surprise.

The cramped closet was hot and stuffy, filled with the scent of cleaning chemicals and stale air.

Luka stood facing Ana. He slipped off his shirt in one swift motion, leaving it to fall unnoticed on the floor. His arms were pressed tight with tension against the wall on either side. His bare, muscled chest filled her vision.

His skin was damp with sweat, and his eyes had a look of predator in them as he looked down at her. He had not cleaned up. It did not matter to Ana, as this was the sort of thing that made her stomach flip-flop in a way she couldn't entirely explain, even to herself.

"What- what are you doing?" Ana asked, keeping her voice low. "You can't be serious. Someone might see us here."

"Then I guess we better be quick," he said. His eyes glinted in the dim light as he gazed at her. "I want you now... I want you here. Isn't that what we agreed?"

She struggled against him, pushing his hard body off her. "No, we didn't. Not like this." In her attempt to free herself, she landed a slap on Luka's cheek.

His face whipped to the side with the impact. There was a stillness in the air as he slowly turned and shot an intense gaze at her.

"I'm sorry, I didn't mean–" the words caught in her throat as she closed her eyes tightly, her face contorted with fear as she shuddered at the thought that he might also try to hurt her. She braced herself for his response.

His brows raised, "Next time, use your fist if you want to make a real impact, but for now, we had an agreement."

In the next second, he grabbed her wrists and pinned them above her head as he shoved down her pants until she was naked from the bottom.

She gasped, her skin tingling as his fingers left a trail of warmth in their wake. Her mind was clouded with lust; there was no way for her to stop what was happening. In the back of Ana's mind, the worried thought persisted.

He spun her around, Ana's hands pushed against the wall, trying to hold herself up as Luka kicked her legs apart.

She felt his dick and pressed it against her entrance and with one hump, he pushed it in.

He leaned in close, and through gritted teeth, growled, "I fucking own you. My fuck toy for me to use, where ever the fuck I want."

Luka's thrust felt deeper and harder than the last. His cock almost came out of her pussy before he buried it deep inside of her. Over and over again.

"Please... sir, slow down."

His voice went low, as he murmured in her ear, "But you take it so well...such a good girl."

Those words.

They caused a sudden surge of adrenaline through her veins, her breath coming in short, sharp gasps. Her hands curled around Luka's body. She couldn't deny the desire that pulsed through her, even as she tried to resist it. What was wrong with her? How had she come to this? All of her strength and self-respect were stripped from her with such ruthless precision.

She felt pleasure building inside of her, but every time she thought she would reach an orgasm, she forced her focus elsewhere.

Ingrown hair. Her great aunt with a messed up eye. Molds. She didn't want to give in... to let go.

Ana understood that Luka had no regard for an emotional bond; This fact had been clear from the beginning and because of the money involved, it felt like a service. Should she let herself enjoy a little intimacy? Even though it felt like a long answer to a prayer she didn't know she needed. It triggered an internal battle between what her mind desired and what her body wanted.

His grip on her waist tightened and brought her body closer to him. The sound of skin slapping against each other filled the small room.

Laughter and footsteps echoed in the hallway. Her hands clasped over her mouth to keep herself from making any noise.

His stubble scratched her cheek as he leaned forward. "You are mine, you understand?"

"Yes... sir."

With a loud grunt, Luka collapsed against her, gasping for breath.

Finally, Luka managed to break free and staggered backward, panting and sweating. Ana's knees almost gave way as she leaned against the wall.

So much for being professional, there was no hope if Luka planned on having his way with her as he liked.

And she was going to let him —because she too was broken, too touch starved, too damaged maybe even more than him— but at what cause?

CHAPTER 9

After a long day at the facility, Ana looked forward to returning home and relaxing. She had been on her feet for hours, and the activities of the storage closet had left her feeling somewhat aroused.

When Pavel poked his head into her office, "Hey doc. Any plans for the evening?"

"No, why?"

"We have a house party to attend, we are celebrating the retirement of Gerry."

She must have had a questioning look on her face because Pavel explained further. "He used to be our defender but he is a cool dude... you should come with us."

She gave a nervous chuckle. "Nah. I think I will just go home and rest."

Caleb, the team captain, joined Pavel, pushing the door wider. "Think of it this way. It can be like a way for you to get to know the players better."

Ana paused. As the newest member of the team, she knew that forming relationships with her coworkers could be beneficial to both her professional development and her overall wellbeing.

When she looked at Caleb, he had a warm smile that reached his eyes. His messy mop of dirty blond curls somehow gave him an inviting air, like he would go out of his way to make sure everyone at the party was comfortable.

She thought about it for a moment. "Will Luka be joining?"

"Nah. He doesn't really socialize outside the rink and he doesn't drink." Pavel answered. "I think he said something about beer being the devil piss and his body deserved the most expensive thing or something like that."

"Okay enough." Caleb retorted. Turning to her, "Come with us. You will have fun."

She took a deep breath and made a decision. "Sure, why not." She said, returning his smile.

•.¸♡ . ♡¸.•

As Ana exited the training center, her heart raced and her brain swirled with a mix of feelings. It was a pleasant surprise that the bar was only a few blocks away. She quickened her pace, eager to get to the bar and to see her colleagues in a different light—as people rather than coworkers—and to learn more about their lives outside of work.

But at the same time, a knot of nervousness formed in her stomach. As a new staff member, what if she said the wrong thing or didn't fit in with the group? What if they didn't like her? Someone had taken a chance on her and chosen her as the physiotherapist of one of the most prominent teams in the nation. She was determined not to make any mistakes.

The warm glow of the living room lamps cast a cozy atmosphere over the gathering. Lively chatter and laughter filled the air, mingling with the sounds of clinking glasses and the gentle music playing in the background.

"Hey, look who's here!" Pavel called out, waving Ana over with an enthusiastic grin. "I was just telling the guys how you helped me with that nagging shoulder injury."

Ana smiled, her initial nerves melting away as the group welcomed her arrival with cheers and applause. A rush of excitement coursed through her as she was introduced to each player, their friendly banter and easy camaraderie immediately putting her at ease.

"Glad you could make it!" boomed Pavel, his voice tinged with the happy buzz of someone already well into their drinks. He ushered her into the living room and made space for her on the plush sofa. "What can I get you to drink?"

"Maybe I could have a non-alcoholic drink?" she ventured, hoping it wouldn't dampen the mood.

“There isn't any, don't worry you will be fine,” he left before she objected.

She knew her limits – alcohol never sat well with her, leaving her stomach churning and her head pounding. But this was a new group, a chance to build friendships, and the last thing she wanted to do was seem like a buzzkill. Maybe just one drink wouldn't hurt. It was a chance to loosen up, let loose, and truly enjoy the company.

She forced a smile, accepting the beer with a murmured "thanks." The condensation on the bottle felt icy against her palm. Taking a tentative sip, the bitter fizz sent a jolt through her system.

Ana felt welcomed into the festivities by Pavel, Caleb, and the rest of the team, the free-flowing drinks and atmosphere quickly putting her at ease.

It was then that Gerry, the guest of honor himself, materialized at her side, a sloppy grin plastered across his ruddy face. He reeked of stale beer and cigar smoke as he leaned in far too close for Ana's liking.

"Well, well, if it isn't the pretty new physio!" he crowed, giving her a lingering once-over that made her skin crawl. "Gotta say, when they said, you are beautiful, i didn't know you were this beautiful."

“Hello, My name is Ana.”

“You can call me Garry but I have to say why did you have to show up when I've retired.”

Ana forced an uncomfortable laugh, trying to subtly create some distance between them without causing a scene. But Gerry seemed oblivious to her discomfort, stepping even nearer until she could practically taste the whiskey on his breath.

“Okay, chillax hombre. She is not into old guys.” Pavel came between them, his hand around Ana.

Garry looked offended. “There is not much age difference between me and Caleb.”

“Hey don't bring me into this.” Caleb teased, “and also let her be.”

Garry shook his head. Don’t mind these guys. You know, a tough old vet like me could always use a little... physical therapy, if you catch my drift," he said with an exaggerated wink.

His comment sent a wave of nausea crashing through her. She opened her mouth to voice a sharp retort, but the words died in her throat as the nausea intensified. Before she could control it, her body lurched forward, and she doubled over, the vile contents of her stomach erupting directly onto Gerry's expensive leather shoes.

A hush fell over the immediate vicinity as Gerry sprang back with a disgusted shout. Caleb quickly guided the mortified Ana away, murmuring apologies over his shoulder, while the rest of the group erupted into raucous laughter at Gerry's expense.

Ana could feel hot tears of humiliation stinging her eyes as Caleb and Pavel half-carried, and half-dragged her out of the living room, toward the hallway bathroom. As they passed through the crowd, Ana happened to make eye contact with Luka.

He was leaning against the wall, arms folded across his chest, watching the scene play out with an inscrutable expression. Their gazes locked for just a moment before Ana ducked her burning face away.

Caleb being the responsible captain he was, got her situated in the bathroom, rubbing her back soothingly as she violently expelled the remaining contents of her stomach into the porcelain basin. When the wrenching convulsions finally subsided, she slumped back against the cool tiled wall, drained and mortified.

"I'm so sorry," she croaked, "I've ruined everything."

"Don't be ridiculous," Pavel countered firmly. "He's the one who should be apologizing for being a lecherous old goat."

"Yeah, I should just go home," she mumbled, her words tumbling out in a jumbled mess.

Her legs wobbled like jelly as she attempted to stand.

A wave of dizziness washed over her, and she stumbled. Caleb reached out to steady her, but she swatted him away with a weak laugh.

“No, you are not.” Caleb guided her out of the bathroom and said. “Great you are here. Can you take her home?”

Ana lifted her head, her vision blurry but enough to make out Luka's scowl. It felt like a physical blow. He must see her as utterly repulsive, a stain to be discarded. The weight of his disapproval felt suffocating.

“So she could puke all over my car. I would rather not.”

“Then you have to take care of Jude.”

Jude was the twenty-two year-old goalie who joined their roster not too long ago. His face fell flat on the table. The guy was 190 pounds and can take heavy hits but gets knocked out by a couple of beers.

“I will take the doctor.” Luka said.

CHAPTER 10

Under the cloudless, clear night sky, Luka frowned as he led Ana to his car, keeping an arm firmly around her waist.

She could barely walk straight and reeked of alcohol. He opened the passenger door and hesitated. A part of him was worried she might throw up or pass out in his car.

Caleb called out. "Thanks, man."

Luka sighed. He couldn't very well leave Ana here in this state. As gently as his patience allowed, he helped her into the seat, leaning her chair back once she was inside.

"Do not fucking puke your guts in here or I'm going to punish you when you sober up."

"Are you going to spank me?" she turned to him with a wide grin across her face.

"What?" Not what he meant but the image of bending her over and 'punishing' her seared into his mind.

"You are funny." She laughed at whatever joke only she had heard.

Christ. Luka settled her on her seat and buckled the seatbelt.

"Call me if you need anything, I have to deal with the others," Caleb spoke, as the captain and the oldest in the team. He had seemingly taken on the role of the father of the group.

Luka nodded and shut the door, walking around to the driver's seat. This was not how he had imagined his evening going.

He pulled out of the parking lot and remembered he had no idea where she lived or which direction to turn.

"Where do you live?"

Ana mumbled incoherently, next to him.

"This is ridiculous," he muttered under his breath, more to himself than to her. He pulled the car over to the side of the road.

"Where. Do. You live?" he shook her body.

"My house... is pretty far," her words slurred when she called out her address.

He punched the address into his GPS and took to the road again.

"Luuukaaa! You're so sweet, taking me home." She punched his arm. "Maybe you are not all weird."

"Weird? How" he had asked out of curiosity, not that he cared what she thought of him.

"Yes. you don't mind sharing bodily fluids, but you don't kiss. It's strange." The rest of her words are buried in an inaudible mumble.

Luka merely shook his head. He wasn't about to explain his choices to some drunk.

"Also!" she yelled, which caused him to flinch against the steering wheel. "This pregame ritual is stupid. I mean, there is no evidence that having sex before a game can affect the outcome. It's all in your head. You are a good player, but wait — I haven't seen you play well. You are an okay player to be famous, but what do I know about hockey?" She shrugged.

Her voice hiked up as she continued, "Caleb said hockey is a more team effort, so that means your *thing* has little effect."

A part of Luka knew that. Perhaps it wasn't just the sex itself, but a mental thing. Or maybe it all could be a coincidence that anytime he had mind-blowing sex, his next game was equally mind-blowing.

The last game had cemented his position as one of the best players in the league. What if it was not the sex but the woman he had sex with? Luka glanced at Ana as a soft snore escaped her lips. Her head lolled to the side, eyes closed, and spit trailed from her lips.

He tossed that thought out of his head the second it came through.

When he arrived at the location, he shook Ana's shoulder. "Wake up. We're here."

Her eyes blinked open slowly. She gazed up at him, brows knitted in confusion. Luka helped her out of the seat, catching her as she swayed unsteadily on her feet.

The nearby buildings were decayed relics, covered in graffiti and broken windows. The street lights barely lit up the uneven pavement below. A cat darted from one building to another before retreating into the shadows. His footsteps echoed off the damp concrete as he hurried to get her home, down the dark and narrow street, Ana cradled in his arms like a precious gem. Her arms came around his shoulder as she leaned to nuzzle his neck.

In the distance, a dog barked. Tattered flyers clung to the wind, drifting over the ground.

A figure caught his eye, lurking in the shadows beneath a hood that hid their face. He frowned, clutching Ana tighter. Something about this stranger was off - their stillness was unsettling and triggered Luka's senses into alarm. *Why would she live in such a neighborhood?*

He strode up the path and set her down by the door, rifling through her purse for keys. The lock clicked open. Guiding her over the threshold, he led Ana into a dingy room and eased her onto the couch.

His eyes bounced off each corner of the house.

"What the hell?"

The interior of the house matched its shabby exterior. Years of neglect and disrepair had taken their toll. The kitchen cabinets were coated in grime, hinges rusted and doors hanging askew. The sink dripped incessantly, the sound echoing through the rooms, and a musty odor clung to the space.

He could not imagine what her room would look like. What did she use the money he gave her?

It didn't matter. His work was done. For tonight, at least, that would have to be enough.

"Sleep this off," he told her sternly. "You're lucky I was there to drive you home." Luka turned and walked out.

His footstep paused when he reached the threshold, feeling unease over the hooded figure he had seen earlier. It blended into doubts about leaving Ana here for the night unprotected.

He cussed himself for this sense of responsibility- he could not leave her alone in such a place even though she called it home. This was not a home, but a hellhole masquerading as one.

She was fast asleep and didn't seem to notice when he returned to the house and hoisted her up, taking her with him.

CHAPTER 11

Ana stirred, blinking awake as golden light filled her vision. She gazed around the room in confusion at the elegant furnishings and intricate décor surrounding her. The events of last night remained a haze, fragments that didn't align with the luxurious reality now before her.

The room smelled of fresh coffee, adding to her sensory disorientation.

At that moment, realization dawned—this was Luka's home. She jolted upright. Pulled down the duvet. She was still clothed. A deep sigh escaped her lips.

Her eyes fell on Luka, who stood watching her silently.

"Do you think I would take advantage of you? It may come as a surprise, but I like my women sober when I fuck them." His brows arched up.

She unfurled from the bed, not knowing how to respond to that. A part of her believed he would and not at the very least allow her to sleep in his bed without having his way.

"Do you know how much trouble you caused me?" he pointed at her with a cup of what she guessed was coffee in his hand.

She stood still, her hand rubbing at the back of her neck. She squeezed her eyes shut and tried to remember what had happened the night before, but all that greeted her was a searing headache. The pieces of her memory were like scattered jigsaw puzzles that she struggled to put together. She could only imagine the shenanigans she had gotten herself into while drunk. For one night, she relaxed and enjoyed the company of the boys. It made her forget all her worries. Heat rose to her cheeks as the humiliation flooded through her.

"New rules to the contract. Never drink alcohol when I'm not around. Can't have you blabbing your little mouth."

"I understand. I'm sorry." She nodded, acknowledging his concern about keeping their contract confidential.

"Ana.." He began, his voice carrying a touch of intrigue. "Do you do drugs?"

Her composure momentarily faltered as her face flickered with surprise, caught off guard by the unexpected question, her mind racing to comprehend it.

"Excuse me, I'm–I'm a doctor."

He advanced closer, one of his hands buried in the pocket of his sweatpants. Though his voice was low, it didn't hide the weight they carried.

"How do you live in such a dump with all that money? I pay you 15,000 dollars per night and it should get you something better than that. I couldn't stand to be there for even a second."

Okay, there was a lot to unpack there. Luka had seen her house, and he had been so disgusted by it. Somehow he concluded that she did drugs because to him that was the logical explanation of why someone would stay in such a space.

Who does this man think he was? How can someone be so high up in their glitz tower and judge people? Yes, her house may seem like a crack house, but it didn't stop the humiliation she felt.

Ana swallowed hard against the tears that stung her eyes as she searched for the right words to articulate her thoughts. "I am sorry that my house may not meet your standard of living. Also, I don't do drugs. It's unfair for you to make such assumptions. Everyone has their struggles, and not everyone is born into wealth and privilege."

With a sense of wounded pride, Ana picked up her bag and walked out of the room.

The suddenness of her movement startled Luka, his gaze following her in disbelief. "What the fuck did I say?"

•.¸♡ . ♡¸.•

Ana emerged from the penthouse into the fading afternoon light. Long shadows stretched down the crowded sidewalks. Her heels clicked a muted rhythm, drowned out by the sounds of traffic and commuters rushing by.

The vibrant, bustling city blurred around her as she made her way down familiar roads. When the bus arrived, its doors opened with a welcoming beep. She climbed aboard, joining the motley mix of passengers seeking solace in the shared journey.

She stared at her phone screen, checking her balance and mentally calculating. She had paid Danny tuition fees for two semesters, and bought most of the books he would need. She didn't like being late and wanted her brother to have the best education. He didn't need to suffer like she did.

Then an intrusive thought swept over her, unbidden and uncontrollable. Just how long would she have to Luka's plaything? Before Danny graduated or before Luka grew bored? Which would come first?

Luka's words echoed endlessly, whispers of doubt and questioning her abilities, eroding the confidence she had built so carefully. She was not ashamed of where she grew up, of her home, but to invalidate her hard work with his assumption was something she never knew would anger her like that.

The bus approached her stop. Ana rose from her seat, feeling a tinge of melancholy as she prepared to face the challenges that awaited her at home. She had yet to deal with the issue of the redevelopment program the government was doing in her neighborhood. This was her grandmother's house. It doesn't make sense that they would evict people just like that.

As she walked down her street, she couldn't help but notice the vacant houses, their windows dark and lifeless. An eerie stillness hung in the air, making it seemed she was the sole occupant of the entire neighborhood. A sense of gravity settled within her, revealing the severity of the situation to be far greater than she assumed.

Ana unlocked the front door and stepped inside, dropping her keys in the dish by the entrance. Her heart leaped as she saw her father in the dim light of the hallway.

"Dad? You're back!" She rushed forward and threw her arms around him without hesitation. His clothes were wrinkled and stained, the buttons unevenly fastened, and his body tensed at her touch, but she didn't care.

Ana yearned for someone more experienced, someone she could lean on. All she wanted at that moment was not to carry this weight alone, feeling the burden press heavily upon her weary shoulders. And if it was the man who hated her existence, she didn't care. Sometimes an adult needs a bigger adult.

She stepped back, a chill crept up her spine as she looked up to meet his shifting gaze.

His smile was strained, not reaching his eyes—his face looked like he had been in a fight, and he lost. His left hand was wrapped in a stained bandage, spots of red seeping through.

"What happened to you?" her voice dropped to a whisper. A lump rose in her throat as she searched his face, so familiar yet somehow changed.

He retracted from her, "I'm fine. It's nothing."

She wanted to press further, but held her tongue. If she did, he might yell or something, and she didn't have the strength to do all that right now.

"Hungry? I went shopping yesterday. I can make you something." She dumped her bag on the couch and disappeared into the kitchen.

"Have you heard? They want to demolish these neighborhoods and we might need to move."

"Uhh... yeah. It's been on the news."

"Really?" she continued from the kitchen, "I had the chance to speak with one of the contractors–

"Ana, can you spare some cash?" He cut her off. "I mean, you must have had enough to go shopping."

She glanced at the vegetables and fruits that lay on the counter. They were not much, but it had been quite different from the bread and beans they fed on. There were varied meals she could make with those options. However, her father's preference for gambling and his reckless spending on Danny's welfare benefits hindered their stability. Even when the checks stopped arriving, his gambling addiction persisted without restraint.

"Look, I won't ask you if it was not life and death. These people–these people you don't want to cross them."

She paused, "You were gambling again? With what money?" then she realized. "The contractors said they compensated everyone in the neighborhood and I was sure they didn't give us any money, but... they did."

Ana's heart was torn between her love for her father and the knowledge that enabling his gambling addiction would only perpetuate their cycle of pain.

"I wanted to help our family. Once I cashed the check I got, I thought I would be able to double it."

"Dad! That money was supposed to help us find a new place."

"I would buy you and Danny a bigger house, I just–" he rubbed his bandaged hand across his time-worn face. His tone rose an octave as he spoke. "You must have something. How did you buy these groceries? Did you get a new job?"

"Yes, but I can't keep doing this. I can't keep helping you."

Enraged by her refusal, her father's face flushed with frustration. "Why? I am your father," his voice thundered.

"Then act like it."

In a moment of anger and desperation, he stormed towards Ana's room, determined to find any hidden source of funds. His hands fumbled through the belongings on her dresser.

"What are you doing?"

It happened so fast before she could react that he had found some money she kept in the pages of her books.

She rushed at him. "No, that's mine! I earned that myself!" She grasped at his hands trying to pry the bills from his fingers. He elbowed her away roughly in anger and frustration. "Get off me!"

In the struggle, his elbow knocked her in the eye. Ana gasped, clutching at her face.

Ignoring her, he grabbed the money and staggered out without looking back. She knelt there, tears streaking her cheeks as her faith in the man she had once called her father disappeared.

CHAPTER 12

Luka lounged on the plush leather couch in his lavish penthouse apartment, as a hockey game was playing. He was barely paying attention as it became a background noise to his thoughts. Which were consumed by Ana–the way she had left.

He prided himself for his bluntness and, *I don't care,* attitude. Perhaps he was too harsh on her? Clenching his jaw, he recalled the last words he had said to her before she stormed out - her eyes flashing with anger.

Whatever it was, it shouldn't bother him.

Most women would kill to be in her shoes, to have sex with a world-renowned hockey player, and still get paid for it. He knew many of his puck bunnies in the past were thrilled to jump into his bed.

Luka squirmed on the couch, unable to get comfortable as he tried to rationalize why he was so bothered by her. Sure, he needed her - no, not her- he needed her skills. She was just his physio - nothing more. He couldn't allow himself to feel anything deeper for her. Their work together depended on distance and objectivity.

•.¸♡ . ♡¸.•

The atmosphere buzzed with the sound of clanking weights and focused conversations. The team had a match in the next two days and part of the coach practice was for some gym time.

"Yo, can you spot me?" Jude pulled Luka's attention.

"Are you carrying all that? That's a lot for your weight."

"I made a bet with Pavel." Jude grasped the weight in his hands. He began his set with determination.

Luka stood by his head and held out his hand. He knew Jude won't go beyond ten but it would be fun to watch him try.

At that moment, Ana entered the training center. "Sorry I'm late." Her tiny voice cut through the metal clinking of the gym.

Luka's eyes wandered, drawn to her, for a moment diverting his attention from Jude.

"What's with the thick glasses?" Caleb asked as he and the coach crowded her.

She glanced away, muttering something Luka couldn't quite hear, but the worried tones of Caleb and the coach were unmistakable. Luka narrowed his eyes, trying to figure it out as she took off the glasses.

Ana's face was marred by a bruise, its vivid coloration ranging from deep purple to muted blue. Despite the injury, she wore a wide grin.

Jude's grip on the barbell weakened as his muscles quivered and strained. Rivulets of salty perspiration ran from his forehead, and yet he couldn't let go of the barbell without it crashing down on him.

Luka, oblivious to Jude's predicament, was transfixed by the sight of a petite woman walking across the gym floor with a bruise on her face but still wearing a bright smile.

It was none of his business. Ana was just his physiotherapist - paid to treat his muscle strains and sports injuries. Her personal life remained her own. And yet...

He was quick to notice how she avoided direct eye contact with anyone, keeping her head down. She moved with a tense, hurried energy, eager to avoid more questions or sympathy.

"Bro. Bro. Bro." Jude's strained tone conveyed urgency, which jolted Luka back to reality.

He grabbed the barbell and lifted it back onto the rack. "Sorry," he murmured.

"Sure, no problem. I almost died but no problem." He coughed out, trying to catch his breath.

"I knew you could not do it," Pavel called out from across the gym. "You owe me 20 bucks."

Despite his efforts to appear calm and collected. Luka couldn't shake the feeling of worry that had settled in his chest. He made a mental note to check on her later.

•.¸♡ . ♡¸.•

Later in the afternoon, Luka stood in front of the medic's office. He reached into his back pocket and pulled out the tube of cream for her bruises.

Just give it to her. No need to ask questions. it doesn't concern you what happened to her face.

He opened the door, words of greeting died on his lips. Caleb was already there, being the friendly, all loving, Captain applying a cream to Ana's cheek as she winced. A sharp pang struck Luka's heart at the intimacy of their posture and hid it behind an impassive mask.

"Am I interrupting?" Luka cleared his throat. "I came for my treatment."

Caleb looked up, nodding briefly before handing the cream to her. "She's all yours." He patted Ana's hand with professional familiarity as he stood. "Take it easy - ice and ointment, remember?"

"I will. Thank you, Caleb." She smiled warmly, oblivious to jealousy brimming in Luka.

He tucked the cream back into his pocket as Caleb left the room, waiting until the door clicked shut, before he spoke. "Seems everyone is concerned about you." His voice sounded rougher than intended, annoyed with himself for acting the hero when she didn't require one.

"I have never had someone care for me... it's kinda new." A smile played across her delicate features.

Inside, Luka seethed with frustration at his foolishness in coming here. She seemed to enjoy the attention. Why did he come here? His presence was unnecessary.

"My shoulder." He said with a bored, deadpan expression, and he climbed onto the cot in the middle of the office.

In haste, she got right to work and helped massage and remove the knot. "Does it feel better?"

Luka stared at the bruise on her eye, it had a distinct circular shape. Was she in a fight? The urge to ask what had happened was nearly overwhelming. But he had no right to demand explanations or meddle in affairs not meant for him.

So he remained silent even as his gaze flicked again at the bruise marring Ana's features. It appeared swollen and tender, surrounded by a faint reddish tinge indicating it was very recent. What happened between when she stormed out of his house and this morning?

Luka felt a surge of anger - and something else. But he tamped it down with harsh words. “Did you fucking slip and fall running out of my house last night?”

She said nothing.

He saw the hurt flash across her face but couldn’t stop himself. It was his way of pushing people away when unwanted emotions arose.

“You seemed chatty earlier with the captain.”

“I have a favor to ask of you.” Her voice went soft and cautious.

“Can you give me some advance for next month? I need to find a new place.”

Luka’s eyebrows furrowed.

“What exactly are you trying to pull here?” Luka clenched his jaw. “First you walk out on me, then you come in here asking for more money. Do I fucking look like your personal ATM?”

“No! I don’t think that at all. I’m grateful for what you pay me. It’s just I need to move or they will demolish my house but I’ll drop it. I’m sorry for even bringing it up.”

Luka sighed, running his hand through his hair. Why did she always have to be so compliant? It made his anger fade as quickly as it had risen.

He sat up, tilting her face up with a finger.

“Look at me. You don’t get to make demands. What’s in it for me?”

Fear flickered in her eyes as she swallowed, holding his gaze. “What do you want?”

"I want you to be my toy. I want to play with you."

"Okay," she said in a whisper.

Luka moved his hand from her jaw to fist her hair. "I am not going to be nice. I will break you and put the pieces back together, ruin you for anyone else. There is no going back. Am I understood?"

Ana's eyes flickered, but she nodded. "Yes."

"Yes, what?"

"Yes, sir."

CHAPTER 13

Ana perched nervously on the edge of the massive bed in the luxurious penthouse suite, her hands clasped tightly together in her lap. Her fingers ghosted over her bruises. She was dressed in a red silk button-down shirt, her braids tied in a ponytail.

The last time she was there, she didn't get the chance to take in the shades of cream and gold. It was decorated with elegant artwork adorning the walls. She didn't care much about art, but she knew her brother Danny would appreciate it and that was enough to have a limited knowledge about it.

"Here." Luka stretched out something to her.

It was a towel wrapped around an ice pack.

"Thank you." She pressed the cold compress to her eye. It must have looked pretty horrible for him to go through all this trouble.

Luka turned his back to her as he poured himself a glass of wine, not one but two.

Her uncovered eyes widened in shock as she saw Luka, holding a tall glass with one hand and extending it out to her with the other.

"I think what I have in store for you tonight is best with alcohol in your system."

Now her fears returned. She took the glass, setting the cold compress down. Despite the alcohol that scorched her throat, it couldn't erase the nagging feeling in the pit of her stomach.

What did he have in store for her? Her mind shuffled through several scenarios. Maybe he was going to tie her up or put her upside down and drown her as he claimed her body.

She fidgeted anxiously with her shirt hem, her gaze veering to the man in front of her as she wondered what sort of twisted fantasy he had.

Luka sat in an armchair across from her, his face expressionless, calmly drinking from his glass. Every passing moment seemed to stretch on endlessly, and the silence in the room was deafening.

He tilted his head, studying her. "You don't want to drink? You seemed to like alcohol when you went out with my teammates."

She didn't know how to reply to that. "Can we... get on with it?" There was no use lingering around.

"Eager are we?" He reached for the table beside him for a box, handing it over to her.

She swallowed hard. Her heart pounded against her chest. Slowly, she lifted the lid of the box. Inside was an object shaped like a pipe.

It was pink and shiny, with a bumpy surface. Her eyes widened in shock and surprise as she recognized it.

A cock ring.

Okay, so he wasn't going to have her drown and fuck her. That was great, but still, this was far more intense than she had bargained for. She had never used a sex toy before, and the sight of it sent a cold shiver down her spine. Conflicted feelings swirl with her, but it was too late to back out now.

"I've been imagining all the ways I could make use of this little toy." The corner of his lip curled into a playful smirk.

There was nothing little about it. It was long, seemed stretchy and would cover most of his length. The bumpy surface did concern her. She didn't want to imagine how it would feel inside, paired with his roughness.

Luka grasped her chin, tilting her face to his. "Having second thoughts?" His eyes glinted with heat, but his tone was serious.

"What color is the sky, Ana?"

She paused, holding her breath. If she said blue... everything would end. Their agreement, the sex, everything. She may as well be out of a job.

"Red."

There was a hidden part of her that thrilled at the thought of Luka using this on her, though she dared not admit that to herself. It was weird, insane even.

Luka Kuznetsov may be the most unemphatic sex-crazed maniac she ever met—she hadn't met any—-but she liked how he took control over everything.

"I'm not having second thoughts," she murmured. "I'm yours, to do with as you please, remember?"

"Take everything off and get on the bed."

CHAPTER 14

Luka regarded Ana as she undone her shirt and stepped out of her jeans one leg at a time. If she was nervous, she did not show it.

He stared at her, taking in the sight of her exposed flesh and tight curves, a sudden wave of tenderness washing over him.

He had imagined she might run out or back out, but instead, she obediently assumed the position he requested.

For the first time, he thought about doing it, missionary style, so he could watch her expression and maybe kiss her.

He paused, wallowing in that thought.

WHERE THE FUCK DID THAT COME FROM?

He had never desired that before. Missionary position would mean looking into her eyes as she moved against him, it would mean they would make love and not just fuck. It would open the doors to a lot of blurred lines in their arrangement. And kissing... he had never kissed anyone, ever.

Physical closeness didn't come naturally for Luka. Even his past relationships had been casual. Sex had always been a physical release for him. He never considered his partner's pleasure. Ana seemed different but Luka wasn't prepared to explore why she seemed different.

He pushed those thoughts on the back burner. He needed to deal with matters at hand and right now, that was ruining this woman for anyone else.

Luka got a rope and bound her hands to the bed and he arranged her to the position he wanted.

"Are you going to put that... in me?" She jerked her head to the cock ring on the bed.

"Yes, but first... you need to be punished. You don't get to walk out on me, especially when I have a game in two days."

In one swift movement, he slipped out of his belt and swatted against her butt's cheek.

She gasped at the sudden sensation.

He repeated the motion again and again, each time with a new intensity. Her body quaking.

"What is the color of my jersey?"

"Freaking... green." She said with gritted teeth.

"Beautiful."

She whimpered as his middle finger breached her tight and soaked walls, reminding her that he was the one in charge, the one to give orders and do what he pleased with her body. She held no power whatsoever.

Picking up the cock ring, Luka inched it up his length, feeling the rubber tighten around him.

He teased her entrance, knowing that with its wetness, it would be a smooth ride as he entered her. His growl of pleasure echoed in the air as he thrust into her tight pussy.

His eyes closed, feeling her warmth and almost suddenly his movements became more frenzied and intense.

Ana buried her face in the pillow, gripping the rope that still bound her to the bed tightly.

She bit down on her lips and squeezed her eyes shut, deliberately trying to control her arousal.

Luka told himself he didn't give a damn if she enjoyed this or not and yet he reached forward and tugged on her hair as he kept on grinding his hips.

"Tell me how it feels to have me stretch your pretty pussy?"

She whimpered, not answering.

He couldn't tell if she was really enjoying it or just masking her pleasure. Her body language said otherwise - her moans, her tight grip on his cock, and the salivation at the corner of her mouth all suggested that she was aroused.

"How does my cock feel inside you?" He repeated.

"Is the great Luka worried about his performance?" she retorted.

"Someone is bold." Luka cursed himself for caring one way or the other. He was here to slake his lust, nothing more. Ana's pleasure or lack thereof meant nothing.

The fact she didn't want to say something angered him. Luka slammed into Ana, grasping her hips hard enough to leave marks. His anger and frustration at her response had morphed into an insatiable need for domination; he wanted to take her to her limits until she submitted, pleading for mercy. It may be irrational to think about it–but still. Why did her indifference sting his pride? Why did he suddenly crave whimpers and pleas from her throat—demands that he satisfied the desire he sensed she willfully buried?

He shoved her face onto the bed. Repeatedly pounding in her. The stretchy ring around his length had made it easier for him to hold back from spilling into her.

A guttural sound escaped his lips as she bit down any moans from her mouth and her body contracted around him. It was like she was doing it on purpose.

Somehow it had become a competition. Ana held back and he wanted her to let go.

His mind traced back to the training center when she was standing close to Caleb and something dark overtook him.

His hand circled her neck. "Is this what you wanted? He rasped, biting down on her shoulder. "To provoke me like the little minx you are?"

Ana whimpered as he quickened his pace, each thrust harder than the last. Her breath came in shallow gasps as her body was wracked with exhaustion, yet she never begged for mercy. Never said stop. Never said the word blue.

Would he stop if she called out the safe word *blue*... Luka didn't know. What he knew was that he wanted to own her. Claim every inch of her. Make her scream.

He was too far gone in his quest to break her willful spirit. He wanted her to be enslaved by this wretched hunger that raged in him, and he would not be denied.

When Ana's eyes rolled back, a cry tearing from her lips, Luka grinned in savage triumph. He had driven her to the edge and now meant to shove her right over. To claim her before her defenses could rally once more.

With a final, brutal thrust, Luka found his release in a roar of satisfaction.

"Fuck." His grip eased on her hands as tremors coursed through him—only for her to collapse against the sheets.

She suddenly went limp. Panic seized his heart in an iron fist as he cursed, freeing her hands.

"Ana!"

No response.

Her eyes closed and her breathing was faint and reedy rather than the panting gasps of only moments before. Guilt and self-recrimination flooded Luka. In his anger and need to dominate, he had pushed Ana past her limits. Had hurt her, perhaps permanently.

Fuck. Fuck. Fuck.

Luka fumbled for his phone with a curse. Part of him screamed to call 911, but the very thought sent a jolt of fear through his veins. His celebrity status meant any emergency vehicles outside the gates of his home would draw media attention within moments. There could be no explanation for this that wouldn't destroy Ana's privacy in the process.

CHAPTER 15

Luka's heart pounded with worry as he hurriedly carried Ana into the hospital. He cradled her in his arms, her body limp against his chest, he traversed the hallway until he met the concerned gaze of Doctor Hernandez, an old friend, who had been alerted to their arrival.

The Doctor swiftly gestured towards a nearby stretcher. Luka carefully laid Ana down, "Easy." Dr. Hernandez grasped his shoulder. "Panicking won't help her now. We are going to examine her."

Panicking. That word caught him off guard. He was not panicking. He was pissed. Pissed at himself. Pissed at her. Pissed off by this unfamiliar feeling that made him feel like banging his head into a wall.

Luka sat in the sterile, fluorescent-lit hospital waiting room, he wore a cap pulled low over his eyes, the brim casting a shadow on his face as his fingers tapped on his knee.

Time seemed to stretch endlessly as Luka distracted himself by observing the people around him, attempting to blend in with the ordinary individuals seeking medical care. But his thoughts kept returning to Ana. The image of her limp body flashed in his mind.

Fuck. he did that. He did that to her.

Finally, the door swung open, and the doctor stepped into the waiting room. Luka's eyes locked onto the physician, hoping for some answers. Luka looked up, his eyes filled with apprehension.

"Do you want to tell me what the hell happened here, Luka?" The doctor whispered. "Look, I get it. You like it rough but seriously you gave her a black eye."

"That was not me. I never hit girls."

The censure in the doctor's eyes cut deep. Luka looked away, jaw clenched. "Fine. I may have lost control," he bit out. "Took my anger at her out in the cruelest way. And now..." His breath rattled in his chest.

He shook his head. "I knew it was a matter of time before you send one of your puck bunnies to the emergency room."

Luka wanted to defend himself but decided against it. "Just fucking tell me, Is she okay?"

"We've run some tests, and she's conscious now. From what we can tell, she experienced a fainting spell likely due to stress, anxiety." he glanced down at his notes, " and she is a bit malnourished."

"Malnourished?" What the hell does she use her money for? He knew very well, it wasn't for a new home.

"A little advice Luka, why not take it easy with this one. She is not one of your hockey opponents. Try a little foreplay, some kissing, some tender touches."

Luka physically cringed. God he hated those.

"I mean it. The fact you called me rather than an ambulance shows you realize that it cannot happen again."

Luka nodded, mute with the force of his remorse. He knew his friend spoke the truth. Knew what he had done was unforgivable, no matter the provocation or his own demons.

If he could trade places with Ana now and suffer so she did not—he would do so without hesitation, that was how he felt right now.

"I gave her some intravenous fluids and something to stabilize her condition," the doctor said quietly. "What she needs right now is probably rest."

He took a deep breath, his voice filled with concern. "Can I see her? Is she awake?"

The doctor nodded once more, his expression kind. "Yes, she's awake. You can go see her now. She's in Room 204 down the hall."

He thanked the doctor, his voice sincere, and then made his way down the corridor to Ana's room. The gentle creak of the door marked his entrance, and he was met with the sight of Ana, her eyes heavy with exhaustion but filled with recognition and relief at the sight of him.

Luka pushed open the door to Ana's hospital room with a sense of urgency, expecting to find her resting on the bed. Instead, the room was empty, save for a nurse who was tidying up. Concern knitted his brows, and he quickly approached the nurse.

"Where's Ana? The girl I brought in?" Luka blurted out, his voice laced with urgency.

The nurse pointed towards the exit, "She left a few minutes ago. You just missed her."

Luka's heart raced as he rushed out of the hospital room and into the brisk night air. The city outside was bathed in the soft glow of streetlights, the pavement glistening with recent rain. The late-night air was cool, and the distant sound of traffic filled the atmosphere.

He spotted Ana, her figure standing by a taxi, ready to climb inside. Determination welled up inside him as he reached her just in time, closing the taxi door before she could step inside.

Ana blinked in surprise, her tired eyes locking with his. "What are you doing?"

He took a step closer, the gravity of the situation etched across his face. "The night is not yet over, Ana."

She huffed, her exhaustion evident. "Are you crazy? I literally just fainted."

Luka's expression hardened, "And that's all the more reason I should take you. I can't bear the thought of something happening to you between here and your house."

"Are you worried?"

His brows furrowed. "No." he said sharply. Why the hell does everyone think that? "I'm worried over the fact that tomorrow's headline might read, hockey player Kuznetsov sleeps with his doctor and causes her death." He leaned forward, his tone firm. "Safewords are there for a reason, you know that."

"You are an asshole."

"I know. Now come with me, my car is over there." He turned, taking a few steps forward only to find Ana still in place.

"Say please."

Luka's temper flared, the signs of his frustration evident. He covered the gap between them, his eyes on her, hoping she would back down. She didn't.

Instead she folded her arms, a defiant glint in her eyes.

He breathed a long exhausting sigh. "Let me drive you... please."

"See that didn't kill you." she walked ahead, following the direction he had indicated.

The city lights flickered outside, casting a soft glow on the streets. The weight of the night's events lingered in the air, and Luka stole occasional glances at Ana, who sat beside him, her eyes heavy with exhaustion.

The journey was mostly silent, except for the soft hum of the engine and the occasional sound of tires on the road.

When they reached a red light, Luka's gaze lingered on her. The gentle rise and fall of her chest, the peaceful expression on her face—it was a sight he didn't want to disturb. The light turned green, and the car glided forward, but Luka kept driving in silence, content to watch her rest.

Finally, they arrived at his penthouse, the soft glow of the building's entrance a beacon of warmth in the stillness of the night. Luka shifted the car into park, carefully turning off the engine. He didn't want to wake her.

He unbuckled his seatbelt, stepped out of the car and silently closed the car door behind him. He approached the passenger side and gently opened the door. He marveled at Ana's delicate slumber, her breathing steady and calm. Cradling her in his arms, he ensured her head rested comfortably against his chest as he carried her towards the building's entrance.

The soft lighting in the room bathed her in a warm, golden glow as he laid her down on his bed, her figure a contrast to the luxurious surroundings. He covered her with a soft blanket, ensuring her comfort as she rested.

Luka remained by her side. Unable to do anything else. He sat in the shadows of the room, unable to tear his gaze from her. Luka was alone with his recriminations, his guilt and fear—and the woman who had become the intense center of everything.

His knuckles brushed her cheek with a feather-light caress, only realizing the intimacy of such a gesture when it was too late for restraint.

His hands froze inches from her face. He was such an asshole. Why was he so angry at her? Why did he want to punish her tonight? would this be the straw that would break their contract?

Would she wake up screaming blue, ending their arrangement or perhaps red? The unbidden question gave him no peace

His phone interrupted his thoughts. It was his agent. Luka crept out of the room, closing the door behind him.

"Hello, what is it?" He answered the call with hushed tones, not wanting to disturb the precious sleep of the woman in his bedroom.

"I have been trying to reach you for hours." The woman on the line spoke. "The plane has been waiting for you. These promotional events don't organize themselves, you know. Your sponsors are expecting you in New York tonight for that magazine photoshoot and interview."

Luka squeezed his nose bridge. He had completely forgotten about the intended trip in the aftermath of Ana's collapse and the long night he had spent keeping an anxious watch at her side. His stomach knotted at the thought of leaving now. He was an asshole, but not that much of an asshole to leave her.

"I had..." His hands combed through his hair. "I was occupied."

"Occupied? This photoshoot was part of the celebration of your return to the ice. Will you still make it? I could send a taxi to you in like 5 minutes ...."

"I'm afraid I won't make it," he said at last.

"What do you mean, you won't make it?" A heavy sigh escaped her, signaling the dangerous calm in her tone. "Your return to the ice after such an injury has been heavily publicized. You can't just decide not to show up on a whim."

Luka won't fail to forget that most of the media were the ones reporting negative stories about his recovery.

He could see the headline *star hockey player ends his career.*

Is this the end of Luka Kuznetsov?

Why this shoulder injury may be hard for the star hockey player to return to the ice.

Barely any of them said anything positive. Now he was back. They wanted a story.

"I changed my mind. I will be coming tomorrow with the team instead and head straight to the game."

"What should I tell them?"

"I don't care, just cancel it."

"And the breach of contract fee."

"Can I afford it?"

"Yes but–."

"Then pay it."

Another terse silence. His agent finally spoke up, a trace of worry breaking through her usual irritation. "Okay, is everything all right?"

Luka glanced over at his locked bedroom door. "No," he answered softly. "Not yet. But I intend to fix that."

"Do what you need to do. I'll handle damage control on this end. But the next time your personal life interferes with business, a little warning might be appreciated."

"Thank you, Agatha."

CHAPTER 16

Ana's eyes fluttered open slowly, senses returning one by one. She was lying on something soft - her bed? No, the sheets on this screamed of luxury. A damp cloth was pressed to her forehead.

"Finally the sleeping beauty awakes."

She straightened herself, rising to a seated position. "I thought you were taking me home?"

"I am not your chauffeur neither am I your caregiver."

She remained silent for a moment and murmured, "and yet you insisted on driving me."

"What was that?"

"Nothing." she pushed herself off the bed.

"You know I am supposed to be in New York right now."

"You had a game?" Her eyes widened. "I'm so sorry." She genuinely was. "I can leave, really. Hope it's not too late. I will be out of here in a second... I just need to find my shoes?" she said in a panic-stricken voice as she gathered her things.

Luka pushed himself off the wall and made his way to her. Ana was still talking when he turned her to face him.

Her body stilled. With his tight grip on both her arms, he examined her face. Then he freed her, taking a step back.

"Not a game but It doesn't matter anyway." He pivoted, waving his hand. "Come."

She was hit by the sweet aroma of something cooking. She couldn't quite place the scent, but her stomach grumbled in response, reminding her she hadn't eaten since yesterday.

When she stood in front of the kitchen island. There were two dishes. "This... is for me?"

"Sit."

She hurriedly pushed out a chair and took in the salad and chicken before her.

"This is quite delicious." She said after a couple of bites, "Did you make it?"

He gave a curt nod.

She didn't expect him to answer, but even less expected him to say yes. "I thought Someone like you ought to have a nutritionist or a chef handy and ready."

"I do have a chef."

"So the chef made this?"

"No."

Ah

He had cooked... For her. No one had ever done anything for her. She should faint more often.

She stared up at him, eyes narrowed into slits. He focused on his meals and not spared her a glance. Without warning a thought rang in her head. Could it be that Luka might like... her?

Like he had heard her thoughts, he shot her a gaze, catching her off guard and made the half-chewed chicken get stuck in her throat. She coughed and sputtered, trying to clear her airway.

Luka passed a glass of water to her and stared. His brows furrowed and his expression tightened, like he was trying to figure something.

"Sorry." She said, finally founding her voice.

He sighed, setting his fork down. His hands clasped together as he spoke in a cold tone.

"Last night... I will admit I may have pushed too far, but I will need you to take care of yourself better. I have too many things to worry about and I can't add you to that."

It was understandable. *Her father used to say the same thing. Take care of yourself and your brother. Don't make me worry. Don't be a bother.*

But Luka... he might be mean, cold hearted and an asshole but there was something in those icy blue eyes that told her otherwise. Or maybe it was her wishful thinking, that she had captured the attention of someone like him.

"I have a game in a few days. I don't need you till then, so go home, clean up, or whatever."

She nodded and continued eating, then paused. "Should I come to the game then?"

"Nope. I can't have you fainting on me."

"No, I mean like a medic." She was still his doctor, despite this crazy arrangement they had.

"You won't be needed. Many medical staff will be on site."

"Okay then. Anyway, thanks for this. I did not expect it. I hate eating alone, the silence and I don't know. It makes me think a lot and I don't like thinking a lot."

Luka leaned back, his hand wrapped against his broad chest. "Why do you do that?"

Her cheeks puffed out as she asked, "Do what?"

"Hold back." His hand tapped against the marble counter. "I'm 90 percent sure I haven't made you cum since we started this," he gestured between them.

She set down her fork and finished chewing. "I find it weird if I'm being honest. We are not together and, whether I like it or not, you are paying me for sex. This is business."

Luka chewed the corner of his lips and looked away, not saying a word.

Ana tried to get a read on his expression and couldn't. She had always seen Luka in two expressions; boredom and anger. In this one he wore, his jaw was clenched, but his nostrils flared. This was new. Was he angry? Offended? She quickly added, "It's probably the same reason. I think you don't like kissing, it's easier."

"ya dovol'no konkurentosposoben, ya zastavlyu tebya vykrikivat' moye imya ili umeret', pytayas."

"That's such a long word. What does that mean?"

"Nothing. I get it." He brushed his curls off his forehead and pushed himself away from the table. "Close the door when you leave."

which translated to I am quite competitive. I will make you scream my name or die trying

•.¸♡ . ♡¸.•

Ana had remained in her office at the training center. She had been catching up on Luka's medical records. Screams reached her ears. She knew most of the players were out of town and that only a few staff, Juniors, and college hockey prospects frequented the facility.

"What's going on?" She asked, peeking out of her office.

"The game is about to start," Lily called out.

Lily was the younger sister to Caleb and the self-appointed social media manager for the Crestmont Giant.

She was a few years younger than her and had the most beautiful blond hair.

Ana walked towards them and settled onto the couch in the coaches' office with a few of the other staff, preparing to watch the game on the large TV screen. Though she couldn't be out there during matches, she still felt invested in the team's success.

"I should have been there right now. It is not even far." Lily said.

Apparently the city they were playing in was 2 hours away by car.

Lily continued, "But I just had to have classes and for what? the professor canceled at the last minute."

Ana smiled at the thought of Caleb insisting she prioritize her college education before her social media job. She found it fun watching them bicker like siblings.

Ana settled on one of the chairs and kept her attention on the screen.

The players took the ice for warm-ups. Luka looked focused and ready. She felt pride swell in her chest at seeing the results of long hours of hard work and patience from every member of the team. The comeback of a star like Luka Kuznetsov was sure to electrify the fans.

But when the screen flashed to live coverage, Ana frowned. The players were still milling about rather than taking their positions for the puck drop. An uneasy murmur ran through the assembled staff. After several minutes passed with no change, panic began to claw at Ana's insides.

"Something is wrong." Lily's voice confirmed her suspicion. "Where is Luka?"

The TV cameras showed the players on the bench. They looked confused. They were looking up and turning their heads, trying to figure out what had caused the delay. The commentators talked about what might be wrong. They wondered if the scoreboard had had a problem, if a player had been hurt, or if a machine had broken. But they didn't really know. They couldn't figure out for sure what had really caused the game to pause.

The air strained around the training center as a phone rang, cutting through the tension.

Ana picked the call after finding out it was the coach calling.

"Doctor, you have to get here. It's an emergency."

CHAPTER 17

The Crestmont Giants huddled together in the locker room. Excitement was heavy in the air as the roaring screams of fans could be heard. Luka and the other players adorned their gear, tightening laces, fastening pads, and fitting helmets over their locks of hair while the coach delivered the same motivational speech he'd been giving since Luka's junior league days.

However, Luka found it hard to pay attention, not because of the content but because the coach's voice sounded distant and muted, as if he were underwater. His fingers trembled as he struggled to lace up his skates, fingers numb and clumsy.

Pavel noticed Luka's distressed and for a moment, their eyes met in silence. But Luka quickly averted his gaze, hiding the vulnerability that his teammate had spotted. He clenched his fist, determined not to let his nerves get the best of him. With a deep breath, he pulled up his gloves, masking his inner turmoil with a mask of confidence.

"How about we go in there and show those kids how we do it," the coach hollered. "Kuznetsov! you ready!"

Luka offered a reassuring nod and a small, encouraging smile.

They all got ready and were ushered out of the locker room. The lights had been dimmed in the arena so that only bright green lines on the ice rink stood out from the dark shadows. The smell of fresh popcorn filled the air as they made their way into the tunnel and onto the ice. The crowd roared when they saw them, loud enough to make a person's ears ring. Some people cheered for them, but many more yelled insults.

Luka tried to focus on his familiar warm up routine, they had about 30 minutes to get ready before the actual game would start.

30 minutes was enough for him to push through whatever he was feeling now. He was better, his injuries had been good for months. Why was he still getting panic attacks before every game?

He noticed his stick handling lost its usual precision. Shit. This was bad.

There was a tightness in his chest, making it difficult to catch his breath. Despite his best efforts to stay focused, the doubts lurked in the corners of his mind grew louder and more insistent.

Caleb, the captain, skated over, with a calm "you good?" while placing a hand on his shoulder. "You're sweating man."

The words barely penetrated Luka's clouded mind. The suffocating anxiety weighing down on him. He yearned to take control, to be the star player he knew he could be, but the cheers from the crowd had transformed into an overpowering noise, reminiscent of the haunting voices that tormented him during his lowest times.

Feeling overwhelmed, Luka veered off the rink, heading straight for the locker room. He needed a moment to collect himself. The sounds of the arena faded into the background as he locked himself in the bathroom, his rapid breaths echoing off the tiled walls.

Inside the confined space, Luka stared at his reflection in the mirror. He searched his own eyes for the fire that once burned brightly within him. But all he could see was uncertainty and fear.

"Kuznetsov. What the hell is going on?" the coach asked, finding him in there, his back hunched over a sink.

Luka tried to respond, but his voice came out as a choked whisper. His heart was racing and he couldn't shake the feeling of impending doom that had settled in his stomach.

"You look like crap." The coach came over and put a hand on his shoulder. "You may have to sit this one out."

He closed his eyes and focused on his breathing, taking deep, slow breaths and trying to push aside the fear that threatened to consume him.

"No. Just get the doctor. I need Ana."

CHAPTER 18

Luckily, the game was about 2 hours away from Crestmont city but the fact that Luka's agent had a jet ready, Ana had arrived in ten minutes.

A cab waited for her at the airport and in another five minutes, with lots of traffic laws broken, she arrived at the Arena.

She grabbed her medical bag from the passenger seat, fumbled with her phone, which suddenly began ringing. It fell to the ground with a crack, because why not?

She cursed under her breath–she didn't curse, instead the word she muttered under her breath, "shoot, shoot."

Ana squeezed her eyes shut, breathing deeply to quell the rising panic. You can do this. It's just another patient, even though that patient was supposed to be playing a live game right that minute.

"Hello, coach. I'm here." Her voice hiked up as she answered the phone.

Ana rushed inside and luckily found the coach, who guided her. She was disheveled, her lungs were burning from the rush, but she was doing her best to project professional confidence.

The sight that greeted her brought her up short. The locker room was a contained chaos, with staff buzzing with frenetic energy yet achieving nothing.

Luka sat at the eye of the storm, wearing boredom-like armor as organizers, medical personnel, and who knew who else circled with questions, assessments, and useless chatter.

He wasn't injured, as she had thought. Instead, he looked fine. Perfectly fine.

Why was she called then?

His gaze found hers through the sea of people, one brow lifting as if to say, *Well, what kept you?*

She shot him a confused look, edged her way through the sea of bodies, and crouched at his side. "What seems to be the problem? Did your shoulder act up or something?"

He leaned close, dropping his voice. "There is no issue. At least, not a medical one." Then he gestured for his coach, who came by his side. "I need ten minutes. Get everyone out."

For a moment, the coach's gaze fixed upon Luka, lingering briefly on his star player's shoulder before yielding to a resigned sigh.

"No need for concern, everyone. Mr. Kuznetsov seems in perfect health. Now, perhaps we might have a few minutes of privacy while his doctor checks on him," he announced. "We have fifteen minutes until the game actually starts so no time to waste."

The room emptied with almost comical speed, leaving Luka alone with Ana.

He stalked towards her.

She froze, not out of fear but nervousness and... something else. She wished for numbness, but her senses remained too heightened, anticipating the passion and intensity, her body ached for and her mind fought against.

His touch, his scent, the fire in his eyes as he gazed at her like some conquest.

She took a few steps back, but Luka matched his steps with hers. She was so absorbed in getting away from him that she didn't realize when her back hit a wall.

"Luka... You want to do this here and now? This is crazy."

"Yes. Yes, I am." His hard body pressed insistently against hers.

He gripped her hands, pinning them above her head, and bit down on the fluttering pulse at her throat. He nestled against her neck, nibbling on her shoulders, before moving to knead her breast over her shirt. It didn't take another second for him to reach underneath her shirt. His fingers found the clasp of her bra and unclipped it.

Luka pushed up the hem of her shirt, exposing a round, beautiful breast perked with desire. Leaning forward, he took one in his mouth and sucked gently before releasing it to trace patterns along its peaks with his tongue. Her breath quickened as she felt his warm breath against her skin.

Unhooking his belt with one hand while the other still held hers over her head, Luka dropped his pants to his knees as he couldn't kick them off without removing a shoe or even loosening a lace.

He ran his hands over her, erasing any clothes still left between their bodies.

She braced herself when he reached down between her thighs and slipped one index finger into her entrance. The abrupt intrusion surprised her, but a moment later, he added another finger.

A moan escaped her mouth as he began to move his finger in and out of her, pushing her to new heights.

She was wet, that the sound of his finger sliding in and out of her filled the room. He rubbed his thumb over her clit in slow, lazy circles, driving her insane.

Her eyes glanced at the door, torn between hoping no one would interrupt them, and fearing what might happen if they were caught.

"Eyes on me."

He grabbed hold of her face, none too gently. His fingers sunk into her cheeks as he stared into her eyes.

The tension in the air was more than just an abstract concept; it was a living, breathing entity, manifested in his body as she saw the raw hunger burning in Luka's blue eyes.

Then, without warning, he leaned in and kissed her, his lips meeting hers in a clash of heat and desire.

CHAPTER 19

It wasn't so much as a kiss... more like he devoured her mouth.

Ana froze as Luka wrestled against her tongue. His eyes weren't closed, but his lashes lowered like he still wanted to see her. His tight hands were on her jaw as he forced his tongue into her mouth, taking her breath.

He kissed her with a desperation that felt like it would tear her apart. His mouth moved over hers hungrily, fervently, as though his very survival depended on the taste of her lips.

His hands gripped the nape of her neck, tilting her face up to meet his hungry kiss. She gasped into his mouth, pulse skittering as he nipped at her lower lip with a growl. Heat licked at her veins, pushing aside any lingering doubts or second thoughts.

She stared up at him with wide dark eyes, lips parted in surprise at the raw passion of his unexpected kiss.

Luka turned everything into a competition, and for some reason, this was no different.

He lifted her by the back of her thighs. Her legs wrapped around his hips as he pressed her into the wall, pausing a breath away to stare into her eyes.

Luka would make certain she screamed his name and begged for release. His name, not his money. The thought filled him with a primal satisfaction Luka didn't care to examine too closely. All he knew was that for once in his life, a woman's pleasure suddenly mattered more than his own—and there was no going back from this. No escape from Ana.

"I want you to climax for me."

She clutched at his shoulders, nails digging in as he hoisted her up, her legs around his waist. A lot was going on at the same time. She almost didn't catch his words.

"What?" She breathed out, a bit dazed.

His lips blazed a trail of fire down her throat, the rasp of his stubble sending shivers across her sensitized skin.

"Don't fucking hold back." He grunted against her ears.

"Okay..." The word buried as he kissed her again.

His kiss turned rough and possessive when she whimpered into his mouth. She could feel it, something unfolded within her. There was no time to think about that now, as every touch sent shivers down her spine, and left her trembling with desire. She stiffened at first, then relaxed and moved instinctively in time to each smooth thrust. The dance between them became a dual seduction.

She moved against him, discovering nerve endings that she never knew existed. He withdrew his cock and pushed back in her again- harder and faster until breathing became difficult for both of them.

He broke away from the kiss and looked into her eyes, his own dark with lust.

A flicker of realization passed between them, their defenses were crumbling like sandcastles washed away by the tide, but it didn't matter. The flames of passion consumed them in a fiery embrace that left them breathless and gasping for more.

"Fuck, Ana."

His lips found the nape of her neck, tenderly kissing her soft skin as they moved together. He pounded into her, stealing her breath and coherent thought.

The intensity kept mounting until Ana felt herself tumbling off the edge. As she moaned out in pleasure, he grabbed her tightly and held her against him as her orgasmic waves rocked through her body.

His forehead rested against hers. They breathed each other in, their mouths almost touching in anticipation, restraint hung by a fragile thread.

One hand against the wall, the other on him, her heart pounded, and her mind spun with the aftermath of her orgasm. She had wanted to say something. Her thoughts had been reeling but the words wouldn't come. Instead, she had simply looked up at him.

He set her down to her feet, stepped away and stared at her, a question in his gaze.

A knock on the door.

"Kuznetsov! Your time is up. Everyone is waiting."

"Yes. I'll be right coming out," picking up his jersey and the rest of his clothes, he got himself dressed.

She watched him leave the room without a glance. From his relaxed stride and blank expression, you'd think they'd just been discussing the weather.

•.¸♡ . ♡¸.•

Ana was filled with anticipation as she waited behind the bench of other trainers and assistants. She'd seen glimpses of Luka's practices, but this was the first time she would watch him compete in a real game.

The arena was alive with energy and the sound of fans screaming as the teams hit the ice. Her eyes quickly found Luka on the rink, with the number 24 highlighted on his back. He glided across the ice while displaying a mix of agility and passion, reminding viewers of his commitment to return to the game.

The game moved quickly, almost too fast to follow, but whenever Luka gained the puck, Ana's breath caught in her chest. He dominated the ice as though born for it alone, firing shot after shot at the goal.

During the second, a scuffle erupted into thrown fists. Ana gasped as players shoved and grappled, helmets knocked awry. Before panic overwhelmed, the referees intervened and broke up the fighters. She spotted Luka skating clear, helmet intact, and released her held breath in a rush. She knew the dangers of the game, but seeing such violence shook her.

Late in the third, score-tied, Caleb rifled a shot past the goalie's glove for the go-ahead goal. The arena erupted. Two minutes later, Luka scored a goal with an assist from Pavel.

The final buzzer sounded. Ana cheered until her hands stung, joy and pride swelling her heart.

•.,♡ . ♡,.•

Amid the shouting and cheering, Ana stood off to one side of the locker room, feeling uncomfortable as she watched the players celebrate victory; it was their world, not hers—she could only watch, never join in.

Deep down, Ana longed to be a part of that chaotic family she witnessed in the locker room. It must be peaceful to know someone would always have your back.

The cocky smirk on Luka's face as he received congratulations from his teammates and coaches made her grateful for any small part she had played in his return. Maybe hockey was more than just a sport to him.

A hand grasped her shoulder, startling her from bittersweet reflections. Ana glanced up into Coach's broad, weathered face—usually stern, now creased with a smile. "Well done," he said simply.

She blinked in surprise. "I'm sorry?"

"Don't think we aren't aware who's responsible for getting our boy right on track. He is himself again." His eyes flicked to Luka, now laughing as he twisted free of an exuberant the captain embraced. "You should have seen him earlier. He was a wreck. He owes you more than most will ever realize does this team."

Ana swallowed hard, a rush of warmth chasing away the ache inside. "I only did my job. Luka did the rest."

Her job, God, If only he knew. If only anyone knew.

"Is that so?" Humor deepened the smile lines around his eyes. "You are not the first physio that tried to treat him. Everyone concluded he was fine, but we all saw it, after his surgery he didn't play like himself, not until you. You see my dear, Kuznetsov plays with his head and when something is bothering him, it translates into his game. So maybe all you did was your job as his physiotherapist but it helped." He gave her shoulder an affectionate squeeze before moving off to corral his players.

Across a sea of bobbing heads and spilled champagne, Luka's gaze locked with hers. The riotous celebration faded into the background noise; at that moment, she understood why he was so fixated on his pre-game ritual. Hockey was his life, he could not take chances. She wanted to tell him she would come. Anytime he needed her, she would be there.

CHAPTER 20

Today, instead of going to work early, Ana planned to find a new place to stay. Every day she'd go to work and feared she would return to find her home destroyed. So, after washing up, she got dressed in front of a vintage mirror that belonged to her mother. Her skin had healed and no traces from the bruise, that was one thing she was thankful for. There was no need to pack layers of concealers.

Shuffling into her handbag, she took out a lip gloss and twisted the cap off, bringing the applicator to her lips. As she stared into the mirror, her lips seemed to stand out more, reflecting back all the sparkle from the lip gloss.

It felt as if they were still alive and tingling from Luka's kiss; she remembered how her body reacted when he touched her, kissed her and held her hair in his hand. Never before had she experienced a kiss so intense and passionate.

She paused, and opened her eyes to stare at her reflection. Her mind rang with the questions, What was that about? What had that kiss meant? Luka had never kissed her before. Why did he start now? Did he feel something more for her, or was it just another part of his ritual? Why did it affect her so much? God that orgasm. The thought made her suck her bottom lip between her teeth.

Focus. This was Luka Kuznetsov she was talking about. Despite her wishes, she had let herself go, and he took her to deep depths. She feared she might come out more broken than she was.

Her body jerked when a loud crash sound came from downstairs. Her heart was pounding in her chest, as she strained to listen for any other noise. For a moment, there was only silence, and she wondered if she had imagined the noise. Or were the construction people approaching her house.

Standing at the door of her bedroom, "Dad?" She called out, maybe he had returned.

No response.

She walked down the stairs to the living room and found three hefty men standing, staring up at her.

One of them flashed his golden tooth.

"Ana, go back to your room." Her dad's voice tore through the tense air.

Her eyes shifted towards her father, his face bloody as he cowered beside them.

"Dad?"

"You have such a pretty daughter, and you hid her from us?" the one with a full head of hair took a step. "Come here baby girl, we won't hurt you."

She glanced at her father before turning to run back upstairs, but behind her heavy footsteps pounded and in no time, she was caught.

"Get back here." One of them, she couldn't tell who but grabbed a handful of her braids and yanked her backwards.

A strangled sound escaped Ana's throat, fear and rage leaving her frozen in equal measure as he yanked her back, shoving to the ground next to her father.

They watched as the intruders ransacked the house, tearing apart her belongings and throwing things onto the floor. A sense of violation and helplessness enveloped her.

Her body shook with fear as one of the enormous men loomed over her, casting a menacing shadow. His arms were like tree trunks and his gaze was intimidating. "We don't want to hurt you but you see, your father owes us a lot of money and we caught him trying to flee town." His calloused fingers stroked her cheek, "You must take after your mother because you look ravishing."

"Take her. Take her and leave me." The man croaked.

Ana tossed a look to her father, did he just say that? Her eyes filled with tears but she willed herself not to let a drop fall. She wouldn't shed any more tears for him.

"You see, the kind of person you have as a father. It's not your fault. Fathers are all shitty." Tilting his head to where her father cowered against the wall.

She swallowed. "Please, I can pay you."

A snicker came from another of the men. This one was tall and had a lot of tattoos on his face. "How much can you possibly have?"

She pulled out her phone and showed them the balance. "I was supposed to get a place since this house will be demolished soon."

"I knew you were holding out on me." Her father spat in her direction.

She ignored him. They were in a mess because of him and, as usual, she was the one to help him. What kind of life was she living, if it meant cleaning up her father's mess every five seconds?

The thugs exchanged a glance and handed her the phone. “Send it now.”

Ana’s hand trembled against her phone as she transferred everything she had to the phone.

“Done. So you would let us go right?”

His face scrunched up and he shook his head. “The money was for the boss. Now, what do you have for us?”

His gaze raked her body lewdly.

Revulsion flooded her, a chill settling into her bones. She was trapped, unable to escape the terrible consequences of her father’s gambling. All that remained was a choice between evil and hoping for some miracle, even though it might never come.

“I— I don’t know what—“

“Come on, don’t act coy. Pretty girl like you, having that sort of money.” His hand dropped to her thigh, “let’s have a taste?”

Her phone rang.

"Wow you must be popular?" one of them said as he passed the phone to the big guy.

He chuckled, his gold teeth flashed again. "Who is this? L.K? You got a boyfriend?”

Ana squeezed her eyes shut, silently she prayed for a miracle.

They hung up the phone at the second ring.

CHAPTER 21

The morning sun peeked over the horizon, casting a warm golden glow on the streets as Luka laced up his running shoes. His night had been anything but restful, filled with swirling emotions that left him feeling both exhilarated and confused.

When Luka got stressed, he would exercise, but today was a rest day. The coach had warned the players not to come to the training center, so at 5am he went for a run. He had been jogging for hours now, through the familiar paths of the park, his footsteps matching the beating of his restless heart.

Like a bolt from the blue, images of Ana's face flashed in his mind. The way she looked at him before he kissed her, the softness of her lips against his—everything about that moment replayed in his thoughts like a broken record. He tried to push those thoughts away, to compartmentalize them, but they kept creeping back, refusing to be ignored.

"Fuck. I shouldn't have kissed her," Luka muttered to himself, his breath coming out in short gasps as he picked up his pace. "Don't think. Don't think. Don't think."

The truth was, Luka didn't know how to process what had happened in the locker room . He did what he did best, push it down. Bury it. Run.

So he ran.

He ran to escape his thoughts, to keep himself busy, hoping that if he kept moving, he wouldn't have time to think about a woman he was literally paying for sex. The rhythmic pounding of his feet against the pavement provided a temporary distraction, a way to numb the confusion and uncertainty that swirled within him.

As he rounded a bend in the park, he felt his body protesting from the exertion. He was exhausted, physically and emotionally. For a fleeting moment, the girl who had kept him up all night was pushed to the periphery of his thoughts.

When he reached the end of his run, Luka slowed to a stop. He took a moment to catch his breath, wiping the sweat from his forehead and trudge wearily towards his luxurious penthouse.

The path that led to his building was lined with towering skyscrapers and bustling streets. When he arrived at the entrance of his penthouse, and with a deep breath, he pushed open the heavy doors and stepped inside.

He was ready to get into his shower and spend the day watching some television. All that plan went to smoke when he spotted a man waiting in his living room.

Vlad was an average-looking man, lacking any striking features that would make him stand out in a crowd. He had a medium build, neither too thin nor too muscular, with an unremarkable height that blended in seamlessly with most people.

He had a head of dark brown hair that was neatly combed back, and his clean-shaven face bore an air of self-importance that seemed to match his position as the chairman of the NHL. His eyes flickered with a hint of arrogance, a light shade of brown that matched the color of his hair. It was a look that he inherited from their father, a trait that was permanently etched onto his face like a badge of honor.

Though they were brothers, there was a vast difference between Luka and Vlad. Vlad took after their father with a cocky attitude and Luka took after their sweet and kind mother.

Well, he liked to believe there was a time he was just that.

Vlad rose from the couch, arms spread, a hesitant smile on his face. "Is that how you greet your brother?"

Luka scowled, fighting the urge to turn around and walk right back out the door.

"What are you doing here? How the hell did you even get in?"

His brother's smile faltered, his hand dropped to his side. "If you answered my phone call once in a while, I wouldn't have bothered." At Luka's stony expression, he sighed. "I wanted to congratulate you on your return to the ice. That's what everyone is talking about nowadays. Your win against the bulldogs was incredible, definitely one for the books."

"It was a team effort."

Luka stalked into the kitchen, irritation simmering in his veins. He yanked a bottle of water from the fridge, and took a big swallow, silently wishing it was something stronger.

He approached the kitchen counter, standing opposite Luka. "Look, I am not the bad guy here. In fact, I am actually happy you found your spark back, but as the chairman of the

NHL, I certainly do not appreciate that one of my games was delayed."

Vlad stood there, his hands shoved deep into his pockets as he widened his stance. "Get your shit together or you are off the ice."

"You wouldn't dare."

He nodded. "I could make your life miserable."

Luka scoffed. "It won't be the first time."

"Jesus Christ." He groaned and turned his back to Luka, his shoulder relaxed. "Fine. I screwed up. Get over it. Besides, look around. You made it. You fucking love hockey and, not to forget, you are one of the best players in the league."

"I don't play hockey because I love it," he had said in Russian, their mother tongue. He had been slowly learning it.

Vlad craned his neck, glancing at him over his shoulder. "You are speaking Russian? We have not spoken since mom..." His voice trailed off.

Luka squeezed his eyes shut. The morning had been particularly trying, leaving him mentally drained and emotionally exhausted. The physical exhaustion he had put himself through earlier only added to the weight he was carrying, making it feel as if he were dragging himself through quicksand.

"Just... go."

Vlad sighed once more, walked over to him and tapped on his shoulder. "Dad is expecting you this weekend."

Luka groaned as his footsteps headed out of the kitchen, a door opening and closing moments later.

Luka stood still for a moment longer in his sleek and modern kitchen, frustration still lingering from his brother's visit. The silence that filled his house after Vlad's departure was deafening, and it only served to amplify the unease he felt about the upcoming dinner with his father. The mere thought of being in his father 's presence again made his stomach churn.

Feeling the urge to escape the thoughts of his brother and avoid thinking about... her. He knew that he needed to find a way to release the tension that had built up inside of him.

A distraction.

He couldn't go for a run again, so Luka decided to call his friends. Surely, they'd have something fun to do. He dialed Pavel's number first, half-expecting the wildcat to be out partying despite their coach's instructions to take a rest-day.

Pavel's voice boomed through the phone, confirming Luka's suspicion.

"Hey, man! You won't believe the party going on here!"

Luka shook his head. "Of course."

"What's going on, K-Man?"

"First of all, don't call me that, and second of all, The chairman was just here, and I need some distractions."

"Wow. a personal visit from the big guy himself. Here is a crazy idea. Why don't you join me? These girls are hot for hockey guys."

Sounds of girls' laughs, muffled sounds of music were audible in the background.

He paused, mulling over the thought. He wasn't much of a fan of parties except if he threw them. Then again, Pavel's type of parties were usually a lot. This could be what he craved, the perfect distraction to clear his mind without getting caught up in complicated emotions.

Fuck it.

"You know what, sure. Why not? I will call Caleb and see if he wants to join us."

He hung up with Pavel and dialed Caleb's number.

Caleb picked up the phone after a few rings. "What's up?"

"Where are you now?"

"The center. The coach and I were reviewing the game footage, then I got roped in to teach these junior league players a couple of things. Many of them were asking of you, by the way."

As Caleb spoke, Luka's ears perked up, and he listened in on the subtle sounds in the background. Amidst the buzz of indistinct voices, he picked up on snippets of conversation, like a distant whisper in the wind. A particular phrase stood out from the rest—the coach's voice, inquiring about the team's doctor.

His curiosity was piqued, and Luka interrupted Caleb, asking, "Wait, Caleb, did I just hear the coach asking about the doctor?"

Caleb hesitated for a moment before responding, "Yeah. one of the kids got injured. Thankfully, it's not that bad, but Ana is not here."

Trying to mask his emotions, Luka asked casually, "What do you mean she is not there? It's almost noon. She should be at work."

"I don't know what to tell you man, the Coach was looking for her."

Luka's heart skipped a beat, concern flooded his mind once more. Since Ana started working as the team's physiotherapist, she had never missed a day of work. He couldn't shake off the memory of the only time she had been late—she came in with a visible bruise. Luka's protective instincts flared up at the recollection. He had never asked her about it, respecting her privacy, but it had been on his mind ever since.

Luka's brow furrowed with worry and stared blankly. His mind was torn between the desire to check on Ana and the reluctance to intrude on her personal life. The emotions inside him churned like a storm, uncertain and complicated.

Nonetheless, Luka's mind couldn't help but race with thoughts. Was she okay? What could be keeping her away from work? Was he overreacting?

Caleb's voice brought him back to the present. "Luka, are you there? Did you want us to meet up?"

Luka shook off his thoughts and replied, "Yeah, sorry, got a little distracted here. I'll call you in a bit."

After ending the call with Caleb, he stood there, contemplating what to do next. He would call her, find out if she was okay, and hang up. Nothing more.

He bit his lower lip and ran his hand through his hair, a subconscious habit that surfaced when he was anxious. He punched her number in and waited.

The call cut after two rings, meaning she saw it ringing and cut it off. Frustration and disappointment gnawed at him. He tried one more time but this time, the call didn't go through.

What the hell? Was she avoiding him? That thought fueled his irritation further. He hated the thought of being ignored, especially by her.

In a spur of determination, Luka decided to take matters into his own hands. He needed to know why Ana wasn't answering his call, and the only way to find out was to go to her house in person.

He picked up his jacket and dashed out of his house.

•.¸♡ . ♡¸.•

Before he got out of his car, he slipped on a cap, pulling it down to conceal his face. The last time he was in her neighborhood was at night. The last thing he wanted was to create a ruckus in broad daylight. He was a celebrity after all, and even though Ana didn't know a single thing about hockey; he wasn't sure about the rest of the neighborhood.

The street was filled with rubble as most of the buildings had been demolished. The destruction around him made it difficult to recognize the place from the last time he was there.

He navigated through the uneven terrain, carefully stepping over fallen bricks and debris. His movements became more purposeful, with a faster stride as he approached her house. Fortunately for him, the building still stood tall, amid the destruction that surrounded it.

His hand up, ready to knock before he noticed the door was slightly ajar, and when he opened it, his expression shifted.

Ana cowered in a corner while three massive bruisers loomed over her.

"Mr. Kuznetsov?"

They seemed surprised at the intrusion, but Ana's words caused the recognition to dawn as they spotted him.

"Kuznetsov, as in the famous hockey player?"

Another of the men responded. "Nah, don't be silly."

He took in the situation, the men hovering over Ana, as she curled up on the floor. A heavily bearded man whose face was covered with bruises sat still on the floor. He didn't know what to make of the situation. He knew he came for one thing–her.

"Hey. Who the hell are you?"

Luka ignored their questions and strode right past them to Ana's side, clutching her hands in his. "Are you okay? Did they touch you?"

"I... I am fine."

He managed to keep his expression neutral, but inside, a fiery rage blazed to life as he contemplated the possibility that they were responsible for her bruised eye.

The thugs exchanged a glance, hesitating—until the largest spoke. "We've got unfinished business with the little lady. Beat it, hotshot, before you get hurt." He held Luka's shoulder.

"I just came to take what's mine." He took hold of her hand and pulled her to her feet.

Luka couldn't afford another injury. The playoffs were fast approaching and the last time he played the hero–he paid the price.

Another came forward, pulling him by his shirt. "Who do you think you are? We are doing business here."

Luka glanced down to the man's hand and shrugged it off. "She is my business."

"Boss, this guy might be a hockey player. Hockey players are known to be a bit umm rough."

"Pff. Whatever. This is the real world. This pretty-faced boy doesn't look like he wants to get hurt." He shoved Luka against the chest with every word he spoke.

Luka let go of Ana's hands, turned to look at the man again and he launched himself at the man with a roar, swinging with pent-up rage and anguish.

Luka's fist smashed into his nose, bone, and cartilage crumbling under the impact. The man screamed as blood gushed down his face.

Another rushed Luka, this one seemed like the leader of the trio. Luka was thrown off guard by his speed and ferocity but managed to duck under a swinging arm, slamming his elbow up into a bearded chin. His teeth shattered, and the man went down.

The last of the brutes grabbed Luka from behind in a bear hug. The giant man tightened his massive arms, attempting to crush the life of the hockey player. But Luka threw his head back into the man's nose, simultaneously stomping down on an instep. The grip faltered and Luka slipped free.

Before he could regain balance, Luka was on him. He drove punch after punch into the man's face, feeling his nose crack under his fists.

Luka stepped back, chest heaving and hands slick with blood. The two men lay unmoving at his feet, barely recognizable.

He turned to who he presumed was the leader of the men with fire in his eyes. He remained standing, wiping blood from his mouth, before spitting out what Luka guessed was a gold tooth.

"Leave before I make you look like your friends here."

The man swore before he stumbled out of the house, the door crashing shut behind him.

In the middle of the trashed house, Luka stood, his eyes frantically searching for Ana. The chaos around him was overwhelming, with broken glass and overturned furniture littering the floor. He heard the sound of muffled sobs coming from the kitchen. With a sense of relief washing over him, he hurried towards the sound, his footsteps crunching on the debris below.

He stood at the door. "The coach was looking for you."

She had held up a knife to protect herself and it fell out of her hands the instant she saw him. "Are they gone? Are you hurt?" she reached for his hand, which was stained with blood. "This looks bad, do you think it broke?"

Luka scowled at her. "Stop."

"How would you play?"

"I'm fine." His voice was low and hinted at annoyance.

"How can you say that? You could have been injured?"

"Will you stop?! I'm fucking fine—and I'd be better if you stopped attracting gangsters and getting yourself into these messes!"

She blinked. "I didn't attract them, they broke in, and besides–"

He cut her off. "Right? And your black eye magically appeared. Seriously, woman, do you have some kind of death wish?"

Ana placed her hands on her hips, eyes sparking irritation. "I don't like your tone. Stop scolding me for things you have no clue about."

"Here is a fucking idea. Why don't you stop doing things that give me a heart attack and I'll consider it!" Luka glared at her, chest heaving.

Their eyes locked in a battle of wills, each refusing to back down. Luka could see the fire in her gaze, a reflection of the passion that mirrored his own. The more they stared at each other, the more he realized that it wasn't about her getting hurt but also the heaviness in the heart that followed.

Warning bells rang in his head. He took a step back, his voice was low and controlled as he said.

"If something happens to you, it affects my game too, you know... for my pregame ritual."

Luka caught the subtle shift in Ana's expression, a flicker of hurt that tugged at his heartstrings. A pang of regret washed over him, and he wanted to take them back, to erase the hurt he had caused, but before he could say another word, Ana spoke up.

"Right. Sorry, I forgot." She looked away for a moment, as if collecting herself, and then turned back to face him.

"Ana? Aren't you going to introduce me?" Her father's voice cut through the tense air.

From his vantage point, Luka towered over Ana, his attention was drawn to Ana's father, his badly beaten face twisted into a wide grin as he approached them.

He felt a surge of protectiveness wash over him and he stepped forward, placing himself between her and her father. His broad shoulders and imposing stature formed a wall of protection, a physical manifestation of his commitment to keep her safe.

"We haven't met but I am her dad and- umm... it's a shame we have to meet in this circumstance." He smiled, stretching his hand to him. "Did my daughter mention I used to play football back in the day?"

Luka peered at his outstretched hand, then back at Ana. She didn't spare so much as a glance at her father, but kept her gaze fixed to the floor.

Luka caught on to this and if she didn't care, he wouldn't care. He, of all people, knew because someone is your family and you love them. It doesn't mean they can't hurt you.

"Your daughter is coming with me," he said with quiet authority, leaving the man confused.

Then he turned to look at Ana's injured foot, concern etched across his face. Luka gestured to the foot that hung mid-air. "Can you walk on that?"

Ana had twisted her ankle when they yanked her down the stairs. "I think I can," she winced as she tested her foot on the floor.

Luka noticed the strain on her face as she tried to stand. Without hesitation, he made a decision and circled his strong arms around her body, lifting her up with ease.

"Wait.. what? Where are you taking my daughter?"

"I wasn't seeking your permission." There was a note of finality in his words, a sense that the decision had already been made and there was no going back.

She wrapped her arms around his neck, holding on tightly as he carried her out of the building. Despite her father's protests, Luka remained resolute.

When they reached his car at the end of the street, he placed her in the passenger seat and buckled her seat belt.

He could sense her eyes on him, searching his face for any signs of doubt or hesitation. But there was none. He was determined in his decision to protect her, no matter what it took.

With a serious expression, he climbed into the driver's seat and started the car.

"Where are we going?" She asked, her voice soft.

"My place, so I can keep an eye on you."

CHAPTER 22

Luka readied an ice pack for Ana, who rested her feet on a chair. Yet another moment where she paid for her father's actions. The last time was her brother. Her heart tightened as she recalled how her brother had lost his ability to walk. If her father had been a lot more responsible, if he made better decisions, she wouldn't be forced to send her brother to a boarding school because she couldn't trust to leave Danny alone with him.

Once, she held onto hope that their father, the man who used to make her feel secure, would come back and everything would be okay. He had a way of bringing harm into their lives, whether he meant to or not. It was safer to keep him at arm's length for now.

No matter how much she loved and cared for him, she needed to let her father go and accept that she had no one. Throughout her life, she shouldered responsibility, assuming the roles of wife after her mother passed away and being a mother to Danny leaving little time to live her life.

She had always been the caretaker, holding their fractured home together, but now, there was nothing left to hold on to, and she lacked the strength to keep trying.

Ana hoped to focus more on her life without waiting on the needs and broken promises of a man who, in the end, cared only for the bottle or the bet.

Luka's cold hand on her feet pulled Ana out of her trance.

"Let me." She reached for the cold compressor.

"I got it." He rested her leg on his lap and gently pressed the pack against her ankle.

She reluctantly rested back down against the couch and allowed him. Seeing him handle her with such care and delicateness was a far contrast to what she expected from him.

She looked at Luka closely, trying to understand him. He was hot and cold, rough and tender, all at once. It left her confused and her heart struggled to make sense of the contradictory signals he was sending. It was as if he was a mystery she couldn't quite solve, a puzzle that kept changing shape and for some weird reason she was attracted to him.

"Does it hurt?" His strong, deft fingers kneaded the sore muscles of her ankle, relief suffusing her body.

"Not a lot." She snuck another glance at the man focused on his task, warmth creeping into her cheeks.

He was handsome, all sharp angles and rugged features -stubble-shaded jaw and a lock of unruly hair fell across his forehead, making her fingers itch to smooth them back.

"I came to take what is mine." Luka's voice echoed in her head once again.

Mine. She mouthed the words.

Was she his? She wasn't anyone's. Definitely not her dad's, who only saw her as a bailout card.

The thought of her belonging to Luka comforted her. She would have someone to lean on, and it was oddly gratifying.

Even though that person was Luka Kuznetsov.

She would take it. Perhaps that's why she felt drawn to him - a deep-seated desire to be protected and claimed by someone. But the thought was unsettling, and she couldn't help but wonder if it was rooted in some sort of unresolved issue from her childhood.

She was so lost in her head that she didn't realize Luka had spoken and was now staring back at her. Their eyes met.

"Did you hear what I said?"

it had caught her off guard as she whisked her eyes away, mustered an awkward cough, desperately trying to conceal the embarrassment that had washed over her.

"Sorry... I didn't catch that—

"I said, you should know your place while you are here. The fact I let you stay, doesn't mean you should be lazy."

There was that familiar coldness in his tone again. It was good. She needed to remember her place. One of these days, his generosity would run out soon and what will happen then? She reminded herself not to get used to it.

Not to get used to him.

"Just like in the training center, you will keep up with my physical therapy. Besides, I feel better knowing you are here, anyway."

"Okay..." Her eyes flickered to her leg still on his thighs, his thumb gently stroking her skin.

This had to be the top rank of mixed signal. His harsh words and yet soft caresses against her skin.

"One more thing. You would only go to the training center and come straight here. I don't need to look for you when I need a good fuck. You can use any of the facilities, pool, and whatever, and also don't you think about stealing from me?"

Her brows furrowed, anger seeping into her voice. "I don't steal." She tried to snatch her leg off him.

His vein-etched hands clenched tightly around her slender ankle, forcefully drawing her closer. She slid against the leather couch as her body plunged back. She snapped to an upright position and was cut off to find how close their faces were.

The smart remark she had thought of died in her throat.

There was a long silence as those blue eyes bore into her, setting her body warm.

"What else?" she muttered.

"Don't expect me to play host. You fend for yourself in this place. I'm not here to cater to your whims and also don't invite anyone over without asking me first. This isn't a party pad."

"So, are these rules etched in stone or just written on a sticky note?"

His brows quirked up.

"Fine." She readjusted in her seat, her voice composed that alerted Luka she wanted to say something serious. "Can I ask a question?"

He let go of her leg, his head fell back against the chair. "I'm listening."

"This is crazy, it's just the last couple days have been crazy." She feigned a short chuckle, before she continued. "First you helped me with those gangsters, treated my leg, and now you want me to live here with you. There was the kiss and i know you don't kiss–

"Where are you going with this?" He interrupted.

"I don't know, I was hoping you would tell me."

"Not even for a moment should you believe that I am doing this because I have any sort of feelings for you," he rose to his feet, taking the ice pack to the kitchen area.

Though his back turned to her, his entire demeanor screamed fury.

Just as expected, she must have imagined it all. This was why she wanted to hold back because Luka would never look at her, heck he only saw her as a means to an end.

"I just wanted to make sure we are in the same place. We are nothing other than friends with benefits... although 'friend' is a stretch. Do you know this is our longest conversation that didn't involve you ripping my clothes off?" She teased.

There was a loud bang and Ana flinched.

Luka had slammed his hand against the countertop.

"What? Did I say something?" She didn't understand why he flared up. All she did was ask what seemed to be a reasonable question and then agreed with him.

"What the hell are you trying to do? Play some mind tricks at me." Luka returned, marching over to where she sat.

Leaning down, he held his index finger to her before tipping her jaw up to meet his gaze.

"You are mine. Your body is mine. The only reason you are here is because it will make *my* life easier. Don't try to think of anything other than that. You are nothing more than my toy, a means to get my head on track and a good fuck whenever I'm bored."

She sat still in stunned silence. She should have been offended by his words, but she wasn't. Instead, her body responded to his last words. Right now, she craved a *good fuck*. She craved him. Even if feelings were not involved, she might as well enjoy having him in her.

His brows furrowed, he was angry obviously but there was something in his gaze that sent a tingling sensation down her spine.

In almost a fraction of a second, there was a moment of vulnerability where his lashes lowered to her mouth, his eyes revealing a depth of emotion that left her breathless.

"You confuse me, Ana and it pisses me off." His voice came out low and raw.

She blinked, taken aback. *What does that mean?*

He stood upright and returned to his cold, unfeeling voice. "Your room is the second door upstairs on the right. I'm going to bed." He exited the room with a seething gait, climbed upstairs before closing his door with a loud bang.

God, what was wrong with her? This was absolutely mind-boggling.

She had let him use her in every sense of the word and allowed him to consume her in every way imaginable, leaving her feeling tainted and dirty. But the real torment was his relentless hold on her. Against her judgment, she had let go and let Luka take her to new heights and now she couldn't come down.

Ana slumped back against the leather seat and allowed the silence of the house to envelop her as she slowly came to the realization she was attracted to a man who saw her a fuck toy. She hated herself for it, but she wanted more.

CHAPTER 23

Luka stalked the length of his bedroom in the warm and inviting glow of two elegant lamps on the bedside table, his fists clenching with each turn.

Damn Ana, for putting thoughts in his head he didn't want or need. Their arrangement was simple - sex before every game. There were no feelings involved. None.

He dropped his head against the wall, swore under his breath and raked a hand through his hair. All this started in that locker room.

That kiss...why the hell did he kiss her like he was unable to stand another second without the taste of her lips? And for a moment, he forgot his one rule. No kissing. If it wasn't for his anxiety, he would not have needed her that day.

Now she was here talking about what it meant? Luka didn't know what any of his actions meant when he came to her.

Luka sucked in a sharp breath as memories of the last game against the bulldogs flooded his mind. He waited in the locker room, trying to ease his mind, and everything became a blur until she entered. Her presence was like a beacon of tranquility amidst the storm. Every noise around him faded into the background that day.

He couldn't explain the sudden calm washing over him. It was as though the mere presence of Ana had the power to settle his nerves and ground him in the present.

There had to be a logical explanation, that had nothing to do with love and there was.

It was normal for a patient to be relieved when they see their doctor.

Then how would you explain the living room incident? You wanted to kiss her again?

There was no logical explanation for that one. These thoughts were giving him a headache. This was ridiculous. She did this.

He was doing fine until she started planting ideas in his head, making him worried by disappearing, then appearing with bruises.

It was also in the way she looked at him, it pierced parts of himself, Luka had long kept locked away. He could feel, bit by bit, Ana chipping away at the walls he had built. Walls meant to keep out intimacy, love - anything that might distract him from the goal.

And that terrified Luka. The thought of a stranger having such a power over him and trusting them blindly they don't get tired and leave.

This was why he made these rules. If he didn't care for someone, he wouldn't care if they left.

"God damn it." He groaned, digging his palms into his eyes. Anger seeped into his blood again. His heart battered aching protest against his ribs, something lost struggling to find its way home again.

Damn the woman for slipping under his skin. He felt nothing for Ana. Nothing! He was going to prove it. He was simply just horny–that he could fix with sex. Sex he had managed to keep separate from his emotions for years.

He surged to his feet, strides eating up the distance to her room down the hall.

A swing of her door revealed Ana was in the shower. He slipped through the bathroom door and stopped.

He watched her through the misted pane, a blurry yet captivating scene unfolded before Luka's eyes. His heart raced, pounding in his chest like a desperate plea, at the sight silhouette of her body moving under the cascading water.

His breath hitched as the sound of her soft humming, a melody that seemed to harmonize with the rhythmic drumming of the water, cut through his hesitation like a siren's call. It was a bittersweet invitation that pulled at the threads of his restraint.

Luka's hand trembled as he extended it, tracing the outline of her body on the glass.

The glass, slick with moisture, carried the imprint of his touch, a connection forged through an invisible barrier.

The decision was made in that fleeting instant, a choice fueled by an unwavering pull towards her.

He pushed open the door, his heart a chaotic symphony of emotions as his sight fell on her body slick with soap and water, every inch wet and glistening made his cock ache.

She stilled, aware of his presence. Her back turned to him.

A deep, primal hunger stirred within him, a need that could only be satisfied by her touch.

CHAPTER 24

Luka should never have left his room or gone into Ana's bedroom. He certainly should not have opened the shower door, revealing her soft body that called out to him like a siren song.

Even more, Luka should not have slipped out of his shirt and pants and joined her.

Luka should not be doing a lot of things, but every logical thought was buried when his hands trailed up and down her back while the other traced lines from her hip down the outside of her thigh. His touches were slow; like committing everything to memory.

She turned, facing him, and for the longest time, they stood still under the drizzle of warm water. Their foreheads brushed against each other, the closeness sent shivers down their spines. Lips inches apart and yet separated by a chasm of restraint.Heartbeats, once out of sync, found a harmonious rhythm and a magnetic pull that threatened to consume his every thought.

"Kiss me," she said in a low whisper.

Like he didn't need to be told twice, Luka's mouth dipped to capture hers in a slow, languid kiss, exploring her mouth with his tongue. The water streamed down their faces, mingling with their hot breath. It was a pure, unbridled passion.

In that moment, their senses intertwined—every touch, taste, heartbeat and whispered breath became a testament to how much they craved each other.

He paused, staring deep into her eyes, as if trying to find something he could almost reach. His eyes trailed down, his mind enraptured by the hardening of her nipples.

The full view of her naked body was completely bared to him.

Fucking perfect. He wasn't going to rush this time, he was going to be slow and savor every moment. He caught one taut nipple in his mouth, sucking hard as she writhed and pressed into him. His hand slipped between her legs, thick fingers thrusting deep into her silken walls. She squirmed against his hand, clinging to his broad shoulders.

A small tug on his hair, he pulled back to kiss her more. Her scent and everything else that was her flooded his senses, intoxicating him, pulling him over the edge.

She moaned into his mouth as he dragged his middle finger between her legs, pausing to rub a few small circles on her clit.

She almost protested when he retreated his fingers.

"What are you?..." Her question was interrupted with a low gasp.

He lowered to his knees on the cold tile in front of her.

"I want to taste you so badly."

Luka kissed her stomach, pushed open her legs easily, and buried his head between them. He pushed his tongue between her slit, tasting her. She was beyond what he imagined her to taste like.

Heaven was the closest word to it.

The gushing shower water barely drowned any of her moans as her grip on his hair tightened. Her breaths turned into gasps, and then into high-pitched squeals of ecstasy.

In between those sounds, she whimpered his name, her body consumed by the intense sensations coursing through her. He hummed against her skin; the vibrations echoing through her body in a haze of pure lust.

She tried to squeeze her legs together. "Too much."

Ignoring her, he pushed her thighs apart again, squeezing her from behind, and circled her clit with the tip of his tongue. His gaze remained fixed on her face, observing how her mouth dropped open as he increased the pressure.

Broken whimpers fell out of her throat as he pushed his tongue in and out, a little faster, sliding over her clit each time.

She clutched at him like he was her only anchor in a sea of drowning pleasure. Her body trembled as she screamed, "I think.. I am... Yes. Luka. Yes."

A burst of stars erupted inside her, filling her entire being. Leaning against the tile wall, she closed her eyes and surrendered to the overwhelming bliss, feeling her body and soul soar together.

"Are you okay, baby?"

She nodded, "yes."

He tipped her jaw and kissed her deeply, their bodies pressed together tightly as if merging into one. He relished the taste of her lips, their breaths mingling, and her responses that mirrored his own passion.

His cock in hand, he teased her clit with the head of his cock, moved it up and down on her slit, before pushing it in.

Inch by inch, he entered her until he was inside in a single thrust.

"I'm going to make you come again." He wrapped her legs around his hips and locked her ankles together.

She shook her head. "I can't."

"Yes, you can."

His hands were under her ass cheeks, his fingernails into her thighs. His sculpted biceps bulged as he heaved her up and down his length, digging deep inside her. With each thrust, her clit crashed into his pelvis over and over as the entirety of his cock filled her.

"Come for me baby," he says with his voice cracking.

She sank her teeth into his shoulder. The feelings inside her started to overtake her.

"Let it out. Let me have it."

Her walls clenched around him, her face flushed, toes curled, and he knew she was close and quickened his pace with every grunt.

Luka picked up the pace, making longer strokes. He pulled out and slammed back into her hard.

This wasn't making love. It was raw, animalistic fucking, and it was bringing her to the point of no return.

"*Oh my God,*" she cried out.

"There's no need to call for divine intervention, baby. I've got this handled."

Her moan matched with each of his grunts as he continued his thrust into her. Her orgasm was so hard, he thought she was going to pass out again.

"There you go. I got you."

Her body spasmed against his, lost in waves of pleasure. He let out a ragged groan at the sight of her coming undone before him.

Seconds later, he came, gripping her hips tightly, forcing himself as deep into her as his dick pulsed inside. Pulling out, he saw his cum spilling in her pussy. *"Shit,"* he said, putting himself back inside her.

He set her down on her shaky legs as she almost slumped to the cold tile, but with a tight grip on her waist, he held her up against him. They stood still for a while, under the drizzle of the water, his other hand cradled her cheeks, his thumb brushed her bottom lips.

When they stepped out of the shower, Ana leaned against the sink.

"Look at yourself," he said

She turned to the mirror. She was a mess, with her breasts bare and marked by his lips. "And you?" Her gaze shifted to his reflection.

Luka's hair stuck up in wild disarray where her hands had clenched tight, chest rising and falling with each labored breath. There was something else, he noticed.

His eyes seemed brighter, a spark ignited from within. The hard lines of his face had softened, the hint of a smile still playing about his mouth. He looked... happy. Content in a way he hadn't felt since...ever.

This was meant to be a simple release, a transactional exchange of pleasure to meet physical needs. He caught his own reflection. The truth hit him with sudden and undeniable clarity, and there was no more denying it.

He pushed the distracting thought aside and snatched a fluffy towel from the rack. Turning back to her, he knelt down and gently pressed the cloth against her skin, starting at her sides and gradually working his way down to her legs. As he moved the towel over her curves, he couldn't help but marvel at the smoothness of her skin.

"I will get one of my shirts for you."

She picked out the one he had tossed to the floor. "What about this?"

"I can get you one that is probably cleaner."

"This one will do fine." She pulled the collar closer to her nose, a soft sigh escaped her lips. "It smells like you," she murmured, her voice laced with an undeniable fondness.

A slow, tender smile graced his face as he watched as she slipped on his shirt. The hem brushed against her thighs, teasingly short, a daring testament to the provocative allure she effortlessly emanated. Right then Luka found his next favorite thing that came close to hockey, seeing Ana in his clothes.

Luka pulled up his pants and proceeded to carry her petite form over to the bed, tucking her under the soft covers, ensuring she was warm and comfortable. Her injured ankle served as an excuse, a reason to hold her, to feel her presence, one more time before he reluctantly pulled away,

"Luka?" her voice, soft.

hmm

"Thank you, for earlier. You know those guys."

Luka gave a small nod.

He was fighting his own battle as several thoughts rang in his head. He didn't want to be bothered with trying to untangle any of them.

Luka walked out of the room, his steps measured and purposeful, not daring to look back. His head whirled with uncontrollable thoughts and emotions. When he stepped in his bedroom, he went directly to his private bathroom, his hand resting on the sink's edge for balance. He closed his eyes and took a deep breath as he bent over the cool, marble surface.

Luka caught his reflection one more time, and it stared back at him almost mockingly.

There he stood, shirtless, disheveled and sated, looking for all the world like a man satisfied in both body and soul.

Like a man in lo... *No. Not that word.* Even though his heart knew it, speaking them would only complicate things, and he'd be damned if he'd even allowed himself to think about it.

That didn't stop as the realization hit. Luka Kuznetsov was falling in love. *No screw that.* He had collapsed, head first without control, helplessly in love with Ana.

Ah... fuck me.

CHAPTER 25

Luka's kitchen was opulent and spacious, with wide windows that let in the morning light. It cast a warm glow over the pristine marble countertops.

He moved with precision among the gleaming stainless steel appliances, his fingers dancing effortlessly as he prepared a healthy breakfast.

His broad shoulders, clothed in a fitted black tee, and his long, dark hair tied in a loose bun at the nape of his neck.

The rhythmic sound of a knife meeting the cutting board punctuated the air, the blade gliding effortlessly through vibrant produce - ruby-red tomatoes, emerald kale, and bell peppers.

Ana descended the grand staircase, her steps faltering as she took in the scene. Her gaze fixed on him, captivated by the quiet confidence that seemed to radiate from his every movement.

Her presence washed over Luka, causing him to turn around, meeting Ana's gaze.

"How is your ankle?"

"Better." She stretched her foot out.

He put together a plate of a kale salad, a poached egg on a bed of quinoa, and a drizzle of balsamic reduction that looked promising with a touch of freshly cracked black pepper added to the decadence of the dish, making it a healthy masterpiece.

Luka set Ana's plate on the elegantly set table.

"This looks wow..." She sat down and took a bite, "okay not bad. Where did you learn?"

A moment passed before he answered. "My mom." Silently he hoped she wouldn't press for more questions about his mother. He wasn't ready to talk about her.

The sound of porcelain and silverware clinking softly echoed as they enjoyed their breakfast.

Ana's gaze wandered over to the living room, where she spotted a packed suitcase. "Are you going somewhere?" she asked, her voice tinged with concern.

Luka's response was calm, his eyes never leaving his plate. "Russia. Family stuff. I'll be back soon." After a long pause, he peeked through his lashes and asked. "Will you be okay staying here by yourself?"

"Believe it or not, I've spent a lot of time alone. I'll be okay," she reassured him, though Luka could tell she was forcing a smile.

Luka's hand disappeared into his pocket, producing a sleek boxed phone.

"Here."

Her eyes widened in surprise as he extended the gift to her. She raised her outdated phone with its web-like cracked screen. "I do have a phone," she murmured.

"Yeah, and whenever I call you, you don't pick up. Use this."

He reached across the table, grabbed her hand, and placed the box in her open palm. His fingertips lingered for a moment before he withdrew his hand, flexing it slightly as he watched her open the package.

"It's the latest model. I've already saved my number in it." He said, trying to keep his voice steady.

"Thank you."

"And also make sure to keep this phone near you. I don't want to fly back here thinking something happened to you."

She chuckled and then glimpsed at the firm expression on his face. "Oh, you are serious, got it. I will have it near me at all times."

Their breakfast had concluded, leaving behind a comfortable silence that wrapped around them like a warm embrace.

Luka paced back and forth in the living room, a hint of awkwardness in his movements. He gathered his things, meticulously checking and rechecking to make sure he hadn't forgotten anything important.

He wasn't forgetting anything, but he was nervous about leaving Ana. He had never left a woman in his home before. They always left before he woke up and for the longest time, he preferred it that way.

Now Luka was faced with a quagmire. Should he kiss her goodbye, wave... or maybe a high five?

No, that was weird.

A concierge appeared in the doorway, a professional smile on his face as he took Luka's bag and patiently waited by the elevator.

"The car is ready, sir."

Luka's attention shifted briefly to the concierge, his movements slowing as he acknowledged the presence of the man who had come to take his bag. Their exchange was brief, a nod of agreement and a few quiet words before he turned his focus back to Ana.

He resisted the urge to reach out, to touch her, to trace the contours of her cheek or hug her. Instead, he let his fingers curl inward, his hand retreating to his side, a silent testament to his battle against the torrent of impulses that threatened to consume him.

"Are you certain you will be okay?" The words slipped from his lips, soft and hesitant, that echoed the depth of his feelings.

"I will be fine." Ana's lips formed a comforting smile, her gaze unflinching as it connected with his. Her hands were clasped behind her, fingers intertwining as if she were unsure of where to place them.

He nodded and turned to leave, following the concierge. The elevator doors slid closed, not before Ana's voice called out.

"Wait!"

Luka's reflexes kicked in, his hand darting out to intercept the closing doors, halting it just in time.

"Yes?" He poked his head out, a little too eager.

Ana stalked closer, her steps fraught with an uncertainty that mirrored his own. Standing on her tiptoes, she planted a small, innocent kiss against the corner of his mouth.

"Safe flight," her voice, a mere breath, held a promise that stirred something deep within him.

She took a wide step back and the elevator doors closed.

Luka stood there, his ears tinged with a rosy hue as he fought back the smile that threatened to surface.

He caught the concierge staring at him, and he straightened up, feeling a bit self-conscious.

His heart raced as the warmth of her lips lingered on his skin. The kiss was unexpected. He wasn't sure what to make of this sudden gesture, but he knew that he liked it.

He had come to the realization last night that he was falling in love with Ana, but now there was the possibility that she loved him too.

Could this be what it felt like? To be in love? He pondered, grappling with the inexplicable pull that Ana held over him. He had navigated a world of sex and desire, but this emotion, so delicate and profound, was entirely foreign.

"Do you have a girlfriend?" He shot a glance at the man beside him.

Clearing his throat. "No sir. A wife."

"You love her?"

"Yes, sir."

"She loves you?"

"I believe so, yes, sir."

"How do you know?"

"Sir?" the concierge turned to face Luka's puzzled expression.

"I'm asking how, do you know, she loves you?"

"Can I be straightforward, sir?" He waited until Luka gestured before he continued. "It's not always easy to know if someone loves you. Love is different for everyone. The best way to find out is by talking openly and honestly with each other. Share your feelings, intentions, and what you expect. Listen carefully to each other and try to understand how you both feel. Also, pay attention to how they act and behave.

Love is complicated and changes over time, so it's important to have these conversations."

Luka slowly bobbed his head then glanced down to his name tag. "Thank you, Mr Newton. You've given me lots to think about."

Luka came to a decision. He would tell her about his feelings, tell her how much he wanted to expand the parameters of their relationship and make it more official.

After his trip, he would ask her to be his girlfriend.

•.¸♡ . ♡¸.•

Every year, Luka's father imposed a tradition of having a family dinner. Luka did not think much of it until he suggested they have this year in Russia. His childhood home. Everything about the trip was a hassle. Not only was it an 11-hour flight, for a dinner that would probably last for... 30 minutes tops, before they got at each other's throats.

Luka's plane landed in Kaliningrad. His parents met in this very city, their short-lived love story woven into the fabric of its streets.

From the airport, a car waited for him, ready to take him to his childhood home.

The streets hummed with the activity of everyday life.

The scent of warm, freshly baked bread intertwined with the refreshing tang of the sea breeze, a symphony of aromas that painted the atmosphere. The car drifted along the meandering roads. The vibrant city scene retreated, replaced by expanses of serene open spaces and stretches of lush greenery.

As he approached his father's house, the atmosphere seemed to shift, enveloping him in a sense of anticipation.

His heart was pounding as he prepared to face his father. It had been years since he set foot in this opulent mansion, and yet nothing seemed to have changed. The manicured lawn was still immaculate, the hedges perfectly trimmed. The grand facade of the house loomed over him, a fact to his family's wealth and status.

The teenage version of himself would have been thrilled to come back home, but now the very thought of his father's presence brought him dread.

Stefan Blackwood, a cutthroat entrepreneur driven by ambition, made Luka believe he never cared for his mother, or understood the impact her absence had on Luka, especially as a child. He strode into the grand dining room, his steps echoing on the marble floors.

Vlad and his father were already seated, surrounded by a small army of staff. The air was thick with the scent of rich food and expensive wine. He took a seat, his eyes flickering around the room. Nothing had changed since his last visit, which was... possibly 10 years ago.

His father greeted him with a small nod, his eyes betraying no emotion.

Despite being such an influential man in the country, Stefan Blackwood preferred to keep a low profile and operate discreetly, making him somewhat of a mystery to the public eye.

And that meant pushing everyone else to do his bidding.

Luka slipped into his usual seat, nodding briefly at Renaud. The chef had been with them since his childhood, at least the food and drink here promised to be excellent, if nothing else.

"We assumed you wouldn't join us." Stefan set aside the evening newspaper with a snap of folded pages, pale eyes cold. "Good to see you still value tradition."

Luka accepted a glass of wine from a server, taking a bracing swallow of the rich Cabernet. "But I am curious why you choose here and not the many other mansions you like to hide away and pretend mom never existed."

"Oh, my God. Come on, we just sat down." Vlad said.

Renaud, the chef, brought over a trolley loaded with appetizers. He placed a tray of smoked duck and mushroom tarts on the table, each one exquisitely made.

"I could never forget your mother existed, not when you took after her. Determined, strong, and stubborn." He picked delicate pastries, taking a bite. "This is good. You should try some."

Luka wanted to respond, but his brother beat him to it.

"Did you hear? Luka's team qualified for the Stanley Cup this year."

His father couldn't look any more interested as he said, "That's nice. I'm glad you're doing well." He took a napkin from the table, wiping his mouth. "But you realize hockey isn't everything. Honestly, I expected you would give up after the accident."

Memories stirred within him as the accident was mentioned, triggering an involuntary shrug—a silent echo of the shoulder injury.

"The accident had nothing to do with hockey."

His father retorted, "You were in an accident, busted your shoulder, and kept quiet just to play the next day, only to lose."

"I didn't want to let my teammates down, that's what you do for people that count on you... you show up, battered, bleeding and broken. You show up for them." He continued, "I'm sure the concept may be a little foreign to you."

"Are you trying to say something?"

"Luka?" Vlad warned. "Dad please."

"No, let him talk. Is this about your mother? It's been years. What exactly do you expect me to do? Life moves on, we adapt."

Luka's voice grew louder. His hands gripped the edge of the table, his knuckles turning white as he tried to contain his emotions.

"Jesus fucking Christ, it's not that simple. You shut us out. We were children, Vlad and I needed you. I needed you. But you buried yourself in work, in this cold, empty mansion, and you left us to fend for ourselves."

Mr. Stefan's voice sharpened, its pitch rising a notch as a subtle edge of annoyance crept into his tone. "Fend for yourselves? You were provided for, weren't you? We had maids and servants to take care of you. Not many people are lucky enough."

Luka's brows furrowed, frustration and sadness echoed through his cracked voice. "We needed you, not just material things! We needed your love, your guidance. Instead, what did you do? Like some sort of twisted game, you made Vlad and me fight against each other, pitting us to vie for your attention."

Mr Stefan looked away. "I had my reasons, Luka. I wanted you both to be strong, to succeed in a world that doesn't wait for anyone."

"Strong? Is this your version of strength? Turning your back on your own sons, denying them the love they deserve? Mom's absence shattered me, and instead of helping me heal, you pushed me further away."

"What do you want from me, boy?"

As his father's question hung in the air, Luka felt like a balloon slowly losing air. His heart sank, and he struggled to find the right words. What did he want from him? Validation? Acceptance? Love?

He knew that he shouldn't seek validation from others and that he should be proud of himself and his accomplishments.

But it was hard, so hard, to ignore the voice in his head that whispered, *You're not good enough. That's why she left.*

Just say it, he silently pleaded, his heart aching to hear the words from his father. *Tell me it wasn't my fault.*

"Nothing. I want nothing." Luka resigned to say as he swirled the crimson liquid around before downing it in one go. The wine had become his refuge, a temporary escape from the palpable unease that permeated the room.

Anguish sliced through Luka's mind. If he couldn't make his mother stay, the woman that birthed him... who would stay?

Vlad had long stopped eating, his fingers gently massaging his temples with an expression of weariness and frustration.

Their father, who sat at the head of the table, his face hardened as he chewed his food. The sound was amplified in the quiet room, a reminder of the underlying intensity that hung in the air. His eyes remained fixated on his plate, avoiding direct eye contact with anyone else.

Stefan perked up, "You know my good friend, Senator Gregory. He has introduced a business opportunity, and it's a good thing for the family."

"That's great," Luka replied, sarcasm laced in his tone.

"It is, especially because I want you involved."

Luka frowned. "I don't understand."

"I need you to quit hockey and come join me in this business."

The unexpected words struck him like a blow, rendering him speechless. His mind reeled as he tried to process what he had just heard, a thousand questions arising but none making it to his lips.

"We do not have the best relationship in the past, I want us to use this opportunity to mend our relationship. Let go of the past and let's look to the future."

His eyes shifted between his brother and then settled on his father.

"So tell me, boy, what do you say?"

CHAPTER 26

"No. Absolutely not." The forceful tone and resolute expression on his face made it clear that his stance would not be swayed, no matter what.

Stefan met Luka's intense glare. "No?"

The air in the room seemed to thicken as the tension between them grew. Luka had been doing everything he could to please his father, but his efforts had gone unnoticed and unappreciated.

"I can't keep–we can't keep doing this. You wanted to control the NHL, you got Vlad in the seat, you wanted a famous hockey player, I became that thinking maybe he will finally be proud of me and now you want me to quit, because what? You suddenly want me to get into some business."

"Luka, if only you could see beyond the rink and realize the opportunities that lie outside of hockey."

The conversation fell into an uncomfortable silence, leaving Luka feeling disheartened and misunderstood.

He pushed away from the table, "thanks for dinner. Goodluck in your new venture. I'll be flying back first thing tomorrow." And he strode out without a backward glance.

•.¸♡ . ♡¸.•

Luka sat on the edge of the narrow bed in his old room, the one he had slept in as a child. Not much had changed - the walls were still covered in hockey posters, trophies lined the shelves. But a fine layer of dust coated everything, reminding him how long it had been since he called this place home.

He ran his hand over the quilt his mother had made, remembering nights she would come in to check on him after a bad loss or argument with his dad.

"It'll be okay, Luka, you did your best." She would whisper, smiling in that way that made all his troubles fade. He could even hear her soft laugh, which stirred a warmth within him.

On impulse, he pulled out his phone, punched in the numbers he knew by heart, fingers hovering over the call button.

Ana's name glowed on the screen.

He stared at her name for a long time, torn between longing for the peace she offered and fear of history repeating itself. Of letting her in only to lose her, the way he lost everyone in the end.

His whole life had shown him time and again that nothing good lasted. The ice was the only thing that never abandoned him - so he had given himself to hockey without reserve.

Without thinking, he clicked on the call button.

The phone rang for so long that Luka feared she wouldn't answer.

"Luka?"

When her voice came in, clouded with sleep, the ache in his chest eased. He wanted to say something, but he couldn't bring himself to open his mouth.

"Are you there?" she asked.

He could picture her sitting up in bed, brow furrowed.

"I... yes, I'm here," Luka managed.

"How was your flight?"

"Long but It was alright."

There was a silence again, and in it a thousand unsaid things hung between them.

Ana whispered, "I'm glad you called. Are you enjoying your visit?"

Luka leaned back against the bed, letting her words surround him. "No."

"Do you want to talk about it?"

Luka didn't answer, not sure how talking would help.

"Do you want me to stay on the phone?" Ana asked after a few minutes.

Her quiet understanding was enough, an anchor pulling him back from the edge.

"Yes, please." Luka said, then cleared his throat. "If - if you don't mind."

"Of course I don't mind."

He could hear the smile in her voice and shyly smiled at himself. She made him feel like a teenager again, experiencing this kind of care and connection for the first time.

They stayed without speaking for a long while, the silence comforting in its intimacy. Luka held the phone close to his ear, his attention solely focused on the gentle sound of Ana's breathing. The rhythmic inhalations and exhalations, soft and steady, created a soothing backdrop that enveloped his senses.

With her, the shadows of the past didn't seem quite so dark or close.

He shook his head, in disbelief at just how much she found her way into his life and his mind, the broken places inside he was afraid to reveal.

"What were you doing?" he asked.

"I was asleep when you called."

"Shit. Sorry. I didn't check the time." He fell back onto the bed. "Then... what did you do while I was gone?"

"Worried I would steal something?" Ana's words came out lighthearted but her words struck Luka like a physical blow.

His stomach dropped as memories of his hurtful words flooded back. His hand grazed his face, anxiously scratching at the stubble growing there as regret welled up inside him. "That. I was being a jerk. I should never have said that, I am sorry."

"For this one thing or everything you have done in the past."

He paused to think. "Everything." The word came out as a choked admission.

Almost as if she could sense his growing discomfort, Ana changed the subject.

"Anyway, I took the liberty of checking the place out. I'm not sure you know this, but you have a massive house."

"Trust me, I'm aware. The place is ridiculous. Half the time I feel like I should put up signs so I can find my way back to the front door."

"Oh, my God. Did Luka Kuznetsov just make a joke?"

She chuckled with delight, the soft sound easing the tension in him. A grin slipped across his features. Her laugh was infectious, chasing away the melancholy that so often dogged his steps. When she laughed, the world seemed somehow lighter.

"Hey, I can be funny."

"No. You can not. You made one joke, not sure that's enough to consider you funny." She said between laughter.

Damn, he wanted to make her laugh for the rest of his life. Luka exhaled quietly in relief and gratitude. Even though they had not started in the most practical way, he hoped in time he could truly earn her forgiveness, because right now all he wanted to do was everything to keep her by his side.

"Who got you smiling like that?"

Luka propped his head up to find his brother, approaching him.

His voice came out in a firm tone. "Have to go now, have a goodnight." Then he hung up.

"No one." He tucked the phone in his pocket. Luka adjusted as Vlad settled beside him, making the decade-old bed creak.

"You knew what this stupid dinner was for?"

"I told him, you know. That you would not throw your life away, to wear a corporate suit."

He shook his head in disbelief. *This was not happening.*

Vlad chuckled, his hand up as if to paint the picture. "Oh, he has everything planned. You were going to make the perfect family man. That was the only condition to have you on."

Luka scoffed. "Well I am not interested in whatever plan he has."

"Will you ever tell me?" Vlad asked.

"What?"

"Why do you still play hockey? The last time I was over, you mentioned something about not playing hockey because you love it. Why are you still holding on?"

Luka sighed. He had never told anyone this but if anyone were to understand, it would be his brother.

"I have been trying to find our mother, but no hope. You know it was her favorite sport, I figured the more time I spent on magazine covers or on TV, she would find me."

"Ah. That explains why you insisted on using her last name. I thought you wanted to piss dad off."

"It's both. You know, I have tried everything. It's like our mother just vanished into thin air."

That information did not faze his brother which stirred some suspicions in Luka.

"Is there something you're not telling me?" he asked, his voice low and serious.

Vlad shifted uncomfortably in his seat, avoiding Luka's gaze.

Without a word, Luka leaned in even closer, his eyes locking onto Vlad's. The message was clear: he wanted the truth.

He hesitated for a moment, then sighed. "Okay, fine. You should know everything dad has done is to protect you, even if it may not seem like it and also the truth is that mum did not *exactly* leave us."

Luka knew all too well the painful truth about his parents' marriage. It had been filled with constant fighting and turmoil, until one day his mother decided to pack up and leave. Luka still remembered that day vividly, even though he was only seven years old at the time. He had stood at the window, watching as his mother walked away from him and his father, her figure growing smaller and smaller until she disappeared from view. It was a moment that had stayed with him all his life, a wound that never fully healed.

"What do you mean? I was there, I saw her as she walked away pulling her bag."

"I think you should talk to dad."

•.¸♡ . ♡¸.•

Luka marched over to his father's study. The room was a blend of old-world charm and rustic elegance, with antique furnishings. The walls were lined with deer heads, their antlers reaching out like bony fingers towards the ceiling. The fireplace was made of stone, and a fire crackled in its depths, casting flickering shadows across the room.

"Where is she? Tell me. I want to know the truth."

Reaching for his silver cigarette case, Stefan extracted a thick Cuban cigar and clipped the end.

He lit a match and puffed the cigar to life, savoring the rich smokiness as it filled his lungs.

"You know what I want." Just as expected, if manipulation didn't work, Mr Stefan usually moved to negotiation.

"Fine. I will quit hockey, if you promise to tell me the truth. Everything."

"You finally come to your senses." He pushed himself up, and he paced across the room. "After this season, it would make sense to respectfully get yourself out, you know, win the stupid cup and retire."

He continued, "We would probably organize some gala event where I would introduce you to the right people, then you will give a speech or two on the tv, talking about whatever the public are interested in these days, climate change or whatever. Don't worry about it, I have everything set."

Luka's brows furrowed as he listened to his father talk. Of course, the man had planned his future, every second of it right down to the color of his tie he would wear on the first day of the office.

"And you say, this is a chance to mend our relationship."

"It will be." Stefan continued, "And then maybe in a few months, we will announce your marriage."

That pulled him out of his mind. "What?"

"Yes, Senator Gregory wants his daughter to be involved so yes, marriage and don't worry, you will like her. I know your generation is against arranged marriages but this is why I'm telling you now, you have a year to get to know her."

His fingers fidgeted, dancing in subtle gestures that mirrored the turbulence within his mind, his words trembling with the weight of his secret love. "What if... I already have someone I want to—

"Oh Luka my boy. I know all about those whores you pay for sex. We can't have any of that. This girl is Senator Gregory's daughter and she is a famous celebrity, I'm sure once you meet her, get to know her, you will like her and if you want to still have your flings on the side you can too."

The room grew quiet, anticipation hanging in the air, as a hush fell upon them

"Do we have a deal?"

CHAPTER 27

Ana took a deep breath as she turned the corner onto her old street, soaking in the nostalgia while anxiety twisted her stomach. Ana heard whispers about the redevelopment team's impending arrival and her fears were confirmed when she turned the corner. Where once there had been a bookstore that sold second-hand books, now there was nothing but rubble. The construction crew swarmed around it, their tools clanging against the hard ground as they placed metal beams in position. Her heart sank at the sight of it, though there was small comfort in seeing that her home still stood unscathed for the time being.

Sprinting from room to room, Ana grabbed whatever she could — Danny's paintings, art supplies, old photographs — all while avoiding glances at the destruction outside.

Ana's gaze swept across the room, taking in the sight of her beloved romance novels lining the shelves. Each book held countless hours lost in dreamy tales and fictional worlds. She reached out to touch the spines, tracing her fingers along the titles until she realized that she couldn't take them all with her. As she left the room, she made a mental note to get it delivered to Luka's penthouse.

Ana scanned the room one last time. She had grown up in this house and experienced joy and heartbreak within those walls. With a sigh, she closed the front door behind her, leaving behind a chapter of her life as the redevelopment team continued their work outside.

Despite the sadness she felt, there was also a sense of anticipation in her heart as she walked away, ready to start a new chapter in her life.

•.¸♡.♡¸.•

She walked ahead the two strapping men who had carried each of her book-filled boxes up to the luxurious apartment. She thanked them for their hard work, suppressing a wince as she noticed a slight tear in one of her boxes. The books inside were fine though - they had packed them carefully.

About 403 books, if she counted right. Her mind flashed to her father's words, "*You could sell these. Why do you have so many?*"

These books made her escape, they saved her. They let her dream and made life a little more bearable. They muted her suicidal thoughts. He wouldn't know that. He never cared, all that concerned him was money to feed his gambling.

She feared Luka's reaction. The entrance of the house stacked the boxes. She would have to find some place to keep them before he returned.

Ana made herself a cup of tea and settled into the plush leather seats, admiring the grandeur and opulence of his house. It was filled with modern furniture, beautiful artwork, and big windows that showed a stunning view of the city at night.

Even though the house was luxurious, Ana couldn't shake the feeling that something was missing. There were no family photos or personal mementos.

The absence of these personal touches made the house cold and impersonal, as if it had been designed only to impress guests rather than to reflect the warmth and personality of its owner

She knew Luka had been focused on his hockey career and had little time to settle into the penthouse fully. But seeing the emptiness emphasized the sacrifices he had made, the aspects of a normal life that had been put on hold.

Deep down, she pitied him.

Perhaps they weren't so different after all.

The only things she saved from her home were her books and her brother's painting materials. She didn't keep any photos either, except one of her and her brother that was safely tucked in her purse.

Taking a sip of her tea that slowly lost its warmth, she couldn't help but wonder what Luka truly desired amidst all the fame and success.

She knew what she wanted, which was family. Stability. She wanted to be surrounded by friends. Those were the pieces she envisioned fitting into her life's puzzle. Yet, as certain as the sun's rise, doubt clouded her hopes, casting shadows that refused to be dispelled.

The spacious rooms echoed with loneliness she couldn't escape. It would be easy to crawl back under the covers, hiding from the world until the black dog of depression retreated again. But she had grown tired of its snarls and snapping jaws, keeping her caged and complacent for days at a time.

Not tonight.

Her shoes sat by the door where she had kicked them off earlier. Maybe she should go for a walk, those usually help. Of course, she never dared to think of walking this late at night in her old neighborhood, but she thought this place would be safer.

With sudden resolve, she changed into comfortable clothes, slipped on her headphones, and laced up her shoes.

The elevator door closed as Ana left the penthouse, reveling in the vibrant pulse of life outside and seeking fresh air and solitude. The moon cast a gentle glow as she strolled along, content with the peace that surrounded her.

However, as she turned a corner, a flicker of unease washed over her—a nagging sensation that she was being followed.

Her pace quickened, and she stole occasional glances over her shoulder, convinced she saw shadows darting between buildings.

Her heart pounded in her chest as she imagined many ominous scenarios, her mind conjuring up an elaborate chase straight out of a suspense movie.

Ana's paranoia reached its peak. She got a tap on her shoulder. Startled, she spun around with wide eyes and threw a punch at her pursuer.

"That will teach you not to follow people."

The man groaned, his back hunched over as he pressed against his nose.

"I was not. Ana, it's me." He shot his head up and bloody nose.

Her eyes widened in surprise as she caught sight of the person standing in front of her. A gasp escaped her lips before she could help it, her cheeks flushing with embarrassment at the unexpected reaction.

It was unmistakable: the midnight kinky hair that snuck out of his beanie, bronze skin, and hazel eyes. It was David, her old friend from her school days.

"D-David? Oh my goodness, you scared me half to death!" Ana exclaimed, a mix of relief and laughter escaping her. "Your nose?"

"No. It's all good. You might have fixed it," he joked. "Where did you learn how to throw a punch like that?"

She ignored that question and asked instead, "What on earth are you doing here?"

He shrugged, his mischievous smile still intact. "You know, visiting some friends in the area. I saw you and I tried calling you, but..." He pointed to the headphones in her ear.

"Sorry." She took them out.

"Do you stay around here?"

"No," she snorted, "Are you kidding me? I can't afford a place in this neighborhood. I am currently staying with a coworker. It's temporary though."

Co-worker? Well, they weren't friends. And lovers, seemed to be too much information for someone she has not seen in several years.

"I know a really good cafe around here. We could get something to eat."

She smiled, considering it. It would be good to catch up with a friend. "Why not."

•.¸♡ . ♡¸.•

"So, how have you been?" David asked, breaking the silence.

"I've been good. Just keeping busy with work and stuff," Ana replied.

"What do you do now? I bet it is something amazing. You were always the smart one in school."

Right. Smart one... she was the smart one till she dropped out because her father needed her to stay at home and be a mom to Danny. By the time she returned, her classmates had all moved on without her, leaving her feeling lost and behind.

Still, she was proud of how far she had come, from working as a waitress to being a cool doctor, but deep down, there was an underlying concern that she didn't earn it - nagging guilt that followed her everywhere. Would she even be working if she weren't sleeping with Luka?

"I'm a doctor, physiotherapist, to be exact. I'm working for a hockey team." She tried to sound excited.

"That's... kinda dope." He cast his gaze downward. "I guess you must have lots of guys falling over you."

She snorted. "Guys? As in Plural no."

"Okay, then guy, singular."

Her mind went to Luka. Sure, they were having sex, but they weren't together. They would never be, not because she didn't like him, but because a loving relationship with a man like Luka seemed like an impossible dream. Someone like him would probably get tired of her soon enough and marry some model or actress or any other person with their life in order.

"No, I'm single and I don't see myself dating a hockey player, anyway."

She would have sworn his shoulder slumped like he was disappointed, but she didn't want to dwell on that. She asked with a hint of nostalgia in her voice. "Remember when we used to hang out at that park near your house?"

"Yeah, those were good times. Life was a lot easier when we were kids. By the way, how is your brother?"

"Good. I visited him today, maybe you can come with me next time. He will be thrilled."

"I would love to." David hesitated for a moment before speaking again. "I have to admit, Ana, I've thought about you a lot over the years. I miss us."

Ana felt her throat clench and her chest tighten. They had dated in the past, but it had ended abruptly and they had lost touch.

"Are you seeing anyone?" she asked, still not sparing him a single glance.

"I've been on a few dates, but nothing serious. I guess I've been waiting for the right person to come along." He looked up at her, smiling.

"How is your mother? It's been crazy long since I last saw her." Ana asked, shifting the topic of conversation.

David leaned back against his chair and nodded slowly, like he could see right through her.

"She's been asking about you."

They drifted to familiar topics that ended in laughter and reminiscence, solidifying the bond between them.

"We have to do this again. Let me give you my number."

Ana handed him her phone.

He typed his number and paused, his eyes flicked up to her.

"You must get paid a lot. This literally just came out." He commented. Ana let out a nervous chuckle and took a sip from her drink, not answering.

CHAPTER 28

Luka entered his apartment, weary from the long trip. He craved solitude and silence, and didn't expect the light that spilled from the kitchen and the air heavy with savory aromas.

It was far from the cold aura that usually welcomed him anytime he traveled.

Luka stopped at the entryway to watch and was struck by how domestic the scene felt. It was as though he had stumbled into someone else's home, a place where people lived and loved and cooked together. He had always thought of his own home as a refuge from the chaos of the outside world.

There was a sense of longing for something he had never known as he watched Ana move across the tiled floor, apron tied securely around her waist. Her hips swayed to a low hum as she prepared a meal, pots clanging gently together as she set them down on the stove.

Ana's presence filled the sprawling, empty rooms with life and warmth. His chest tightened at the certainty that she belonged here like this was her home - their home - instead of his private purgatory.

Then his father's ultimatum struck his mind like an unwanted reminder.

His heart clenched at the realization that in the madness to come, their arrangement would have to end. No longer playing hockey meant he would have no reason to have her by his side. The thought twisted like a knife, that in reaching for one truth, he stood to lose another only just found.

Ana caught sight of him hovering in the doorway, a smile fading into concern as she read the conflict written on his face.

"Hi... welcome. How was your trip?" she spun, spatula in one hand. "I wanted to make you something. Is that okay?"

His fingers unconsciously weaved through his tousled hair, strands slipping through his grasp as if mirroring the chaos of his thoughts.

"Thanks. I need a quick shower."

He climbed the stairs with quick, determined strides.

Now refreshed and rejuvenated from the long shower.

He had slipped into a simple black tee and some shorts. The black tee accentuated his broad shoulders and highlighted the contours of his physique, while the shorts offered a relaxed fit.

When he stepped back into the living room area, "What's this?" He asked, pointing to the boxes in the corner.

She came forward, whipping her hands with a napkin, and set it on the countertop. "Ah yes. My things from my old home. I will get them out of your way. The canvas all belongs to my younger brother, and I could not leave it there or it would be destroyed."

He made his way and found some paintbrushes. "Your brother?"

"Yes, he is in a boarding school for exceptional learners. He loves to paint and draw. He is really amazing at it."

"Why isn't he staying with you? Isn't that expensive?"

"At first it wasn't. We signed up for this... umm...Assistance Program. I was barely paying anything and I could work the whole day without rushing to return home."

"I'm guessing the financial support for that stopped."

"Some bill that was passed crushed that." She shrugged. "Anyway, I was stuck. Let him remain there and finish his last semester or bring him home where I'd be forced to reduce my work hours to care for him, risking both of us starving." She smiled like it was no big deal.

Luka was quick to notice how she said "I" not "we". Meaning her father never helped out. From the little he knew about the man, he understood why she was taking everything on.

He reached for a worn paperback novel, its cracked spine revealing signs of frequent use with slight curves and folds in certain spots.

"These belong to your brother, too?"

She squeaked in dismay and lunged to snatch the book from his hands. He raised it up and away from her reach.

"Those are mine. I will get them out of your way once I can."

She reached for it one more time, but he yanked it out of her hand.

"Why are you shy about it?"

"Me... shy?" she took a step back, hands on her waist. "I promise you I am not. There is nothing in there that is not natural and common."

Luka nodded as he began flipping through the book. Random underlines, annotations, and notes in the margins. "Lots of highlighted pages in here."

"They are second-hand books so I didn't write those."

"Really?" He arched his brow.

"Okay, maybe I may have doodled a little here and there." She wished she could crawl under a rock and disappear.

Luka read the steamy scenes and chuckled at the cheesy dialogue.

"What? He looked at her with hooded eyes. What the fuck?" He said, laughing. "explain."

"That is... umm... the eyelids dropped and the hero is staring at the heroine, thinking about kissing—" then stopped and suddenly realized how close Luka was to her.

"Go on." He urged, leaning closer.

"You are doing it."

"Doing *what*?"

"You know what!" She shoved him and buried her face in her palms.

"Wow, Ana," he said, looking down at the book one more time and grinning.

"Okay. okay. There is nothing embarrassing about reading a romance novel. Now can I have it?"

She made one final attempt to get the book out of his hands, but he looped an arm around her waist and drew her close, brushing his lips against her neck in a flirty manner.

"Is this what you like? I'll have to study those novels thoroughly for research purposes."

"You're incorrigible." She swatted at his chest, unable to hold back an answering grin, and teased. "If you think you need tips from those books, clearly I've been too subtle!"

Luka swept her up into his arms, carrying her to the couch. His body hovered over hers as he gazed down at her, warmth flickering across eyes usually so guarded. She reached up to brush an unruly lock of hair off his forehead, her heartbeat quickening in response.

At that moment, the teasing humor faded as realization dawned - they were developing an emotional bond neither of them could hide anymore.

The connection between them had gone beyond the physical, building on the trust that had been created during their quiet moments to create an intimacy they were unprepared for.

Ana's fingers stilled against his stubble.

He leaned forward and took her lips in such a way, her heart stopped.

Luka hovered above her, enveloping her in warmth, allowing her to dictate the rhythm. His gentle touch moved from her jaw to her hips, then her thighs, lifting her skirt and creating a delicate exploration that sent shivers down her spine.

There were no demands, no urgency now, no desperation in the way their mouths moved together. Just the tender reconnection of lovers who knew they had all the time in the world.

The taste of her lips lingered on his tongue, left him craving for more. With each passing second, their kiss deepened, fueled by an intensifying passion that coursed through their veins. Their lips moved with a growing urgency, like they were trying to convey unspoken words, to communicate their feelings.

There was no doubt that she could feel his erection against her legs as their bodies pressed closer, hands roamed, fingers tangled in hair, and bodies intertwined in a passionate embrace.

He broke the kiss and stared at her, his brows furrowed. A strange tension strained the space between them. The air was charged with things left unsaid, bonds still too new and fragile to give voice to.

"I missed you." The soft unexpected confession hit Luka with the weight of a thousand pounds.

He stared, not blinking, not saying a word. He should say something. What should he say? That he missed her, too? Of course, he missed her, he missed her so much even when she was near, his body ached, as if each cell yearned to be fused with hers.

The truth was undeniably painful. Yet, alongside it, there was another truth that remained.

They had no future.

He should say something. He had been quiet for too long.

"I—

"It's okay. I'm not sure what came over me. It's just being alone in this big house, I guess I miss having someone around. Don't freak out. It's nothing."

Now Panic set within him. *Did she not mean it? Why did she take it back? Was he alone in this… or perhaps she didn't like him. .*

Fuck. His mind screamed at him. There was a lot to think about. One thing he was certain about was he didn't want to string her along on a path he wasn't sure of.

Ana deserved so much more.

He had to put up a wall, now and fast. This was getting too real. This was why he didn't do love–it always seemed to complicate things. *What did that guy in the elevator say? Be honest?* He could do that.

Luka pushed back and stood, taking a couple of paces around the room before finally stopping in front of her.

"I will be quitting hockey."

He winced at his cowardice, the inadequate words tumbling out instead of what he burned to say.

"I'm quitting hockey to marry some stranger in an attempt for my father to expand his business in exchange to find out the truth about my mother's disappearance."

Ana blinked, confusion and worry mingling across her features now.

"Quitting? But you love the game. What's really going on?"

"My father wants me to quit."

"It's not what *you* want?" She stood.

He had agreed to abandon hockey and take up the family business legacy, despite its absurdity. Why? Because his father was a manipulative bastard who treated everything like a good damn negotiation. This decision meant him finding out the truth about his mother's disappearance and he had been on this road for too long to give up now.

"It doesn't matter what I want. Instead, you should be aware that this season will be my last and after the playoffs..." His voice trailed.

"After the playoff, you won't need me." She formed a smile.

Luka would give anything for a glimpse into the mind of Ana Sheen.

"Ana..."

She continued, "No. No. I get it. Trust me, I know we are doing this because of your games, and it makes sense that we would end it once you stop playing. You've been clear about your intentions and feelings from day one. "

His face contorted in a mix of irritation and helplessness, like a tightly wound spring on the verge of snapping.

His hand clenched at his sides. "I just want to be honest with you. I can't assure you of anything other than what we initially agreed on."

Like my heart.

"Look, I get it. We are adults. We had a deal, no strings attached."

No strings. No strings. But there were strings. Lots of it and he felt it tugging his heart toward her.

"So we go back to having sex only before your games," she continued.

"Ye... err. Sure. sure. That's what we agreed on." Luka bobbed his head repeatedly until his mind drifted to when the next Crestmont Giants game was.

Shit. Two weeks. He was going to spend two weeks having her near and not touching her. *Why did he agree to this? He was really looking forward to a welcome back sex with her.* Well that plan was out the window.

He cleared his throat and shifted his weight from one foot to the other. "Just wondering if this is okay for you?"

She snickered, "Me? I will be fine."

Of course she would.

She gestured to him. "The question is, would you? I mean, you were the one that joined me in the shower a couple of days ago."

"And you kissed me when I was leaving or there is also the fact you said you missed me a couple minutes ago."

She groaned. "I literally just explained that or have you forgotten, you made it your mission to make me orgasm."

Luka opened his mouth ready to speak but nothing came to mind, then resigned to say, "Look, we can agree to disagree as long as you *agree* that you like this," he gestured between them, "more than you let yourself admit."

"Want to bet?" her hands folded across her chest.

"Bet what?"

She paused, "You can't go two weeks without your hands on me... heck without kissing me."

He bit his lips. "First of all, how did you know my schedule? Obsessed with me?"

"I work there." She rolled her eyes.

"Right. What would be the wager then?"

Ana took a long pause. "A question and the loser have to answer honestly."

He nodded, taking two steps closer to her. “Fine. No touching, no kisses.” His eyes glanced down to her mouth, “Nothing, till the game.”

“Deal.”

CHAPTER 29

Ana could not hold anything against Luka. She knew he wouldn't give himself to her, but that didn't stop the fact, it still hurts.

He had been honest. Too honest.

In an attempt to make it not weird between them, she suggested the betting game and was quite surprised he was on board.

Besides, maybe if they keep the lovemaking to a minimum, it would help her tame her growing affection for the man.

When they were in the training center, it was easy to stay apart. She simply secluded herself in her office or hung out with Lily.

Gradually their playful challenge had become a test of their willpower and turned to ways to make each other fall.

Ana stood by the side of the gym, her gaze diverted from her conversation with the coach and drawn to the sight before her. Luka was doing pull-ups. With the flexing of his biceps, his arms glistening with sweat, it was impossible not to be captivated.

She bit her lip, hastily tearing her gaze away as she realized she was supposed to be having a conversation with the Coach.

"You've been doing an excellent job with the players' recovery," Coach Thompson was saying, his voice a low rumble that she struggled to focus on. "We're lucky to have you on the team. That's why I think you should join the team on the road for their away game in a few days."

"Thank you, Coach. I'm glad to contribute in any way I can."

As he continued to speak, Ana's attention wavered once more, her eyes drifting back to Luka who was now wiping his face with a towel, his chest rising and falling with each steady breath. She cursed herself for being so easily distracted, her heart racing at the sight.

Just as Ana tried to recentre her thoughts, Luka approached, his strides purposeful and confident. Did he catch her staring? She can't lose. It was far too early.

She swallowed, her fingers tightening around the clipboard she held.

"Hey, Doc," he greeted. His lips quivered into a half-smile, his eyes sparkling with a playful glint. "See something you like?"

Ana couldn't help but smile in return. "I'm just concerned you don't strain yourself, especially with those pull-ups and your shoulders."

"Oh, I'm not bothered. I love a challenge."

"Really?" her eyes narrowed.

Coach Thompson glanced over, curious about the exchange. "Everything cool with you two?"

Luka and Ana exchanged a swift glance, a silent understanding passing between them.

"Just talking about some new treatments, Coach. You know how it is."

Ana nodded in agreement, her expression composed. "Absolutely. We're focused on his game."

Coach Thompson shrugged, accepting their explanation. "Good to hear. Keep up the hard work."

As the coach moved away, Luka turned her attention back to Ana, a hint of anticipation in his gaze. "So... turned on yet?"

Her eyes twinkled with subtle amusement. "Come on, sweaty-flexed muscles won't work on me."

His voice dropped a fraction as he leaned in even closer. "Oh? Are you saying you didn't imagine me picking you up right now, right here, your legs around me while I fuck you till you cry out to heaven?"

The way Luka's eyes devoured her, filled with a hunger that sent her senses into overdrive. She bit her bottom lips. "You want to play dirty? See you at home," and cat-walk back to the office.

His eyes were drawn to her backside as she walked away. There was an air of grace that enveloped her every move bewitching Luka completely. *"Yeah this was a fucked up idea."*

"Lunch is here, boys!" The sound of Lily's voice cuts through his thoughts.

The self-appointed social media manager of the Crestmont Giant and Caleb's younger sister, bustled into the gym area, arms loaded with bags from the deli down the street.

Minutes later, everyone shuffled out straight to the coach's office, which was not big enough to contain all of them, but it became a tradition that they eat together once in a while and none of them seemed to be bothered.

Luka usually joined in team lunches, preferring their easy camaraderie during lunch than when they were nose deep in alcohol.

Most of them were on a strict diet and preferred to eat salads, but Lily had made sure to include some variety in the meal. She had ordered sandwiches, wraps, and salads, along with some healthy snacks like fruit and nuts, except for Jude. He was the worst eater and fed on the most unhealthy stuff ever.

The boys crowded around the table, eager to grab their share of the food. Lily smiled as they dug in, their faces lighting up with delight at the sight of the delicious treats.

Lily sorted through the bags, pleased she had remembered Luka's favorite - hot pastrami on rye, extra pickles.

"Here. I got it from that one place you liked. It was a 2-hour wait but..." When she turned, lunch in hand, stretched out to him, he was unpacking a wrapped parcel from his bag instead.

Caleb glanced at his sister. Her face fell, disappointment piercing before she could mask it.

The others regarded his homemade meal with surprise.

Jude elbowed Luka with a grin, stealing a chip from the open bag. "What's with the pack, huh?"

Luka shrugged and answered in a flat tone, without any thought. "Ana made it."

He watched his teammates' expressions change from disbelief to shock. He realized his mistake.

"Ana? As in the physio?" Jude asked.

He ignored the question but focused on unwrapping his lunch with care and he slowly came to the realization he didn't regret the mistake. Sure he wanted their arrangement to be confidential but that would only make Ana be more approachable to these guys. The last thing he wanted was another man to think she was available.

"So what does this mean? Are you guys dating?"

Luka paused, his spoon halfway to his mouth. His first instinct was to say yes, a possessive need to stake his claim and ward off potential rivals. But the word lodged in his throat, doubts and complications crowding in.

Were they dating? He shifted in his seat, uncertainty etched on his face. Memories of their passionate nights together flooded his mind, leaving him yearning for more. There was also what he had told her: their agreement would end after the playoffs.

There was also his arranged marriage his father was planning. Even though he had agreed to his father's request, he can't imagine going through with it.

Ana would certainly not make a bad wife.

He would find a way to get out of this entanglement. How? he had no fucking clue.

"Earth to Luka." Jude snapped his fingers in front of his face.

Luka set his lunch aside, his appetite fading as a headache began to form in his temple.

"It's... complicated," he stated.

"She rejected you," Caleb stated, "must be because of your shitty personality."

Luka shook his head. Only Caleb could jab at him like that. It brought some laughter to the room.

"This is why I don't hang out with you guys. The doctor and I have an understanding," Luka said calmly. "Nothing more."

Pavel laughed. "An 'understanding'? What is this, a business deal?"

Luka bristled at the knowing looks exchanged between his teammates. His relationship with Ana was complicated, undefined. But that didn't mean he would stand by while they spoke of her with such disrespect.

"Let me be clear on one thing," he said coolly. "Ana is mine. Whatever is between us stays that way. She's off limits to all of you - if anyone here was considering stepping up to take my place." His pointed stare left no doubt as to the warning beneath those words.

Luka didn't care. They could think whatever they liked, as long as the message was clear. Ana belonged with him, whether either of them could define exactly what they were to each other.

"Message received," Caleb said with a grin, raising his hands again. "Ana's all yours, man."

Pavel leaned forward eagerly. "Is she as hot as she looks under those scrubs?"

Luka's jaw tightened, a spark of irritation surging through him at Pavel's question.

"Caleb?"

Right on cue, Caleb who sat beside Pavel knocked him on the head.

"Hey what did I say?"

"This is no place for locker room talk. There is a girl here." Jude chimed in.

Pavel rubbed the back of his head, then glanced at Lily who sat still like she was in a trance. "Who? Lily? She is not a girl."

He reached and poked her, taking her out of her long trance.

Lily flung to her feet. "Oh my gosh, will you leave me alone. Can't you tell when someone is not in the mood for your jokes." She yelled and stormed out of the room, her face contorted with unmistakable anger.

"What's her problem?" Jude asked with a mouthful.

Luka, seemingly unfazed by Lily's emotional outburst, continued calmly eating his lunch, his eyes fixed on his plate while everyone else's eyes followed her.

"Seriously, man, cool it with the jokes," Caleb said.

"What are you guys doing later?" Luka asked, getting the boys' attention.

"Pavel was going to introduce us to some underground dungeons. It's supposedly filled with girls ready to explore their kinks and shits."

"Yeah, I hate every word of that sentence." Luka leaned back in his chair and crossed his arms.

With a hint of accusation in his voice, Pavel retorted, "Funny how you say we never invite you, but when we do, you cancel at the last minute."

Jude added with a mouthful, "Yeah, you never hang out with us."

Luka's eyes narrowed, and his voice carried a touch of frustration. "That's because you guys never pick anything fun. It's either a club or a bar."

Pavel, unable to resist a comeback, "Where do you want us to go, a fucking museum?" he snapped back.

"It wouldn't kill you to learn some culture."

Pavel rolled his eyes then clapped like a memory clicked. "What about the car show? We went to a few months ago? You bailed on that too."

"It was on a Tuesday."

Pavel tossed his hand in exasperation.

Caleb reached for a bottle of water, taking a sip to compose himself. "I don't know why y'all can't see that Luka is an introvert," he chimed in, his voice carrying a touch of understanding.

"I'm more of an ambivert," he replied, his voice holding a touch of self-reflection.

With a smirk on his face, he quipped, "And what's that, some kind of bug?" The room erupted in laughter, fueled by Pavel's jest.

Luka shook his head, a combination of amusement and resignation on his face. He ran a hand through his hair and chuckled softly, "I can't deal with you guys."

•. ,♡ . ♡ ,.•

Luka was making dinner and Ana insisted on helping. When she said, "*See you at home,*" she wasn't kidding because his body had turned into a battleground of longing.

Every casual touch, innocent in its intention, ignited a spark of electricity.

Fingers brushed against one another, sent shivers down his spines. Their hands grazed as they reached for shared items, a subtle reminder of the connection he was trying so hard to suppress.

Luka prided himself on being able to control himself, but in the last couple of days, he realized he wasn't addicted to sex, but he was addicted to Ana. Her scent, her touch, the feel of her lips against his.

He was sure she wanted him to break his composed attitude to the point of begging for just a taste of her because he was very much close to the edge of doing so.

It was silly. Even the most mundane activities became charged with unspoken tension. Like when she had her bedroom door opened, and he caught her arranging her bookshelf.

Luka had one made to accommodate her books but her choice of attire, a simple pair of shorts, seemed innocent enough, but it drove him to the brink of madness.

As she reached up, exposing her slender legs, the curve of her hips, it awakened a primal hunger within him. That was a sight he would definitely picture when he was alone in the bathroom with his hand on his cock for the second time that day.

He might end up on his knees sooner than expected.

later that evening...

Luka descended the stairs. His footsteps were light and cautious. The air crackled with suppressed desire as the challenge of their bet lingering in the periphery of his thoughts.

He settled on the couch adjacent to Ana, who was reading one of her shirtless guys' cover books and pulled out his phone, seeking a distraction.

"Doing okay? You've been in the bathroom a lot."

He answered, his eyes on his phone. "I went for a run, I sweated so naturally, then I had to take a bath."

She snapped her book shut and her cat walked to the kitchen area.

One second, he took his eyes off his phone to glance over and catch her luscious lips wrapped around a spoon coated with Nutella.

"What are you doing?"

A moan of pleasure escaped her, the rich chocolate hazelnut spread melting on her tongue. Luka's breath caught in his throat, his eyes transfixed by the sensual act unfolding before him.

"Nothing, suddenly craving something sweet, that's all."

His eyes fell to her lips as he thought about how the hazelnut would taste coming straight from her. Luka's body instinctively reacted to the sight. He tried to ignore the hardening of his cock pressing against his pants.

Her tongue swirling around the spoon, sent a jolt of electricity straight to his core and gave him ideas. He wasn't going to last; he knew it.

Closing the distance between them, he advanced towards her, a visible sign of frustration filled his expression. His fingers found their place at the nape of her neck, tangling in the intricate braids that adorned her hair as their lips met in a kiss that ignited the very core of their beings.

Pressed together, their bodies seemed to meld into one, a fusion of heat and need that left no space for uncertainty.

"You cheated." he breathed against her lips.

"I did not–

"Get on your knees, Ana and take my cock like a good girl."

She lowered to her knees and unfastened his belt, With a mischievous glint in her eyes, Ana began to explore the cock. Her pink tongue darted out like a curious butterfly, making a tentative lick before she wrapped her lips around the throbbing head of his cock.

He looked down at her, his eyes entranced and locked in a hazy gaze, as though she possessed a depth of complexity he had never before encountered. Every subtle movement of her tongue, every delicate nuance of her expression, held him captive.

It was as if the world around him had faded into insignificance, leaving only her as the sole focal point of his existence.

She noticed his eyes squeezed shut tight, and he was gasping for breath like he was trying to hold back. The sound of his whimpers, strained and desperate, filled the air. "Your mouth feels good."

His free hand remained entangled in her hair, revealing the depth of his surrender, a testimony to the intoxicating power she held over him.

"Oh fuck. You are doing so well."

Hers were heavy-lidded, high off of the sounds and reactions coming from him.

Tongue teasing the underside of his cock as his breath began to pick up again. A heavy sigh fell from his lips as her hand stoked most of his length. The prominent veins pulsing in her mouth made her eyes roll to the back of her head.

"I can't hold on much longer." His leg jerked, but she pushed down on his hips and took his entire length. Her head bobbed up and down on his cock, with each lick, a small dribble of saliva trickled down her chin, forming tiny, glittering droplets that hung precariously on the edge of her lower lip. The sticky, salty-flavored his pre-cum beckoned to her like a tantalizing treasure.

"I can't– fuck.. Ana..."

His big, mesmerizing blue eyes were fixed upon her, filled with an unspoken plea. "Ana... I'm going to cum." Her name falling from his lips like his saving grace.

The combination of his tender moan and the pleading gaze painted a vivid picture of a profound expression of his desire for her. She was proud to watch him crumble under her as she worked harder on him.

He pulled out and spilled over her face. His chest rose and fell quickly as he tried to regulate his breathing as his semen cascaded down her cheeks.

"I admit defeat. I can't keep my hands off you any longer. But just so you know, sweetheart. You weren't playing fair."

He kissed her.

She tried to push him off. "That's gross."

"Which is it? Kissing you or having cum on you?"

"Kissing me with your cum on my face."

He smiled, "Exactly mine." He kissed her one more time, before grabbing a soft white rag from the countertop.

Dampening it with a touch of cool water, he held her chin and delicately brushed the cloth across her cum-speckled cheeks, like an artist restoring a masterpiece, creating an oddly intimate moment.

Luka's eyes met hers, and a shared laughter bubbled up. It was a lighthearted testament to their closeness and an underlying passion between them.

"So, what's your question?"

"Right, my question. Remember, answer honestly."

"I'm all ears."

"Do you believe in love?"

Luka released Ana's chin, his touch lingering as his eyes flashed with a range of emotions. His parents' marriage left him with an unmistakable fear of abandonment, a lingering shadow that cast doubt on the lasting impact of love.

With a gentle sigh, he took a seat beside Ana on the kitchen floor. His voice carried a touch of melancholy as he responded, carefully choosing his words.

"Love... it's a beautiful concept, something that has the power to bring immense joy and deep connection. If I'm being honest, I've never seen it in a way that convinces me it's real."

Pausing for a moment, his gaze shifted, as if lost in a labyrinth of memories and emotions. The scars of his childhood echoed in his words. "When someone you loved dearly leaves, it can be difficult to trust in love's permanence."

With a subtle shift of focus, he directed his attention to her. "However, I suppose love has the power to overcome those fears. It requires time, patience, and a willingness to open one's heart in the face of the past's shadows."

"Luka? Is that a yes or a no?"

A jovial smile graced his face. "Yes, I do believe in love. I believe in its capacity to heal, to mend broken hearts. But for now," he hesitated, lowered his eyes. "I need to navigate my fears and hope that one day, I'll find the strength to share my feelings with the person who has captured my heart."

"Oh."

A moment passed, before Luka spoke, "Can I ask a question?"

"Sure. It's not how the wager works but I'm actually curious so go ahead."

"What do you want?"

She looked at him. "What do I want? In what? Life."

"Yeah."

"Stability. A big Family. I liked to have loud chaotic family Sunday breakfasts or a get-together." She chuckled. "Invite friends and family. I don't know, I want to host those kinds of things."

"Why chaotic?"

"Maybe not chaotic-chaotic but definitely not quiet or me sitting alone."

Be patient with me. We will have those chaotic Sunday moments.

She adjusted to face him. "My turn. Tell me who is that person that captured your heart?"

"You said, one question, Ana."

CHAPTER 30

The month of April brought new life to the world, with its gentle warmth replacing the cold of winter.

The beginning of the hockey season added to the excitement. The play-off for the Stanley Cup had kicked off. Luka and his team were hyped up. Ana didn't know much about hockey before taking this job and even knew less about the playoffs.

What she got from her research was that each team had to win four games to qualify for the next round and it was a total of seven rounds, with the top team from each conference facing off in the Stanley Cup Final to determine the NHL champion.

The Crestmont Giants had qualified for the playoffs and had to travel to Seattle for their first game. Ana followed them. It wasn't unusual for a doctor to follow athletes. She had kept her distance and remained professional so as not to raise suspicion that they lived together or slept.

Unsure how that would look professionally and if she was honest, she didn't want to find out.

After the flight, they boarded the bus ride to the arena in Seattle. The team had been talking about the new addition to the Seattle Seals. This person was a sharp player and new to the roster. Luka didn't seem fazed by the concerns of his teammates and that was enough for Ana to dismiss them.

Ana and Lily walked into the spacious hockey arena. The sleek ice rink stretched out before them, surrounded by towering metal bleachers.

She watched as Lily took out her phone, bent down to take a video of the players as they walked in. Lily worked hard on her job and it fascinated Ana how much she did.

When it got to Pavel's turn, he walked past, not before flicking Lily's hair.

Lily twirled and attempted to kick him on the calf but his strides were too quick.

"Seems he is always bothering you a lot." Ana stated.

"You have no idea, he is so freaking annoying— crap Luka is coming." She quickly returned to the position to capture what seemed to be a perfect shot.

Luka walked passed without a glance at the girls, mentally getting himself ready for the game tomorrow.

They leaned over, watching the video, replaying it on Lily's phone.

"His post always does the best."

Ana was quite aware of that fact. She might have stumbled on the team's social media page once or twice. The videos, photos, and everything looked good. The fans loved it.

Mainly out of curiosity, she checked out Luka's picture. It had been a candid photo where he poured drinking water over his hair. The number of comments, especially from female fans, was overwhelming.

One thing was sure. Ana wasn't the only one who thought the cold-hearted hockey player was hot.

The arena echoed with the sounds of pucks slapping against sticks and skates carving into ice as the team practiced the day before the playoffs. Rows of empty seats rose around them, waiting to be filled with cheering fans. Sunlight filtered through high windows, giving an almost cathedral-like atmosphere to the space.

They arrived early in Seattle for a photo shoot for a sports magazine. Ana settled in the corner watching the photographer set up bright lights and a tripod, ready to capture promotional shots showcasing the players' prowess.

Ana had joined Lily and they stood on the sidelines watching the players.

The team lined up, sticks at the ready. Caleb, their captain, grinned as the camera flashed, basking in the spotlight. Then each player took their solo shots, each giving the camera a bit of their personality and a cocky smile.

"Look, Luka is not feeling it."

"He doesn't like his pictures taken?" Ana asked.

"Kind of. He easily gets bored of things that aren't hockey. Maybe that's what makes him attractive. His dedication to the sport."

Ana noticed a blush rising in Lily's cheeks and the way her eyes lit up when she spoke about him. She realized Lily may have a crush on him.

"There is something that has been bothering me for a while now."

Ana turned to face the bright-faced girl, waiting for her to continue.

"Is there something going on between you and Luka?" Lily blurted.

Startled, Ana went mute, eyes wide.

"I mean he basically told the guys hands off."

"He did?" Ana's composure shattered like fragile glass, leaving her floundering for a coherent response. "No, No. There is nothing– we're just friends."

She gave Lily a reassuring smile, trying to tamp down a twinge of guilt for lying.

Relief washed over Lily's face and her posture eased.

"That's good. I was hoping...never mind."

Pavel skated over to the girls. "Did you see my pose, cool right?" he skated around them,

Lily rolled her eyes. "Save your energy for the game tomorrow."

"Oh, those Seattle seals won't know what hit them. Even with their newly drafted players, I'm sure we can kick their ass in their city."

Lily took out her phone once more. "Excuse me, I have a job to do."

Pavel grabbed it. "You didn't take pictures of me!"

"I don't need to. Pavel gave it back."

He took off with the phone, skating away, the camera mode on as he snapped a couple of shots of himself.

Ana's laughter echoed around the ice rink as she watched Lily chase Pavel, their cute but weird frenemies-ish relationship brought a smile to her face. When she looked up and saw Luka staring at her from across the rink, all her laughter died away in an instant.

He wasn't paying attention to the photographer but had all his attention to her. An intense blue that seemed to tear through her own dark eyes. She noticed the hint of a smile tugging at his lips.

The room around them blurred into nothingness as she felt her face flush with warmth. Now they lived in the same four walls, and the feelings between them seemed to become more complicated. She didn't know what it was or where it would lead, but something inside of her warned that she was in too deep.

She felt her heart thumping in her chest as Luka skated towards her with a stony expression on his face.

•.¸♡ . ♡¸.•

Luka's eyes remained distant and lips set in their usual firm line.

The photographer sighed, lowering his camera. "Come on Mr. Kuznetsov, you're killing me. Give us a simile"

"Take the damn picture."

Ana's bright laughter rang out, echoing off the metal railings and plexiglass surrounding the rink. His attention shifted to her, taking in her smile.

His stern look softened instantly into an almost bashful grin, tension melting from his broad shoulders.

The photographer's frustration turned to delight as he captured shot after shot of the smiling Luka, at ease now. "That's perfect! Keep that look."

Ana met his gaze, his crinkling in a smile meant only for her - a smile that slipped away as soon as his gaze slid back to meet the camera lens.

"Wow. The ruthless icy king smiles." The photographer chuckled then frowned when Luka glared in warning.

"Sorry." He turned and yelled, "Who is next?"

Luka glided over to the edge of the rink where Ana stood, his hand tightened around his stick.

Luka leaned against the barrier, pretending to watch the photographer directing other players into different poses and expressions.

He leaned down, his voice a low whisper meant only for her, "Room 618. Thirty minutes."

The numbers hung in the air between them like a secret code.

Her eyes flickered at him, a hint of surprise crossing her features before she quickly masked it.

He straightened up and skated away.

The photo shoot continued around him, but his mind was elsewhere, filled with anticipation. He felt a thrill rush through him, knowing they were sneaking around right under the nose of the entire team.

His mind raced, thinking of feeling his hands on her body, kissing her soft lips, the passion they shared.

•.¸♡ . ♡¸.•

Luka was usually never ruffled, but as he paced the hotel room for the hundredth time, checking his watch anxiously, he felt a knot of dread in his stomach. He had said 30 minutes but she ought to be here by now. He glanced at his watch again.

Just as he was beginning to feel restless, there was a soft knock at the door.

He opened it in an instant, "You are late."

She slipped inside the room in the next second, "Are you sure this is okay?" Ana whispered. "What if someone sees me?"

The door clicked shut behind her.

"I don't care. I've wanted to do this all day," he murmured as he backed her against the wall.

His eyes darkened to the color of a black storm cloud as his gaze dove into hers, and then his mouth descended on hers in a kiss like fire, hot and consuming.

He kept her captive to his kiss, devouring her lips hungrily as if driven by desperation. His hard body pressed against her and the heat of his desire filled the air.

He loved hearing her moan as his lips trailed hot kisses along her neck and collarbone. He wanted to thirst every bit of her, it was like he was drunk and somehow couldn't get enough.

He broke away from her neck and looked into her eyes, his dark with lust. "You want this?" he asked, his voice hoarse.

She nodded, unable to form words as he slipped his hand between her legs, teasing her with his fingers. She arched her back, pushing herself against him, desperate for more.

He chuckled, enjoying the way she squirmed under his touch. "Patience," he murmured. "We have all night."

And with that, he lowered his mouth to hers, kissing her deeply as they both lost themselves in the throes of passion.

Without warning, Luka's hands roughly grabbed her waist and swept her off her feet, carrying her over to the bed where he set her down gently but with unmistakable intention in his eyes.

CHAPTER 31

Ana's body rippled with pleasure as Luka's lips trailed down her neck. His hands explored her body slowly, like he was committing every line and curve to memory. Somewhere along the line, their love life had taken a turn. What used to be frantic and almost aggressive had softened into unhurried reverence.

His hands, once grasping and impatient, now moved with tender purpose. The fire between them still smoldered, hot, but was tempered by affection.

Their lovemaking mirrored the growth of their relationship – a blend of passion and devotion, intensity and comfort. Every caress and kiss whispered a language they had crafted through countless nights spent together.

She liked this new version of Luka.

This Luka was slow, sensual. His caresses were unrushed, his kisses deep and languid. He lavished attention on her, wringing pleasure from her body with an expertise that left her breathless. But it was the tenderness between them, the intimacy in the way he looked into her eyes, that threatened to undo her.

The sensation of his entire body against hers, the roughness of his hands, and the softness of his lips - it all created a conflicting combination that only increased her longing.

Moments like this made her wonder if there could be something real between them. She dared not to hope that it was more than just a "contract relationship," as Luka had called it. Like every contract or agreement, it has an expiration date.

They had an expiration date.

She knew even when they parted ways, she would crave this intimacy between them. No one had made her feel so alive as Luka in the past few months.

She had to stop thinking. It wasn't helping. Not right now.

He grasped the hem of her shirt, dragging it up and over her head in one smooth motion. Her breath caught as his hand skimmed up along her side, clever fingers unhooking the clasp of her bra.

He slid the strap down her arm, leaning in to press a hot, open-mouthed kiss on the newly bared skin. She arched into him with a moan, fingers clutching at the sheets.

With exquisite slowness, Luka's hand came up to cup Ana's breast, his thumb teasing back and forth across the stiffened nipple.

His hands began to move lower, tracing the contours of her body until they found their way to her underwear. He worked to take them off, reveling in the anticipation of what was to come. His fingers graze her clit before plunging his finger inside her. She closed her eyes and bit her lip, trying to stifle her groan. When she looked down at him, his eyes were wild with lust, and beads of sweat were forming on his brow.

"Luka," she gasped.

He ignored her plea, intent only on stoking the fire building within until it threatened to consume her utterly.

His passionate kiss seemed to move over her like a wave, starting at the top of her head and slowly making its way down her body. Everywhere his lips touched, they left trails of fire in their wake.

In an instant, he rolled her on top of him and inserted his length into her. Luka clung to her body as he thrust in and out from underneath. His fingers dug into her with a strength that both surprised and excited her.

"Never been fucked like this before, have you? "

Her thoughts scattered like autumn leaves in a gust of wind as his touch enveloped her, leaving her breathless and devoid of coherent reasoning.

"Still fishing for compliments, but if you must know, I had better," she taunted breathlessly, looking down at him through narrowed eyes.

"The last time you said something like that, you fainted."

"It won't happen this time."

He pulled out and shoved her off him.

Ana almost protested until he said, "Get on your knees. Ass in the air. Hand on the headboard. I am going to punish you right now and maybe next time you will think twice about saying shit like that."

She did as he commanded.

"Remember your safe word?"

"Yeah."

"Good and also don't be afraid to use it, Ana."

"What are you going to do with me?" when she noticed his stern expression. "Fine. I will say the safe word when I need to. Happy?"

He slipped off his belt and looped it around her neck like a choke chain. Her neck pulled upward, the breath choked from her, and there was also even greater tension in her arms.

"So what are you going to do?"

He smirked, "You will soon find out."

Ana didn't mind the choke; she was anxious about exploring this side of herself, but what she did mind was the waiting. Every passing moment intensified her ache, a yearning that etched lines on her face. She desperately needed him like the earth craved the sun after a long, dark night—desperate, essential, and without compromise.

Luka took his time, positioning himself behind her.

Ana gritted her teeth the moment she felt the pressure against her entrance. Then with a single, powerful stroke he drove in its full length as she let out a piercing cry, the sudden ecstasy of this swift intrusion too much to contain in silence.

He began thrusting. It didn't take long for him to quicken the pace, tugging at the belt loop around her neck at the same time.

"What's the color of the sky?"

"Green," she uttered with gritted teeth. Her body rocked back and forth. With each motion, she let out a squeal. There was a measure of sharp pain initially, mixed with the pleasure. But, for her, that pain somehow stimulated the pleasure, deepened it.

"Is this what you want?" he rasped. "For me to take you without mercy until you scream?"

"You'd like that, wouldn't you?" she taunted. "To pretend I'm just another one of your conquests, overcome by your skill?"

From her peripheral vision, she saw Luka's reflection. He was smiling. He was enjoying the game they were playing. Her teasing only fueled his urge to break her stubbornness, and she liked it.

"You are going to be begging for release very soon," he promised darkly. "And we'll both know those pretty lies won't shield you any longer."

He leaned forward to kiss her, conquering a plunder of lips and tongue as he began to move.

Her body trembled with pleasure, waves of ecstasy building and crashing within her in a series of intense climaxes.

It was a sublime and electrifying release she desperately needed. Ana clung to the feeling, chasing the high only he could give her.

She reveled in the thrill of his touch, letting her worries drift away. Their contract relationship, while profitable, was a source of constant anxiety. Was this all there was? Did he not have feelings for her? How can one kiss another in such a tender way and not want to keep them? Was she not enough? Was she only good for his bed and not his heart?

While she had tried to protect her heart...she may have already lost it to this beautiful, complicated, emotionally unavailable man.

He did as he said. He had ruined her for any man.

•.¸♡ . ♡¸.•

Ana sighed, nestling deeper into Luka's embrace. His arms encircled her as she drifted off to sleep, one hand gently caressing up and down her arm.

The weight of exhaustion pulled at her eyelids. "I should be leaving." Her words were slurred. "You know, before... someone sees me."

He held her tightly, cherishing the warmth of her presence, her gentle curves molded against him with a familiarity that whispered of a perfect union, as if she were made to be nowhere else but there, in his arms. The steady rise and fall of Ana's chest and her faint, even breaths were a soothing litany.

"Stay for a couple of minutes."

"Okay, just five minutes." She mumbled in a sleepy tone.

After a short while, "Ana?"

"Hmm."

A beat passed,

"I think I underestimated how much I fell in love with you," he murmured.

When he glanced down, Ana had gone. Hopefully dreaming of something beautiful as a small smile spread across her face.

Luka pressed a kiss into Ana's hair, breathing in the familiar floral scent that lingered there.

•.¸♡ . ♡¸.•

The arena thrummed with energy as fans filled the stands, awaiting the start of the game between Crestmont Giants and Seattle Seals.

Ana gave herself a mini tour around the arena, taking pictures to show Danny. He would be excited to see them.

Up ahead, a tall brown suited man holding a hydrogen flask caught her attention.

"David?"

"Ana. Hi. What are you doing here?" He came in for a hug.

She returned the hug. "My hockey team...um... they are playing here. Do you work here or something?" Then she took a long stare at his suit one more time. "David? What are *you* doing here?"

"Yo. David, the coach wants to see us," someone called from behind.

"I got to go." He stepped backward. "Are you watching the game?"

She nodded, still confused.

"I will look out for you out there."

CHAPTER 32

The battle was on, a fierce contest of skill, strength, and strategy.

The arena seemed to hold its breath, every spectator captivated by the impending clash of wills. In that moment, just before the puck dropped, time appeared to freeze.

It was a collision of determination, a fierce clash of ambitions, as both teams fought relentlessly to gain possession of the puck.

Skates dug into the ice, sprays of frost filled the air, while sticks clashed, creating a symphony of resonating echoes that reverberated throughout the arena.

Luka, with his masterful stick handling, danced through the Seals' defense with a grace that left onlookers in awe.

The Seals' left winger possessed a lightning-fast speed, a force of nature as he weaved through the Giants' defensive lines. In that fleeting display of skill, the crowd held its breath, captivated by the spark of brilliance emanating from the players.

Neither team had yet found the back of the net, but at that moment, the air crackled with anticipation. Everytime they seemed to get control of the puck, it would be intercepted by this new player.

Luka skated to Caleb. "Who the fuck is that guy?"

"David Doku. He is their new left winger. We were literally just talking about him earlier."

"Well, I don't like him." He bit down on his mouth guard.

"You have to admit he is a sharp-shooter."

"I don't care... lets bring him down to earth."

Midway through the first period, Davidson received a perfectly executed pass, burst into the offensive zone, and unleashed a blistering slapshot that beat the Crestmont Giant's goaltender, sending the puck soaring into the top corner of the net.

David raised his stick in celebration and was mobbed by his teammates.

Then he skated across the rink, flashed a smile and tossed a kiss to the crowd — directly at Ana. Players do that all the time. Take someone random in the crowd and wave or whatever, but Luka's stomach twisted into knots when Ana seemingly responded with familiarity.

This wasn't someone random.

She smiled, clapping, her gaze fixed on the Seals' celebration.

Red misted across Luka's vision, jealousy and rage boiling in his veins.

He would not let the seals or this new character *David Doku* ruin their chances of winning tonight. The Crestmont Giant had regrouped and was ready to continue the game.

Barely ten minutes later. Another cheer went up as the Seals took control of the puck again. But then a skirmish broke out near the net. It was now Luka against David, both players struggled for control of the puck.

The buzzer sounded, signaling David's goal for the opposing team. Before David could celebrate this time, Luka slammed full-force into him, knocking the player off balance and sending them both crashing to the ice.

Luka tore off his gloves and helmet, throwing them aside. He grabbed the front of David's jersey and threw a punch into his uncovered face. Blood erupted from David's nose as his head snapped back from the force of the blow. Each punch carried the weight of pent-up anger, fueling the power behind every impact.

Howling in anger, David grappled with Luka, wrestling him to the ice. The two tumbled across the slick surface, landing blow after blow. Nearby players hurried to pull them apart, but both were fuelled by adrenaline and refused to relent.

The referees blew their whistles frantically and waded into the melee. It took four teammates each to drag Luka and David off each other, still swinging at each other. Both were sent to the penalty box, nursing injuries as the crowd erupted into boos and cheers over the dramatic fight.

Fury coursed through Luka's veins as his eyes, burning with intensity, remained fixated on Davidson, who sat in the opposing box.

The team's momentum was disrupted, and the Seals capitalized on the power play, scoring a crucial goal to extend their lead.

The Crestmont Giant lost.

The final buzzer echoed throughout the arena, signaling the end of the game and a bitter defeat for Caleb and the team.

As the Crestmont Giants and the Seattle Seals lined up to shake hands, a longstanding tradition in hockey, Luka found himself face to face with Davidson, the player he had confronted earlier in the game.

Caleb leaned down and whispered. "Be nice."

Luka took a deep breath and extended his hand.

He accepted the handshake, and for a brief moment, they held each other's gaze. Luka's grip tightened ever so slightly, a subtle sign of the competitive fire still burning within him.

David, sensing Luka's determination, squeezed back, acknowledging the fierce rivalry that had played out on the ice.

The handshake line concluded, and the Giants made their way back to the locker room, their heads held a little lower than before. They had tasted defeat.

They entered the locker room. The echoes of the game began to fade, until it became silent except for the sounds of gear being shed.

Luka slammed his stick into the wall, emotions spilling over at last in a rage. His teammates gave him a wide berth as he paced, circling endlessly in a futile attempt to drain the anguish from his veins. He rose to leave the locker room but halted his steps when the coach walked in.

"That was a shitty game. What are you fucking children?" he started to say, but Luka's mind had already wandered off to a certain dark-haired young woman in scrubs who was smiling at someone she shouldn't have.

"Kuznetsov!"

Everyone in the room stared at him. "What the hell happened out there? We lost because of your antics."

"Sorry, Coach," he muttered, schooling his expression.

"What am I going to do with you?" pressing his hand against his temple like he was wading off some headache. "It's no problem, also the press wants an interview with you."

He hated the media and he was in no mood to speak to any of them. "Isn't that the captain's job?" he pointed to where Caleb sat, untying his skates. The last thing he wanted was to fake a smile and give some sound bites to those soulless reporters.

"They don't fucking care. They are looking for some drama and they want to speak to you," he emphasized. "And one more thing, don't give them the drama."

•. ¸♡. ♡¸.•

Luka took a deep breath and stepped forward, facing the barrage of reporters.

The room buzzed with anticipation, the air thick with the collective curiosity of journalists eager to dissect his performances, to unravel the stories hidden within their weary expressions.

His eyes betrayed the weariness and frustration he carried when he met David joining him on the podium.

This was ridiculous. He knew this tactic, the media now trying to pin them against each other. This was another reason he rejected the role of captain years ago, and now here he was wasting his time when he should be... finding Ana.

God. The thought of it all made his jaw clench, muscles still coiled in tension that had yet to fade. Maybe the journalists knew what they were doing when they asked for this joint interview.

The press had gathered around them, microphones and cameras at the ready. They fired away with their inquiries, probing for answers about what went wrong and how the Giants found themselves on the losing end.

Luka sank into the chair, his shoulders slumping with dejection.

"This is the first Crestmont Giant lost since you returned, how do you feel Mr Kuznetsov?"

He paused for a moment, collecting his thoughts, before he began to speak.

"It's a tough loss, no doubt," His voice tinged with disappointment. "We came into this game with high expectations, and we fell short. There's no sugarcoating it. We didn't execute our game plan the way we should have, and the result reflects that."

"Congratulations on the win, Mr David Doku." Another reporter started, microphone poised in hand. "The Seals played with remarkable energy and speed tonight. What do you think gave your team the edge over the Giants?"

David leaned forward, a knowing smile playing on his lips. "Thank you," he replied, his voice carrying a hint of satisfaction. "I suppose our team's youthful vigor and agility played a significant role tonight. I mean, there is no denying that."

Did this fucker just go there? Luka chewed the inside of his mouth in an attempt not to say something people would consider stupid.

The room nodded in agreement, acknowledging the Seals' reputation for their fast-paced style of play.

Another reporter, sensing an opportunity, directed the next question at Luka.

"The Giants are known for their veteran presence and experience. However, tonight the Seals seemed to outpace your team. Do you think the Giants' age is starting to show on the ice?"

"I believe the Giants' experience is an asset, not a hindrance," Luka responded firmly, his voice carrying a note of defiance. "Despite the outcome of tonight's game, hockey is a dynamic sport with many factors at play. Our team of experienced players brings knowledge and leadership to every game. We'll regroup, analyze, and adapt to maintain our advantage."

Another reporter stood and asked, "As the newest player to the Seals, how does this win make you feel?"

The question was directed at David and, with a cocky smile, he answered, "I feel really great. This was a good opportunity to prove myself to my new teammates. We are going home smiling, and I was hoping to learn one or two things from... the experienced players."

With every question posed, Luka's frustration grew more palpable, his responses becoming increasingly curt and clipped. The reporters sensed an opportunity, eager to extract any hint of drama to spice up their reports.

"Mr. Kuznetsov, you seemed to unravel in the final minutes. What went wrong?" A man asked from the back row.

"We... I mean, I was distracted." His pointed look across the table made it clear where blame might lie for wanderings of mind and gaze.

David chimed in, his tone irritatingly calm and moderate. "Every team faces obstacles. We were fortunate to take advantage of a rare mistake on Mr. Kuznetsov's part, but the Crestmont Giant remains a formidable opponent."

What does that mean? Was he mocking them after calling them old?

Luka could take no more, professionalism stripped away as he replied, obviously irritated. "The only reason you fucking won was because I was locked in the penalty box."

"And whose fault is that? You started a fight because you couldn't stand getting your butt kicked. It's okay, there is still a chance to win the Stanley Cup, although not as long as I am playing."

A shocked silence fell over the room, tension thick enough to suffocate.

Camera shutters clicked incessantly, capturing every moment of the interaction between David and Luka. Reporters leaned forward, eager to witness any sparks that might fly between the now rival players.

Luka's hands clenched on the table, a visible display of the restraint he exercised. His knuckles turned white, betraying the internal struggle between his desire to defend his team and the need to maintain professionalism. This was why he didn't want to do this interview.

It didn't take long for one of the team staff to pull Luka out of the scene, putting an end to the interview.

The reporters were ushered away, every one of them packing up their microphones and equipment.

In passing and out of any camera's eye, behind the media booth, Luka said to David. "Stay away from Ana." The words were low but carried every threat he intended.

His lip twitched and Luka instantly held himself back from punching the smile off his face.

"Is that what this is about? Too bad, I don't plan to."

"Seems the punch i gave you earlier didn't do it for you?"

These sudden rivals players found themselves engaged in a heated argument. The noise of passing staff and players created a chaotic backdrop, adding to the tense atmosphere.

"Tell me, what exactly does Luka Kuznetsov know about Ana Sheen? Hmm?" he asked, stepping forward, his expression defiant and met Luka's gaze head-on. "Do you know she cries herself to sleep? Do you know she is literally the kind of person that would set herself on fire if it meant warming up someone she cares about? Do you know she hates being alone because of how dark her thoughts can be? Do you know her dreams? hopes?"

David's words echoed in his ears, and a deep sense of inadequacy settled upon Luka's shoulders. How could he, in his self-assuredness, claim to love Ana when he had failed to truly understand the depth of her emotions?

The revelation hit him with a force that left him speechless, grappling with the realization that he had been blind to her hidden pain.

Images of shared laughter, stolen glances, and tender moments flashed before his eyes, but now they seemed hollow and incomplete. A surge of regret welled up within

Luka. He had been captivated by her vibrant spirit and had failed to see the cracks beneath the surface.

"It's obvious you don't know shit about her." David scoffed, shook his head, and turned to leave.

"You are right." Luka blurted out. "You are absolutely right. I don't know everything about Ana," he admitted, "But what I do know is that I love her. And from this moment forward, I vow to be there for her, to truly see her, and to be the one she can lean on, no matter the struggles she faces, so back to my original statement, back the hell off."

CHAPTER 33

Ana hadn't expected a brawl to start out on the ice and even least expected David, her old friend, to be a hockey player. Last she could recall, the David she knew was terrible at sports, but this David scored most of the goals for the Seattle Seals, leaving the sour taste of defeat on the tongue of Luka.

Her mind was transported back to that moment on the ice, reliving the intense fight with vivid clarity.

Luka had unleashed a flurry of punches at David, totally unprovoked.

The resounding thuds of fists meeting flesh reverberated through the arena, intertwining with the deafening chorus of the crowd's raucous cheers and jeers.

After the game, she tried to catch Luka to talk to him and try to understand what was going on in his head. For some reason, she couldn't get him alone.

When they got to their hotel, she went straight to his room. Ana knocked on Luka's door, her anger barely contained.

The door flew open. Luka stood before her, tension radiating from every rigid line of his body.

"Come to lecture me?"

The hallway buzzed with chatter as Ana pushed through the door. She refused to succumb to the pressure of needing to justify her presence in his room.

"We need to talk."

He whirled to face her before she let another word out.

"Do you know this, Davidson fellow?" Luka's scowl returned at the mention of his name.

She kept quiet for a moment. Her eyes darted away, avoiding eye contact, as if seeking an escape from the intensity of the question. Her fingers fidgeted, tapping a nervous rhythm against her thigh.

"Ana?"

"We used to live in the same neighborhood for a while until his mom got a new job and he moved."

"Did you guys date?"

"When I was a teenager." She waved her hands in the air, as if trying to clear up her thought process. "Wait a minute. Is that why you hit him?"

Luka turned away, stalking across the room. "Nothing quite like defending what's mine to liven up the game."

"Yours?" Her eyes widened, mirroring the surprise that coursed through her veins. "Is that how you see me, as something you own?"

Luka whirled at her, eyes blazing. "Yes, that's exactly how I see you!" He advanced until they were toe to toe, looming over her with hands clenched at his sides. "I thought I had been clear about this. You're mine, Ana. I'm tired of pretending otherwise. Fucking tired of hiding."

She shook her head in disbelief. "You don't get to have it both ways, Luka! You told me once the playoffs end, we end this. Now you're acting like some possessive beast."

Her words made Luka flinch. He looked away, jaw clenched and hands fisting at his sides.

Ana fought to steady her voice. "One minute you're telling me we have an expiration date, the next you're defending my honor like a jealous boyfriend! You tell me we are only friends with benefits and then kiss me like..." she reigned into a sigh.

"It's... it's complicated."

"Complicated?" She looked up at him. "You have a serious issue and I can't deal with this right now." She moved past him, headed for the door.

"No. No. You are not walking out. We are talking about this." He twirled and blocked the door with his full frame.

"Talk about what, exactly? How I'm good enough to sleep and not good enough to keep."

His heart sank, and a flicker of anger ignited within him.

"Ana. Sit the fuck down," he snapped.

She bit down on her lips, her arms folded and flopped down on the bed.

He stood before her, staring distantly, the distress evident in his eyes. His voice, low and husky, revealed the depth of his emotions as he finally spoke the truth that had been tormenting him. "I don't like it when guys look at you and I don't like it even more when you smile at other guys."

"But we are not in a relationship, you said so yourself."

"I didn't mean it! I only said that because..." He trailed off, hands fisting at his sides. "Because I'm terrified one day, you'll realize you deserve far better and walk away."

He wanted to remain silent, shield his heart like always. But the words built inside until he could contain them no longer. "I recognize I don't deserve you," he said in a low voice. "But I can't help that I am selfish enough to want to keep you."

Ana frowned, confused.

Luka took a shaky breath and continued, "You are perfect - beautiful, smart, kind-hearted. And I was just..." He shook his head. "Broken, and lonely with lots of emotional baggage. When I met you, I knew you could mend all the jagged pieces of me in a way no one else ever could."

Luka advanced until he loomed over Ana. His eyes filled with raw anguish.

"No matter what I said before...we belong together. My heart, my life, my everything belongs to you," he whispered hoarsely. "Tell me you know that. Tell me you're mine. I want to hear it from your lips."

Ana stared up at him. The depth of emotion behind those fierce words rocked her to the core. She rose to her feet, her hands came up to clasp Luka's face, gently. "I'm yours."

She beamed with pure happiness, her hands reached for his cheek, waiting until she met his eyes once more - eyes which held not anger but understanding, and a grief to echo her own.

"You foolish man," Ana whispered. "You lost the game."

"I don't care about that."

"You don't really mean that. You like hockey."

"I like you more." He gazed at her intently and tucked a stray lock of hair behind her ear. "Before I met you, hockey was all I had - but now when I'm on the ice, all I can think about is getting back to you."

"Luka..."

"Do you have any idea what you do to me?" he murmured. His thumbs stroked along her cheekbones, igniting sparks beneath her skin.

Luka leaned down, giving her time to pull away. But she had no intention of going anywhere. Her eyes drifted shut as Luka's lips met hers, soft as a featherlight caress.

He kissed her once, then again with a tender passion that deepened by aching degrees. His mouth moved over hers, each kiss sweeter and more intoxicating than the last. Ana's hands grasped at Luka's shoulders, pulling him closer until he groaned against her lips.

His tongue teased along the seam of Ana's lips, coaxing them to part. She opened for him willingly, a thrill coursing through her at the first deep, searching taste of him.

They lost themselves in each other. The world beyond faded away until all that remained was this - Luka's hard, athletic frame pressing her into the wall, their mouths and tongues dancing together in a lover's embrace. Heat sparked between them, burning where their bodies met from chest to hip.

When at last the kiss broke, her body aching from his passion unleashed.

Luka gently pressed his forehead against hers, his breaths coming in ragged bursts. A smile played upon his lips, slightly swollen from their passionate kisses, while his eyes fluttered open halfway, radiating a satisfied gleam.

"Tell me... what do I do to you?"

A low laugh rumbled through Luka's chest. "You undo me completely," he whispered against her mouth.

His raw honesty and emotion stirred her in a way she couldn't explain. She realized with sudden clarity that she wanted him - every part of him. The cold, charming, cocksure man the world saw, and this Luka who hid from all but her. The rough, possessive man who takes what he wants. She craved every part of him.

His hands slid down to grasp Ana's waist, pulling her close against him. She gasped at the feel of his body fitted to hers, firm and wanting - hers for the taking, just as she had always belonged to him.

Deep down, Ana wished she could bare herself like he did. If Luka knew her past and her struggles. He might look at her differently, and that scared her.

She needed to stop thinking, to silence all of her loud, anxious, nagging thoughts of guilt and uncertainty and lock them away in her mind for another time.

Things are different now. She was different now. Different from her teenage self. She would enjoy this... she deserved to be loved.

Luka stilled, regarding her as she took a step back and sat on the bed, hiking her skirt up to reveal her thighs.

He took a step.

"Stop." She held her hand up.

He froze, confused.

"Remember my novel, that page you read?"

"You want to recreate it?"

She shrugged one shoulder like it was no big deal.

Tongue in cheek, Luka considered it. His eyes narrowed when Ana slipped off her panties and tossed it to the side.

"You are killing me." The bulge in his pants was now particularly obvious.

"Kneel."

"I bare my heart to you and you are already abusing power."

"Oh, I plan to abuse my power over every inch of you." She gasped as her finger slipped in her pussy, biting her bottom lips, then said in her most sultry voice. "Are you kneeling or... "

Without hesitation like he was under compulsion, Luka dropped to his knees.

"Now crawl."

CHAPTER 34

He hesitated. Part of him wanted to edge her, curious to see what she would do. Would she deny him from touching her? Well, that was a double-edge sword, that none of them was coming out of it.

His grin widened further when his gaze fell between her legs. His mouth hung open, his eyes never blinked, and he licked his lips as he stared at the glistening flesh, bordered by and splattered with fine, dark hair. He wanted a taste of her, to run his tongue over her, to savor her with his teeth and his lips.

Fuccckk

She touched herself, biting her lips as her fingers pushed inside and out, showing him her juices.

She was wet. Wet and willing for him.

"Crawl," she said, reiterating her words.

He was already on his knees, so he did. Then took her fingers into his mouth, sliding his tongue between her fingers.

Luka glanced up to find her watching him through half-lidded eyes, pupils blown wide with arousal. A wicked impulse seized him. His arousal thrummed hot in his veins at the feel of her against him - but her satisfaction came first.

He grasped her hips, leaning in to trail heated kisses along the sensitive skin of her inner thighs. Further and further he went until he was between her legs.

Ana shivered at his touch, her soft gasp of pleasure firing his blood. He teased higher with lips and tongue, teeth grazing sensitive flesh until she whimpered.

She moaned as his tongue flicked over her clit, sending shivers through her body. He worked her with his mouth, bringing her closer and closer to the edge.

He knew every way to please her, reading her body's responses with ease. Her fingers kneaded at his scalp as he pushed her closer to release, each stroke building upon the last. She was nectar and ambrosia; Luka lost himself in her pleasure, determined to wring every shudder and cry from her lips.

When her orgasm hit at last, he gentled his caresses, drawing out her release until she went limp with sultry repletion.

He slipped a finger into her as his tongue worked its magic.

Her eyes opened at last, still dark and drowsy. "Oh, Luka."

He smiled back wolfishly, triumph and tenderness mingled. His name slipped from her lips like a benediction; her pleasure was his own, a passion that bound two bodies and lives as one.

She was spent, but Luka had yet to be done. She swallowed as he took her in, his gaze intense and hungry. His hands roamed over her breasts, cupping them roughly before pinching her nipples. She moaned at the sensitivity, arching her back to press herself closer to him.

"You like that?" he breathed against her neck, his lips tracing a path down to her chest. Without waiting for an answer, he took one of her nipples into his mouth, swirling his tongue around it before biting down lightly.

She writhed beneath him, her hands tangling in his hair. He moved to her other breast, lavishing it with the same attention.

But she wanted more. Needed more.

Pushing him back, she grabbed his shirt and yanked it off, revealing his chiseled chest. He smirked at her, his eyes filled with desire as she straddled him.

She wanted to see his eyes. Wanted him to see hers. Her fingers grazed over his abs, feeling the ripple of his muscles under her touch.

"What do you want to do?" his breath caught, and an intensity flamed in his eye.

Ana smirked as she lowered herself onto his rock-hard cock. Settling herself onto his hips, burying him deep inside her.

"Shit. That's sheer perfection." He groaned as he watched himself slowly disappearing into her.

His hands now cradled her ass cheeks to push her further down his length, but a smack against his hand prompted him out of the lust-filled daze.

"No touching."

"What?" Luka asked, confused.

She took his hand and pinned them above his head. "I'm in control now."

"Okay. Cool." He swallowed, "Fine."

She eased up and lowered herself back agonizingly slow to the pained arousal of Luka.

Every movement of her hips teased his senses and stirred a deep hunger within him. "Ana... this is torture. I beg of you." he whined, the words came out with more air than actual noise.

She worked her hips back and forth, feeling him touch the walls of her pussy.

Luka's hunger grew more pronounced. The sound of her low moans, the way she closed her eyes in bliss, and the slight smile that played upon her lips only intensified the ache within him. The desire to have her pinned underneath him and fuck her into the bed had become almost unbearable.

"Please let me touch you at least." His fingers twitched.

"*Shh*, I want to tease you."

Each second stretched into an agonizing eternity as Luka endured the torture of watching Ana, unable to satisfy his voracious appetite.

Her grip on his hands loosened and it would seem that's what he was waiting for.

In one quick movement, he spun her around and she was under him.

"I said no touching." She laughed as her arms wrapped around him, kissing him passionately.

"To keep me from touching you, you're going to need handcuffs next time, baby." Luka withdrew his cock back and gently forced it back in with each thrust he added, "I'm going to be rough right now."

"Sure. yeah."

She squirmed, but he held her down, his firm hands gripping her hips as she pounded in her. She loved every second, wrapping her legs around his waist. He was thrusting into her short little pumps, grinding the base of his cock against her.

"Don't stop.... right there." At some point she began thrusting back at him, her back arching as she grind into his pelvis from underneath him. Her orgasm swept through her as she dug her nails into his back. Ana was sure she had drawn blood, but he didn't seem to care.

She screamed and her body shook. He felt her orgasm around his cock and it triggered his release.

He leaned down and kissed her as he came, calling out her name.

Spilling inside her not before taking out his cock and watched as the thick ooze of his cum flowed out then shoved it back in again.

"That was so good," she whispered breathlessly.

Luka rolled over, reaching for the phone beside the bed.

"What are you doing?"

"Calling room service. I thought you might need some food and maybe some alcohol for what we are about to do."

•. ¸♡. ♡¸.•

Sunlight streamed into the hotel room. Ana stirred from sleep slowly, a delicious sensation teasing at her senses. She blinked awake to find Luka propped on one elbow beside her, a lazy smile curving his lips.

"Why are you staring at me like that?"

"Do you know you snore when you sleep?"

Her eyes flared open. "I do not."

"How would you know? You are asleep." A gentle laugh rumbled in his chest as he chuckled. "It's weirdly cute and comforting. I don't mind it."

"Only you would find my snoring cute and comforting."

"I find everything you do cute."

"Thank goodness for that."

His free hand skimmed along her collarbone, down between her breasts, tracing idle patterns across her stomach. Each brush of his fingers left sparks in its wake.

"I want to know everything there is to know about you."

"That's not what I expected you to ask, like months into sleeping with each other."

"I'm serious, Ana. I want to know all there is to know about you."

"Fine. What is it you want to know?"

"Everything," he said softly. "Your hopes, your dreams, the little moments that make you smile when you think no one is watching. I want to know what makes you laugh until you cry, what makes you angry, and everything that has shaped you into the woman before me now. The little and mundane, significant and trivial, past and present. I want it all, Ana."

His lips curved, playful yet sincere. "So you see when I say everything - I mean precisely that."

"I don't know," she whispered, her words laced with a tinge of sadness. "I have never had the chance to know myself." Her eyes were glassy with tears as she slowly came to the realization. "I have always been Ana. Sister and daughter. I'm sorry."

"To me, that is more than enough. You need not apologize for that." He tilted her chin and gazed deep into her eyes, willing her to see the sincerity of his heart laid bare for her alone.

"You made me remember colors I had forgotten even existed. You're a fucking rainbow, Ana - bright and vivid and beautiful. That is who you are. My whole world is better because you're in it."

"No one has ever said that to me," she whispered, nestling deeper into Luka's embrace.

"Then everyone is color blind."

Her shoulder quaked as a round of laughter came out of her.

There was a knock on the door.

"Luka? hello? Everyone is waiting."

That was Lily.

CHAPTER 35

Ana rolled off the bed and started scrambling for her clothes in haste.

"This is bad. This is bad," she said in a hushed tone.

"Remind me, why would it be bad?" Luka leaned back on the bed, his hand underneath his head.

Ana slipped on her shirt and her skirt. "Oh, let me think," her brow furrowed with concern. "Perhaps people who have feelings for you, like Lily and all the other admirers, might come after me."

"You are exaggerating about the fangirls." He waved his hand, got to his feet, and picked up a towel, tying it around his waist. "What's this about Lily?"

"She likes you."

He blinked.

"You didn't know? I mean, everyone can see it. How could you not?"

"I don't see anyone but you." He smirked, and his gaze dropped to her unclad body.

Ana bit her lips, cleared her throat and willed her mind to the matter at hand. "I am merely concerned that if people find out about us right now, they are going to frame the narrative that I got the job because I slept with you." She zipped up her skirt. "Even though it's not far from the truth,

I don't want the team to treat me weirdly, I'm allowed that and I like Caleb and the guys."

His tone now serious and firm, he added, "I won't let the team disrespect you."

The knock came again. Harder this time.

Luka went for the door.

"What–where are you going?" Ana asked in a hushed tone.

Luka reached for the handle. She dashed to hide behind the door, clutching her shirt against her unclad chest.

"Lily, easy with the knocking. You are going to give me a headache," he said, opening the door.

"You haven't gotten dressed yet?"She moved an inch, attempting to enter the room, but Luka blocked the entrance with his body.

"Is everyone ready?"

Lily was a bit distracted, peering into the room. "Umm.. yes. We need to leave now or we will be late for our flight. Did you perhaps throw a party here?"

He tossed his eyes back to the empty wine bottles. He and Ana had ordered more and made love for the rest of the night.

Geez, what had he become? Made love.

He slid a short glance at the girl hidden behind the door, the same one who had managed to slide and nettled in his heart.

"You know, because of our loss yesterday. I just needed a drink...or four."

"Don't beat yourself up." She turned to leave, then stopped. "Any idea where Ana is? I checked her room, but she wasn't there."

"Ana? I believe she's still recovering from last night's... activities."

"I don't understand."

"Something about not being able to walk straight."

Lily brows furrowed.

"Tell the coach I will right down." He slammed the door shut. Stepping back with a wide grin on his face.

Ana shot him an intense glare. "Why? Just why?"

His eyes slid down and then settled on her face. "The fact you are standing tells me I may have not done my job well last night. Want to go for another?"

She bit her lips, hiding her smile. "It's too early for this. I'm leaving." Her fingers gripped the door handle, waiting.

Luka moved around the room, picking his clothes. "I thought you were leaving?"

"I just want to make sure Lily is not out there."

"Or we could simply let everyone know..."

"No," she said firmly before leaving the room.

•.¸♡ . ♡¸.•

Ana rushed towards the idling hockey team bus, her cheeks flushed. The coach and several teammates were gathered outside, concern written on their faces.

"Where have you been?" The coach demanded. "We were worried sick that something had happened to you!"

"I'm so sorry, I..." Ana stammered to a halt. She couldn't possibly tell them the truth of what had kept her. Or rather, who - a certain charming rogue she found impossible to resist, even with the threat of missing their flight looming...

Caleb strode over, frowning. "Are you hurt? What's going on? Lily said something about you getting hurt or something."

"Oh, I tried using the gym here and um... she laughed. "Let's just say I am not a gym person, but I am fine, walking perfectly straight." Ana insisted, avoiding his eyes. If they caught so much as a glimpse of the real reason for her delay, she would die on the spot. "Just... got held up. I'm sorry to have worried everyone," she called out.

If there was anybody that should be dead, it was Luka for putting her on this childish prank.

Lily didn't look convinced, staring at her from the window. Jude and the others were still watching in confusion and concern, murmuring amongst themselves.

Luka propped up from the bus, looking out to the window. "For heaven's sake, woman, at least call next time if you're going to be late! We're on a schedule here."

Fighting back a smile. "My bad." Ana stepped onto the bus, her sights landed on Luka sitting near the front.

Luka's eyes gleamed with amusement, his face lit up in a smile at the sight of her, burning right through her like a hot coal.

"Lily." Pavel tried to get her attention but she ignored him and went straight to Luka.

Settling beside him. "Hi... you don't mind," her finger twirled around her golden locks.

Of course, she'd take the open seat next to Luka.

A bitter taste of envy coated Ana's tongue, leaving her with a lingering sense of discontent. Even though it was her request for them to remain a secret, she couldn't help but feel jealous at the sight of Lily's closeness to Luka.

It was just a seat. You had his tongue in you a couple of hours ago. Twice.

She bit back a sigh, made a beeline to the back of the bus and settled for vacant seats.

A moment later, someone dropped into the seat beside her. The familiar smell of strong perfume filled her nostrils. She didn't need to look up to know the identity.

Caleb nudged her shoulder. "Alright, out with it," he demanded in an undertone. "How long have you and he been hooking up?"

"How did you find out?"

"You mentioned 'walking straight.' I didn't. Lily also said Luka mentioned exactly the same words which means when he had said it, you were there. My little sister may be a bit naïve and blinded by her crush on Luka, but I'm not."

"It's a bit complicated."

"Funny. He used that word too. Maybe you two are made for each other." A smile slipped on Caleb's lips. "I don't know if you guys are keeping it on the down low, but you are doing a terrible job at it, especially him."

He stood up and returned to his seat.

Ana glanced ahead to where Luka sat, Lily had settled beside him. Like he could sense her gaze, he turned back to her.

She gave him a small smile.

Lily was chatting animatedly to Luka, oblivious to the undercurrents at play.

He turned his attention back to Lily and said a few short words before he slipped on his headphones.

Beep.

Ana's phone emitted a gentle vibration, announcing the arrival of a text message. She glanced at her phone, her eyes absorbed the words etched upon the glowing screen.

"Seriously? Him? Anastasia Sheen, we need to talk." — David.

CHAPTER 36

Luka hummed to himself as he stirred the pasta sauce on the stove, the aroma of garlic and herbs wafting through the kitchen. Dainty arms wrapped around him from behind, and he leaned back into Ana's embrace.

"I could get used to this, you cooking for me." She murmured, dropping a kiss onto his neck.

Luka replied jokingly, "Well, I know how to cook five things. I hope you don't get bored."

"Never."

"It's almost ready. Why don't you set the table?"

She gave him another quick squeeze before moving to grab plates and cutlery. Luka watched her out of the corner of his eye, heart swelling with affection.

Who would have thought he could be so domesticated? He cherished every moment of normalcy they had together like a present, almost like he got a glimpse of what their life would be like if they were... together, in more of a permanent sense.

The issue about his supposed arranged marriage loomed at the back of his thoughts, Luka knew he couldn't hide that from Ana for long. He had to tell her... no. He had to talk to his father instead.

"What plans do you have today?" she asked, interrupting his thoughts.

"What? Sorry you said something."

"What's going on with you... you've been in your head for the last couple days."

He forced out a smile. "Nothing. Just... umm... I don't want to quit hockey."

Her brows raised then followed by a small chuckle. "That's what you've been thinking about."

"Yep."

"What about your dad?" she leaned over the countertop. "Have you told him yet?"

"No, but I will." He turned off the cooker, and picked up a rag, wiping his hands. "So what are we doing today? Want to stay in and watch tv and maybe cuddle up?"

"That sounds nice but today I'm taking out my braids and washing my hair so as you can see I'm set and booked."

"Oh. I could help you."

She arched an eyebrow and gave him a puzzled look. "You want to help me take out my braids?"

"How hard can undoing a few braids be?" he crossed his arms confidently.

"If you insist... this should be amusing."

•. ¸♡ . ♡¸.•

After breakfast, they cuddled up on the couch with full bellies and contented sighs.

Ana sat down on the tiled floor with her back to Luka. "Go right ahead then, Mr. Capable. The brush and oil are there when you need them."

She opened her latest romance novel while Luka toyed with her braids, unraveling the strands.

Luka cracked his knuckles and examined her braids. "Right, let's see..." he reached for one braid and started unweaving it meticulously, tongue poking out in concentration. "Almost got it..."

Luka studied the tangled mess of Ana's braids with a furrowed brow. How had he managed to twist them into such a complicated knot? He tugged at one plait, trying to determine where the end began.

She giggled, "How's it going back there?"

He huffed in frustration. "I think I made a knot. I got it."

He squinted at the braids again, searching for the weak point in their defenses. This was more complicated than any hockey play he had encountered, but he wasn't going to give up.

"Your braids seem to be fighting back, but..."

He stretched out the braiding hair, showing Ana. "One down... several to go."

"In all seriousness, though, if it is too difficult, you can stop. I don't want you pulling my hair out over this - literally."

Luka shook his head and smiled. "I have gotten the hang of it. It's not hard or frustrating at all. Besides, this gives me an excuse to be close to you longer."

His gentle tugs on her hair were soothing as she was engrossed in her novel.

"Is that one of your sexy books?"

"I don't read only *sexy books*." Ana tilted her head to look up at him. "This one is a rom-com. You know a sweet love story with a happy ending. I can be sentimental like that."

Luka wriggled his wrist before selecting another thin braid and gently worked it free.

After an hour and a half of struggling, his fingers were sore. He flopped against the back of the couch with a sigh.

"It is finished."

Ana's braids were completely undone, leaving her natural curls unbound in a soft cloud around her face. He ran his fingers through the coils and waves, marveling at their springy texture.

"There now, all done. Your braids put up a good fight, but I conquered them in the end." Luka smiled, pleased with his eventual victory.

She set down her book and picked up the mirror she had placed beside them, her eyes widening. "You did a good job." She looked at Luka, a hesitant smile tugging at her lips.

Luka gazed at her, taking in the natural beauty as he fingered a lock, letting it wrap and cling around his finger. "I love your hair like this, natural and free - like you."

Her expression softened into a smile. "Thank you, my brave knight, for conquering one braid at a time."

Luka chuckled, pulling her into his lap. "In that case, fair lady, your knight could use a reward for his futile efforts. What do you say to a kiss for his trouble?"

He pressed his lips against hers in a lingering kiss, and she responded with an eager sigh. His arms were strong and steady around her back as he explored every inch of her mouth with playfully sweet movements as he smiled against her lips.

The television was on in the background, the sounds of the sports highlights reel filtering through. Luka ignored it until a familiar team name caught his attention. He glanced up just as the announcer's words echoed in the living room.

"What's that?" Ana turned facing the television screen.

Luka sat up straighter, his hands firmly hooked around Ana's waist, eyes peeled on the television screen.

"The seals won tonight - if we defeat the Cougars next week, we'll face them in the finals."

"Is that a good thing?"

"It will be when I beat your ex-boyfriend's ass."

"Luka, no fighting."

He groaned, "Fine. I will try."

Luka's phone chimed with an incoming text. He glanced at the screen and sighed, muscles tensing. It was from his father - the man who had always sought to control Luka's path in life.

The last time they spoke, his father had demanded Luka quit hockey to join his business and marry some socialite bride of his choosing. Luka had agreed in anger, eager to find out the truth about his mother. But that was before Ana. Before he confessed his feelings to her. Before he had gotten used to waking up to the low hum of her snore.

Her soft caress against his cheek prompted him back to reality.

"It's my father. He is in the city and throwing one of his lavish parties tonight and insisting I attend."

"Oh?"

He could bring Ana as his date tonight, to show her off in subtle defiance and make clear in no uncertain terms that his choice was made.

Luka turned to her, "Come with me. These events are tedious without company, and I'd rather have you by my side to help me endure it all."

She pushed herself off him and settled beside him. "I -I - I just removed my braids."

"I'm sure I can get a stylist, one that is familiar with your hair." He picked up his phone, scrolling through his contacts.

"No. I mean, you are ruining my system. I'm supposed to scroll endlessly online looking for a hairstyle for at least a day before I end up choosing probably the same one I just removed."

He smiled, looking at her. "Okay but the dinner is tonight."

She groaned burying her face in her hands. "Also, I don't have anything suitable to wear. I'd feel out of place."

"Don't worry baby." Luka stood, pulling Ana to her feet. "I've been remiss - I should have spoiled you with gifts long before now. Let's go shopping. My treat."

CHAPTER 37

Ana usually preferred braids because it was as easy as fixing her baby hairs and running out the door, hence the thought of straightening her hair and styling every morning was tedious but Luka had other plans.

Luka had arranged a meeting with a renowned celebrity stylist who would transform her hair and another to shop for dresses.

The skilled hands of the stylist, a talented black woman herself, moved with a graceful expertise. Her fingers deftly weaved and intertwined, adorning Ana's natural hair with the transformative beauty of faux-locs. Ana relaxed into the chair; though not usually one for lavish pampering, she had to admit that it felt wonderful.

Ana's hair exuded regal elegance, the faux-locs cascading down her back with undeniable glamor.

Luka stood before her, dressed to the nines in a sleek black tuxedo that fit him like a glove. In the right light, the fabric seemed to shimmer a vibrant celestial blue.

"You look hot," she uttered, unable to contain her admiration.

"I could say the same for you. I love the hair." Luka marveled at the outcome.

"Really? I was thinking i should have gone with a weave or–

"No. This is perfect. You are perfect."

She nodded. "Now we move on to the dresses."

Luka simply waved his fingers, signaling for someone to enter the room. A woman came forward, pushing a large cloth rack filled with garments of all sorts.

Ana pushed herself off the chair and began to scan through the rack, her eyes settling on different bright colors and styles.

She reached out and carefully selected a deep emerald green dress that seemed to have been tailored especially for her.

She entered the dressing room and slipped on the dress. It was a form-fitting silhouette that accentuates her curves, and a flattering V-neckline. The most striking feature is the thigh-high slit on the left side of the skirt, which added sensuality.

Ana stepped out of the dressing room and Luka's eyes darkened with desire at the sight of her in it.

He stood in front of her, tracing her exposed skin. "Maybe we should, you know, ditch the dinner party."

Ana shivered at his touch, heat blooming under her skin. She turned in his arms, eyebrows raised. "You were the one so eager to buy me couture and show me off to your father, were you not?" Her lips twitched. "Perhaps you should have thought twice about spoiling me."

Luka groaned. "Oh baby. I have no regrets spoiling you." He planted a kiss on her neck. His eyes gleam of a wicked promise. "Before this night is over, your dress and all else beneath shall be mine to ravish with pleasure and without delay."

•. ,♡ . ♡ ,.•

Ana sat in the passenger seat of Luka's car, her body tense with anticipation. She wrung her hands together and her fingertips drummed on her thighs.

The window offered her glimpses of the house they were headed to - his father's place. A sense of dread settled deep in her stomach.

She knew little of Luka's family beyond what was reported in the media. They were socialites and influential business magnates. Her mind raced with all sorts of worries and fears.

What if his family didn't like her? What if they thought she wasn't good enough for their son? What if she spilled something on her dress or said something stupid?

Anxiety flared inside her like a fire, but it quickly subsided when Luka reached out to clasp her trembling hands.

"I'm here." He whispered, bringing it to his lips and placing a kiss on the back of her hand.

She smiled, then gazed up at the sprawling mansion in awe. This was no simple family dinner - it seemed Mr Stefan was hosting a lavish party, and many prominent guests were in attendance. Limos and sports cars lined the winding driveway, with valets parking each new arrival.

Luka escorted her inside, firmly holding her hand.

Ana paused in the doorway, her breath catching in her throat as she took in the grandeur of the dining room. Light fixtures twinkled above like stars in a night sky and crystal glasses sparkled like diamonds in the low light. The room was filled with elegantly dressed people chatting and laughing over cocktails, while waiters walked around serving hors d'oeuvres on silver platters. She recognized a few politicians among the well-heeled crowd, their haughty expressions evident even from a distance. This was a world of prestige and power, far from anything she knew. She suddenly felt out of place in her new dress and hair.

Luka squeezed her hand. "You okay?"

"This is not a -meet my girlfriend type of dinner."

"Trust me, here nobody cares, everyone is too focused on kissing my father butt-

"You made it." Stefan strode up to greet them, "You brought a guest, I see."

Luka turned. "Dad, I want you to meet someone, Ana sheen."

If Stefan was surprised, he did not show it. Jaw tightened, but his expression remained politely neutral.

"Charmed," he said, though clearly anything but.

Stefan was a stern, imposing man with an aura of cold authority. His sharp gray eyes seemed to pierce through Ana, assessing and judging her with a single sweeping glance.

No warmth softened the hard lines of his face or the calculating gleam in his eyes.

A younger man approached, grinning at Luka. "I hoped you would come." He turned to Ana, smiling warm and genuine. "You must be the woman who has finally captured this rascal's heart. I'm Vlad, Luka's older brother."

"A pleasure to meet you," Ana said. At least one member of Luka's family seemed pleased to welcome her.

Vlad took Ana's hand, patting it fondly. "The pleasure is ours. Any woman who can tame my wayward brother is a treasure worth keeping." His eyes twinkled at Luka's mock scowl. "Now, if you'll excuse me, I have guests to attend to. We will speak more later."

"I like your brother."

"Well, be careful or he will shove a knife in your back."

Ana didn't know how to take that comment. She followed Łuka led as they shuffled with the rest to the dining hall.

•.¸♡ . ♡¸.•

They were seated among other important dignitaries and celebrities. Chefs milled around preparing dishes table side as waiters poured wine. She had known Luka came from a well-off family, but their lavish home and formal dinners were more than she had bargained for.

She pretended an interest in the conversation, though she couldn't follow all the cultural and political references flying over her head.

Luka sensed her unease and turned to the silvered haired woman seated next to Ana.

"Kristina, this is Ana. Ana, this is Kristina Werner, an old family friend. She practically raised me."

Kristina smiled warmly at Ana. "So lovely to meet you! Please, call me Kris."

Ana smiled back, relieved. "It's nice to meet you."

Kristina effortlessly drew Ana into conversation, asking about her life, hobbies and interests. Her kind, genuine demeanor put Ana at ease.

Soon Ana found herself chatting away, forgetting about the pomp and grandeur around them.

Ana met Luka's eyes with a grateful smile. His small act of introduction had allowed her to connect with Kristina, gaining an ally in that sea of strangers.

Luka's father, Stefan, smiled as he addressed the stunning woman beside him.

"Everyone, please welcome our guest of honor tonight, the lovely Helen Dover."

"I'm sorry, I'm late. I just got in from Paris." The lady settled on the seat beside Łuka. "Thanks for the invite, Mr Stefan."

Ana's eyes widened - the famous actress herself? This was surreal.

"Remember, my son?"

"Yes. you made me a hockey fan," she said, smiling brightly. "I love watching you play, it's so thrilling."

Luka nodded, "thank you."

"My hope is that the Crestmont Giants take home the cup. I'm trying to clear my schedule to make sure I make it to your next game."

Ana glanced at Luka, but his attention remained on his glass.

With the wide grin on Stefan's face and Helen's hand touching Luka as she spoke, there was only one explanation. It made her heart sank as she realized this dinner was likely Stefan's vain attempt to match make.

That stung Ana.

Helen exudes effortless beauty and poise, as though she was born for magazine covers. She had everything from her red hair to her makeup to her designer dress perfectly in place. Everything about Helen is polished and refined, which was something she was not.

"So what do you do, Ana?"

She had been so distracted, she didn't hear where the question came from.

"Ana is the physiotherapist for the team. She is amazing at her job and honestly, I don't think I would have been able to go back on the ice if not for her."

Luka answered with a proud smile across his face.

"Thanks." She mouthed.

Stefan spoke after a bite. "It wouldn't be fair to give her all the credit. What about the surgeons who worked on your shoulder, the previous physiotherapists and doctors who helped with your recovery?"

"I'm not belittling their ability, but they didn't help my performance anxiety and panic attacks. She did." Luka's leg brushed against hers under the table, a subtle reassurance.

"Hmm." Stefan gave a small nod, his stare fixed on her.

His gaze had a way of stripping her bare of confidence and assurance, reducing her vulnerabilities.

Vlad coughed and asked, "How have practices been going, Luka? The finals are coming soon. People are saying the Seattle Seals might come for the cup."

Ana was glad for the change in topic and wanted nothing to do with any discourse. Ana tried to focus on her meal. But her hands shook as she grasped her knife and fork, keenly aware of Luka's father's scrutinizing gaze.

She had the sense Stefan did not fully approve of her. She chewed slowly. Nobody would ask her any more questions if her mouth was busy, right?

"So, Miss sheen," Stefan said in a silken tone.

Oh no.

"How much is my son paying you to fake moans?"

The table went silent. She opened her mouth, but no reply emerged, stunned speechless by his audacity.

Luka threw his napkin onto the table. "That's enough!" he glared at his father. "Ana is my girlfriend and my guest here tonight. I won't have you disrespecting her this way."

Stefan gave a derisive snort. "Come now, son. We both know of your encounters. I don't mind because it's your money you can spend however you wish but surely." His gaze turned scornful as it flicked over Ana. "You could find someone of better breeding and means."

Helen hid her chuckle behind her perfectly glammed up nails. There were a couple of laughs coming from others, but Ana dared not try to look up to find out.

Under Stefan's scrutiny, she felt small and inadequate, as though failing to measure up to some invisible standard of worth.

In the suffocating stillness that followed, Ana pushed back her chair.

She endured Luka's father condescending remarks and subtle insults no longer.

Ana set her napkin down, the remnants of her appetite vanishing. "If you'll excuse me," she said, in a tone as polite as she could muster. Without waiting for a response, she strode from the opulent dining room as fast as she could without breaking into a run.

Once out of sight, Ana quickened her pace. She was overwhelmed, fighting back tears of anger and hurt pride with every step.

What did she expect? That they welcome her with open arms. This was ridiculous. Deep down in her heart, she knew Luka and wasn't compatible. That's why she was scared to tell people about her relationship with Luka. Tonight proved her fears were right.

"Ana!" Luka's voice called out from behind.

Ana strode down the hallway as quickly as possible, eager to escape but she had only gone a short distance when Luka caught up, grasping her arm to stop her.

"Don't leave. Please. Don't leave."

CHAPTER 38

Luka held her close, his touch gentle yet desperate, as if clinging to her presence to anchor himself against the fear that threatened to consume him.

He repeated, "Please... please don't leave." Luka whispered, his voice laced with raw emotion.

His eyes searched her face, seeing the hurt she could no longer conceal and the frustration boiling beneath her skin.

Eyes glassy and filled with tears and somehow not a drop had fallen.

"Why did you bring me here? Did you know Helen would be attending tonight?"

The truth struck home, filling him with self-recrimination.

He had brought Ana with the intention of provoking his father, but didn't realize that he was also subjecting her to the same type of criticism that his father usually directed at him.

When he failed to respond,

"You knew?"

"I suspected."

"I think I need some space." She twisted her wrist from his grip.

The mere mention of space from Ana sent a jolt of terror through Luka. If she walked away now, the fragile remains of his battered heart would shatter at last beyond all repair. He was certain of that.

A shiver of dread crawled up his spine, sending a chill through his body as he watched her reach for the grand staircase banister. Anguished memories of his mother's abrupt departure, reverberating in his mind, force him into a state of panic. His heart lurched with dread at the possibility of losing Ana like he had lost his mother - forever. He could not bear to take the risk.

Without pausing to think, he lunged forward, the sound of his footsteps echoing off the marble floor. His fingertips grazed her wrist just as she began to descend the stairs.

"I messed up. I get it. Please... please don't walk away from me. Yell at me, curse me if you want, but don't leave like this whenever we argue." His voice was ragged. "I can't-I can't- I'm sorry I didn't tell you. I wasn't thinking."

He stopped in front of her, blocking her path. His skin was damp with sweat, and his breath came hard and fast.

She had never seen him so shaken before. "Luka, are you okay?"

"Just tell me you forgive me," he pleaded. "Tell me you're not leaving. I need to hear you say it."

With gentle hands cradling Luka's face, her touch tender and comforting, "I am not leaving you. This... this is not a breakup."

Hearing that eased his heart, but he owed Ana the truth, though the memory still haunts and burns like fire. "She left, my mother. After a huge argument with my dad, she left... That was the last time I ever saw her." His voice was raw and cracked.

The memory had haunted him and since then he had lived in terror of his loved one leaving.

Ana locked eyes with Luka, and a flicker of understanding crossed between them. At that moment, she caught the vulnerability, fear, and anguish etched upon his face. It was as if a veil lifted, and she understood the reasons behind his guarded heart.

Her rage faded, replaced by a desire to assure him. She brushed the tear that hung at the corner of his eye.

Her voice softened. "I'm right here. I will always be here." Ana caressed his cheek softly.

She gazed up at him, her anger fading beneath the warmth of his touch and the love still shining clearly in his eyes for her alone.

Luka hugged her into an embrace, inhaling her scent. She fit so perfectly in his arms. He glanced up briefly, his eyes catching a glimpse of his father at the top of the stairs.

Stefan stood there, observing the scene unfold, his presence a stark reminder of the challenges they faced.

In that fleeting moment, their eyes met, and Luka's gaze held a silent message.

"My father is right about one thing–I should forget about the past and look to the future."

"Hmm?"

He pulled away from the hug and looked down at the beautiful woman in his arms. "You are my future because you are the only woman I see. Not Lily. Not Helen or any other. Only you... Ana Sheen."

Luka captured her lips in a tender kiss.

Ana wrapped her arms around his neck, melting into the kiss.

He dragged his hand down her body, setting off sparks of electricity with each touch. His fingers were like fire as they touched her thigh, leaving a trail of heat in their path as he reached for the hem of her dress and snuck his hand underneath.

Breathless, Ana drew away to gaze up at him. "What are you doing?" she asked, eyes sparkling.

His fingertips ran deliciously around her thigh. She inhaled sharply as he hovered over her lace panties, and plunged them inside her warmth. Her back arched and a moan escaped her lips as pleasure rummaged through her body.

"I'm apologizing." He said as his finger explored deeper.

The sounds of music and conversation still echoed on the stairs.

"Someone might see -"

His lips silenced her objections, demanding her full attention. "Let them see. I want the world to know you are mine - and I am utterly consumed by you."

Luka deepened the kiss with a groan of pleasure as he thrust two fingers inside of her and fucked her hard with his fingers, his thumb rubbing vigorous circles on her clit.

Luka didn't know whether it was because they were in public or if it was the feel of his long fingers plunging in and out of her, but it sent her teetering on the edge and he loved it.

She had her hands on his shoulders now for stability and moaned with each exhaled breath. She moved her hips closer against his finger.

He sensed her mounting arousal and responded by deepening his fingers and making several in-and-out motions.

He loved watching her writhe while she tried not to cry out, her nails burrowed into his skin, her grip on his hair as if it was her only anchor in a sea of pleasure. Her little whimper because she was trying hard not to moan. The little signs he learned meant she was close to orgasm.

"I want you to come over my fingers."

"I... don't want to ruin this dress."

"Fuck the dress. I will buy you a thousand more. Ana, come for me." He applied more pressure with his finger.

She closed her eyes and buried her face against my shoulders to muffle her moans. She started trembling as she approached her climax.

He let his finger slide out of her and out of her panties.

She stood straight, opened her eyes slowly and looked at me and whispered one word, "wow".

Luka inserted his glistening fingers into his mouth for a quick little taste as she watched.

"You are crazy."

"I know."

She glanced down at him and could see him hard, straining against the fabric of his pants.

"You can't go back inside like this? What do you say we do at home and I take care of that?"

"If we can make it home. I might have to tear off this dress in the car."

•.¸♡ . ♡¸.•

Ana slammed the passenger door of Luka's sleek black Porsche, eager to make their escape from the disastrous party behind them.

Luka slid into the driver's seat, grasping her face in his hands. He captured her lips in a burning kiss, drawing her closer across the center console until she was nearly straddling him.

Ana melted into his embrace, the rest of the world forgotten. Her fingers grasped at his silk tie, longing to tug it loose and undo the buttons of his tailored designer shirt. She ached to have his skin against her own, to soak in the warmth radiating off his athletic build.

Luka's hands found the zipper of her sequined evening gown, slowly dragging it down to her bare shoulders as his mouth trailed hot kisses along her throat. "I've wanted to do this all night," he rasped, shrugging out of his suit jacket and throwing it carelessly into the spacious backseat.

A loud ringing broke the sensual spell, Ana's phone buzzing inside her handbag on the floorboard. She pulled away reluctantly, grabbing for it and trying not to tumble off Luka's lap. "My phone."

He nuzzled against her throat, "Ignore it," Luka urged, trying to recapture her lips as his hands slid up her thighs, grasping her hips.

Ana shivered in pleasure and longing but shook her head, pushing at his chest. "I'll just be a minute." She slid back into the passenger seat, digging through her handbag until she located the phone. She glanced at the screen, her expression subtly shifting. Luka, ever observant, caught the change.

Curiosity and a hint of unease mingled in Luka's voice as he asked, "Ana, everything okay?"

With a quick shake of her head, she replied, "You are right. Ignored." She tucked the phone back into her mini purse before returning to reclaim his lips in a desperate attempt to rekindle the passionate connection they had temporarily lost.

Yet, despite her reassurance, a lingering suspicion gnawed at the back of Luka's mind. He couldn't shake the nagging concern that Ana's reluctance to answer the call in his presence hinted at something more.

Trying to silence his inner turmoil, Luka clung to the hope that it was merely a fleeting thought, a baseless worry born out of insecurity. For now, he chose to bury his unease beneath the veil of their shared intimacy, hoping that their love would triumph over whatever came their way.

CHAPTER 39

Ana sighed as she looked over the last paperwork, eager for a distraction from reliving the disastrous events of the previous night.

Meeting Luka's insufferable father at the dinner party had been awkward enough, with his constant disapproving glares and thinly veiled insults.

Her thoughts kept drifting back to her own father's unexpected phone call. She wanted nothing more than to bury every memory of him, but as usual, the man always had a way to ruin the little happiness she created for herself. With Luka by her side, she found strength and courage - but the ugliness of her past was one she wasn't ready to share with him.

Almost like her thoughts had summoned him, her phone rang again. She grabbed it with trepidation. "Hello?"

"Finally, you still answer for dear old daddy." Her father's voice was bitter and cutting. "Though I'm surprised you found the time, seeing as you've abandoned your only family to shack up with some rich man."

His words struck deep, reopening old hurts and guilt Ana had long thought healed.

"You act all self-righteous and for what? You are worse than me."

Tears welled up in her eyes as her father's rage persisted, his words like sharp blades scraping at her soul, aimed to hurt and wound with each syllable.

Finally, Ana found her voice. "Enough!" She drew in a shuddering breath. "You destroyed this family long ago. You offered me to those gangsters!" Angry tears burned in her eyes at the injustice. She had suffered enough heartache at his hands; she would not endure insults now.

"Don't spout your lies at me, girl. I gave you everything, and you threw it back to whore yourself out to the highest bidder!" Her father's tone grew uglier and more enraged with every accusation. "Instead of you trying to help me, you abandoned me. Your father. Your only family!"

"Danny is my family. I don't need to listen to you. My life is my own now - you gave up the right to judge me. The only one who ever hurt and abandoned me was you." Ana struggled to keep her voice level. "Goodbye Dad. I won't allow your venom in my life again."

"Wait — Her father's protest was cut off as Ana ended the call, hand trembling.

Her blood pressure rose as the heat of anger flushed her face. Her breathing came in rapid, shallow gasps as she paced furiously around the office, trying to work off some of the adrenaline coursing through her veins.

The phone blared again.

Ana grabbed it without glancing at the screen, in a pain-stricken voice, "Leave me alone!" she cried. "You destroyed us - there's nothing left to say!"

A startled pause, before a familiar voice spoke her name in concern. "Ana? It's David." He trailed off, no doubt taken aback by her harsh greeting.

A flush of embarrassment rushed over her, pushing aside all the emotions she had been feeling. "I - I'm sorry, David. I shouldn't have... please excuse my outburst." Having taken a deep breath to steady herself, she realized what she had done. "My apologies."

"Do you want to talk about it? I'm in town."

Ana glanced up, Fingers gently tapped against her desk, contemplating his offer. She had known David for years; they came from similar backgrounds, children of broken homes and loss. If anyone understood her family drama, it would be him. But his feelings for her had always been more than friendly, and she was worried confiding in him might give the wrong impression.

Still, she needed someone to open up to or she might burst. Luka could never fully grasp the baggage she carried. David had lived through similar struggles; with him, there was no need to put on a brave face.

"Fine. Ten minutes."

Ana hurried out of her office, glancing at her watch. If she could make it to David's within the hour, she might return before Luka finished with his charity event.

•.¸♡.♡¸.•

Ana pushed open the door to the quaint corner café. A little bell tinkled overhead as she escaped the balmy outdoors for the familiar cool interior. She paused to take in the worn wooden floors, cozy booths along the walls, and the aroma of fresh baked goods mingling with coffee. Sunlight filtered through the front windows.

She hadn't told Luka about David's text message so as not to cause some friction, which was probably not the best way to start their relationship. She made a silent promise to herself to tell him about this meeting later considering It was much better to ask forgiveness than for permission.

David was already seated at a booth in the back, away from the other patrons. He stood with a smile as she made her way over, enveloping her in a warm hug. "It's good to see you again."

"You too," Ana said, sliding into the seat across from him. Her heart fluttered with nerves as she studied his face - still as handsome as always, yet perhaps more careworn. They made stilted small talk until the waitress brought Ana's coffee and the elephant in the room could no longer be ignored.

"I thought you were angry at me or something. I can't imagine who was meant to receive your wrath."

"My father called," Ana said at last, gaze fixed ahead. "He hasn't changed. Still blaming me for everything wrong in his life. You know what he is like."

David's expression turned grim. "I'm sorry. I know how he can be." He searched for the right words. "But don't let him have power over you, Ana. You're stronger than he is - you built a life for yourself despite everything."

She blinked back tears, touched by his support. David had always known what to say to lift her; she was lucky to have him as her friend.

"Thank you," she said softly, bumping his arm with her own. "For listening, and for being there. I don't know what I'd do without you."

David smiled, though it did not quite reach his eyes. "I'll always be here when you need me."

"So, you're playing hockey now?" Ana asked, grasping her warm mug for something to do with her hands. They hadn't seen each other since she saw him play.

"I didn't mean to hide it but-" He glanced out the window at the passing traffic. "When you said you'd never date a hockey player, I didn't want that to destroy my chance before I even had a chance." He let out a short laugh. "Funny how things turned out."

"I.." She started, paused, shaking her head ruefully. "We weren't together officially till a couple of days ago."

"Good, so it's not too late to end it." David's hands grasped hers against the wood tabletop. "Luka's not right for you..." He held her hand tighter. "I know you, and he'll only end up hurting you. Don't you see that?"

She pulled away, anger rising sharp and quick. "But you don't know him."

"I know people like him. If he knew the truth about your past, would he still want you?" David asked quietly, and immediately regretted it.

Ana stared at him, her face fell. He did not just go there.

"I didn't mean it like that."

She folded her hands and leaned over the table. "Are you threatening me? Do you want to ruin my career? Christ, David. When I was young, I made a mistake. I was sick. You, of all people, knew of my situation." Her heart was pounding as she stood.

"I'm sorry I shouldn't have said that." He reached for her hand but she retreated it.

He let his breath out slowly, as if trying to collect himself so as not to say the wrong thing.

"I'm sorry. I shouldn't have brought that up. I care about you a lot, can't you... I don't know... quit."

It would seem everyone had a lot to say about her life and she was getting tired of it. Biting down on her bottom lips, she pushed herself up. "This was a mistake, coming here was a bad idea. I should go, David. Goodbye."

Ana strode from the cafe without looking back, unable to stop trembling. But her path was certain - she had to tell Luka the truth before David's attempt to blackmail her did damage to the new life she was building. She could only hope that Luka's love was strong enough to weather any storm. The past was done, yet the battles were never over... Ana steeled herself, heading home to the man who had found her at her lowest - and showed her she could rise again.

•.¸♡ . ♡¸.•

David sat for a moment as Ana left. Maybe he came on too strong. He did have Ana's best interests at heart. He shouldn't have mentioned her past–it was a low blow and a bitter reminder.

"Hi... you are the new player from the Seattle Seal." A tiny voice cut through his thoughts.

He got up. "Sorry. I'm not in the mood for photos or–

"Oh God, no. I'm a Crestmont Giant girl all the way."

At that moment, David knew. This girl knew Ana. "I should go."

"Five seconds please." She blocked his path. "What can you tell me about the girl that just left? Like.. what's going on there?"

He looked down at the name doodled on her cup, "Lily, is it? Why don't you take your coffee and leave? I don't have time for this."

Lily pulled up her phone at the picture she had taken just a few minutes before.

CHAPTER 40

Luka and Pavel entered the auditorium packed with round tables draped in white cloth and topped with elegant centerpieces.

Dressed in a tailored suit, Luka appeared both sophisticated and out of place, his rugged charm contrasting with the polished glamor that surrounded him.

A string quartet played softly in the background as people mingled and chatted. Waiters glide fluidly through the designer-suited crowd carrying flutes of champagne. The event aimed to raise funds for extracurricular programs and facility upgrades for the school.

"I hate these kinds of gatherings." Luka fidgeted with his suit cuffs.

"Well, it's for a good cause," Pavel added, picking up a glass from a passing waiter. "The money we raised here will be used to help the school."

Luka's agent, Ms. Agatha, frazzled and harried. "You are late."

"Because I don't want to be here."

She gripped Luka's elbow and guided him through the crowd, introducing him to various sponsors.

A portly man in a brocade waistcoat approached with his hand outstretched. "Wonderful to have you!" he boomed. Luka smiled politely and grasped the man's hand.

He had always been wary of such gatherings, believing them to be little more than façades, a way for the wealthy to appease their conscience while bypassing taxes. Yet, he had agreed to be here, driven by a desire to make a difference for the school and its students.

His gaze fell upon Pavel, who effortlessly blended in with the crowd. Pavel's easygoing personality and playful charm made it seem effortless for him to win over even the toughest of critics. It was one of the many stark contrasts between them. While Luka possessed a brooding nature and easily grew bored, seeking solace away from the spotlight, Pavel radiated warmth and humor, always finding a way to make others laugh.

Luka couldn't help but envy Pavel's ability to navigate social settings with such ease. The thought of being trapped in a room filled with superficial conversations and forced smiles made him feel suffocated. He needed a break from the pretense, a moment of respite where he could escape, Luka slipped out of the bustling charity event, seeking solace from the overwhelming crowd.

He wandered through the corridors and found an open classroom. Inside, a boy in a wheelchair was engrossed in painting.

Luka watched quietly, charmed by the scene. He didn't want to disturb the peace but couldn't resist commenting, "That's amazing work."

The boy started, glasses askew, and his face lit up in recognition. "You're Luka Kuznetsov!"

Luka smiled warmly. "Guilty as charged. Why are you here alone?"

The boy's face clouded. "I like the quiet. It's easier..." He trailed off, adjusting his wheelchair self-consciously.

"Yeah, and I bet when you grow up, you will be an amazing artist. Friends will come then."

"I wanted to be a hockey player but..." the boy looked down at his wheelchair. "I'm not sure how, also painting is easier."

"Why can't you do both?" Luka asked before adding. "That hasn't stopped the thousands of people that are playing hockey in wheelchairs. It shouldn't stop you, kiddo. Besides, I can teach you."

"For real?"

"Yep. As long as you give me this," he gestured to the canvas.

"Do you know how to paint?"

Luka scratched his head. "I have seen a Bob Ross video one time."

"Who?"

"Never mind." Luka reached for the canvas. "So can I have it now?"

"It needs a couple of days for it to dry."

Luka nodded. "I will send for it."

At that moment, the door opened. "Danny, what are you doing here?" a teacher wearing a brown vest with a pinched expression which disappeared when it landed on Luka. "I'm sorry if he disturbed you."

Luka quickly reassured her, his eyes twinkling with warmth. "No, he's fine. We were just having a nice chat."

The teacher's face relaxed, and she turned her attention to Danny. "Come on now, it's time to go," she said gently, guiding him away.

"What's your name?" Luka called out.

"Danny. Danny Sheen," came the reply before the door closed, leaving Luka in awe.

The wheels in his head began to churn. Didn't Ana mention her brother attended a boarding school. This was amazing. He couldn't wait to tell her.

Taking out his phone, it began to beep, notifications pouring in. Curious, he clicked on the post that was generating all the buzz. It was a photo of Ana and David holding hands across the table of a cafe.

The photo had hundreds of comments.

"Isn't that the Crestmont giant's new medical staff?"

"Isn't this a betrayal?" another said.

He scrolled until his eyes saw this comment,

"Are they dating? They look like they are dating."

The sight of Ana, his beloved, with another man, pierced through his defenses like a blade. A distant, haunted look clouded his eyes as he stared at the picture again.

It was a stark reminder of the risk that comes with opening oneself to love.

CHAPTER 41

Ana strode into the training center and paused when the coach blocked her path.

"Miss sheen–

The man had barely finished the sentence when Luka charged towards her.

He seized Ana's wrist and led her down the hall to an empty treatment room, shutting the door firmly behind them.

Luka was dressed in a casual yet stylishly disheveled manner - a few buttons undone, sleeves rolled up.

His jaw clenched tight. "Why does the world think you are dating David?"

"What? I'm not dating David. He's just a friend." A chill ran through her as she started piecing the clues together. "How did you find out I met with him?"

Luka sighed, dragging a hand over his face. "There are photos of the two of you laughing together. Rumors are flying that you've been secretly seeing each other for months. His expression turned anguished as he passed her the phone.

Ana sighed as another barrage of angry comments flooded her notifications.

The photo of her talking to David went viral, and Luka's fans had been attacking her online.

@Luka4TheCup: Our physio traitor fraternizing with the enemy! She needs to go!

@HockeyQueen: How much is David paying you to sabotage us, Ana?! We want you out!

@TrueNorthFaithful: Ana's a spy! Maybe she's been helping the other team all along.

@CrestmontGiantPuckbunny342: Someone like her should not be part of the medical staff.

Ana shook her head, hurt and anger warring within her. She had thought dating Luka in secret was hard, but this public backlash was even worse. Everything she did now seemed to warrant suspicion and accusations of betrayal.

"Everyone thinks I am betraying the Crestmont Giant and telling him secrets that could help him win the finals." This was bad. Who knew hockey fans were this passionate? Or that the internet was vicious in spreading baseless rumors.

"Why did you meet him?"

"I— I don't know. I just wanted someone to talk to. It wasn't supposed to go like that."

He ran an agitated hand through his hair. "Do you have feelings for him, Ana? Is that why you don't want to tell people about us?"

"Don't be ridiculous," Ana retorted. "This is exactly the reason I wanted to keep us secret. This, right here." She indicated to her phone.

Luka's eyes flashed with hurt and suspicion. "What am I hearing? You wanted us to keep a secret so you could still see him?"

She was stunned.

Ana refused to feel guilty for something that was not her fault. "I care about you, you idiot. But I also care about my friends."

"Friends that want to fuck you."

She took a breath, willing her voice to stay steady. "You are angry. I get it. I'm angry too, but this is not the place to do this right now."

"Do you realize what's more painful? It's not dating rumors or anything. It's that you have no problem talking to him about your troubles, but you hold your tongue when you are with me. When all I ever wanted was for you— for us to share our burden."

The door slammed open. "Ana sheen! What is going on?" the coach stepped in.

She sighed, "I'm sorry. This... David is an old friend. We grew up together and I swear to you that's it. No trading of secrets, nothing is going on between us." The last words seemed directed at Luka.

The coach shifted and glanced to the window, where Luka stood, back rigid, shoulders tense. His posture revealed the anger burrowing deep, taking root.

His eyes landed back on Ana. "If that's the case, the NHL will have to do an investigation. You should go home. I will keep you posted."

"Thank you, coach."

•.¸♡ . ♡¸.•

The drive back to Luka's house was tense and silent.

Luka had not said a word since leaving the training center, staring fixedly ahead at the road. Ana sat curled up in the passenger seat, barely noticing the scenery flying by as she scrolled through her phone in disbelief.

The comments under the latest gossip coverage of her and David's fabricated romance were vicious. Their "fans" continued to demand answers and call her cruel names.

Ana sighed, dropping her head into her hands. She was trapped in this storm with no escape, every aspect of her life and relationship torn apart for entertainment. And for what - because of a single photo and careless assumptions? Her chest tightened with anxiety and frustration.

They pulled into the parking lot at last. Ana could hardly meet Luka's gaze, dreading another confrontation. The doubt etched across his face cut her deeper than any rumor or tabloid gossip ever could. But as they walked into the elevators, her phone rang — it was the coach.

Ana answered.

After a brief, tense conversation, she ended the call in stunned disbelief.

"What did they say?" Luka's anger seemed to fade in the wake of her distress.

"I've been suspended for causing disruption and drama."

They stepped into the house. She tossed her bag on the floor and twirled to face Luka, her vision blurring with unshed tears.

"This is great. Perfect even. My boyfriend thinks I cheated. I might lose my job. And I just saw someone wishing me death online."

A tear trickled down her cheek, and her once-composed demeanor shattered. She hastily swiped the tear away with the back of her hand, her movements fueled by frustration.

"I am sorry. I am." Her voice was low and cracked. "Meeting up with David was a bad idea."

"Come here." Luka pulled her fiercely into his arms and kissed her forehead.

"Your boyfriend is really shitty for adding unnecessary stress to an already difficult situation."

This prompted a small laugh from her. "He is."

"But he cares about you."

"I know." Her arms wrapped around his waist tightened.

•.¸♡ . ♡¸.•

Next day.

Ana leaned against the doorframe of the bedroom, watching as Luka threw items hastily into his duffel bag.

He was flying out early for the semi-finals against the cougars.

"The PR team didn't even waste time. Already sending out a statement that the matter is being dealt with while I'm on suspension," she said as she scrolled through her phone.

Luka grabbed the phone and tossed it on the bed. "Listen to me, I will fix this. You won't be suspended for long."

Ana sighed, arms folded across her chest. She didn't share Luka's optimism. At this point, the rumor had spread like wildfire, and any attempts at damage control might just add more fuel to the flames. But she bit her tongue, not wanting to discourage him. His determination to fix this mess and save her reputation was sweet.

"Don't worry, baby."

Luka zipped up his bag and turned to face her, frown lines etched across his forehead. "I wish you could come with me. I hate leaving you alone to deal with all this." He grasped her shoulders, ducking his head to meet her gaze.

Ana mustered a small smile, touched by his concern. "I'll be fine. Just focus on your game and try not to get too riled up. I need you in one piece for the finals." She reached up to adjust his collar, stalling the inevitable goodbye. "No injuries allowed."

Luka raised an eyebrow, a smile teasing at the corner of his mouth. "I meant to come as my girlfriend, not as the team doctor." He pulled her into his embrace, kissing the top of her head.

The offer was tempting. If she stayed alone in this house, her thoughts might eat her alive. Being on her phone all day was already out of the question.

"You know what? I might just be there."

"Cool, because I'm going to score for you."

•.¸♡ . ♡¸.•

It was game day.

Ana slipped into the crowded hockey stadium, keeping her head down and letting her locs fall forward to partly conceal her face. The last thing she wanted was to be recognized tonight, surrounded by so many people who likely despised her after the drama and rumors of the past few days.

She found her seat, settling in and gazing out at the ice rink below. The energy of the crowd was electric in anticipation of the semifinals. Ana allowed herself to get swept up in the excitement for a moment, cheers erupting as the teams took the ice. Her heart swelled with pride seeing

Luka, Caleb, Pavel and the rest of the team stride out, focused and determined as always.

The hockey game was fast-paced and physical from the first drop of the puck. Ana winced more than once as players including Luka slammed into the boards, holding her breath each time.

Luka's gaze found her in the crowd, he flashed a smile as he got to his feet and continued the game.

The tension in the rink rose as Luka squared off against an opposing player. With a thunderous clash of bodies, they toppled to the ice in a spicy haze of sweat and energy. As the other player tumbled away, their skates flew up, slicing through the air with purpose - and catching Luka across the face.

Blood sprayed into the air like fireworks, splattering crimson droplets onto the ice.

Her heart sank as Luka fell back.

An eerie silence descended over the arena, broken only by murmurs of shock and disbelief from the fans.

She tried to peer closer, but the officials and medical personnel had surrounded him, blocking her view.

Luka was hurt and she couldn't help him.

CHAPTER 42

Halfway through the second period, an opposing player fell after colliding with his teammate. The cold steel of the players' skate whipped through the air and sliced across Luka's brow.

Pain exploded in his face as the impact caused him to reel backward, almost stumbling to the ground before catching himself dazed and disorientated amongst an eruption of noise. He clutched at the injury, cursing under his breath.

Luka's breath came in labored gasps as the referee's shrill whistles pierced his ears. His vision blurred, spinning until all he could see was a sea of crimson - his blood.

An outburst of anxious shouts surged from the stands, their panic only adding to his determination not to give up. With a determined effort, Luka straightened his posture, willing himself to sit upright despite the pain coursing through his body. He waved off the concerned medic, gesturing for just a moment to gather himself. His eyes darted anxiously through the crowd, scanning faces in search of a familiar presence.

And then he found her in a sea of thousands of hockey fans... he focused on her.

Ana's beautiful face, usually adorned with a radiant smile, now contorted with fear and worry.

Luka's gaze lingered on her. He had to tell her he would be alright — that he *was* alright. With a feeble but determined smile, he raised his hand in a shaky thumbs-up, a silent reassurance that, despite the bleeding, he was still alright.

It was a small gesture.

A brief moment of connection amidst the chaos of the arena was all he needed before he surrendered to the medic's assistance, relinquishing his weight on their supporting arms.

Luka hobbled off the ice. Though battered and bruised, his spirit remained unbroken, fueled by the unwavering support of the woman who held his heart.

The cut stung as the medic cleaned and stitched it, but his thoughts were only of Ana. Each second away from the game was another second for her to fret, imagining the worst. He had to get back out there and prove there was no cause for concern.

His injury was forgotten; her peace of mind was all that mattered.

"Patch me up so I can get back out there. I promise someone I will score a goal," he urged impatiently.

15 minutes later, he strode back onto the ice to raucous applause and this time with a visor on his helmet.

Luka embraced the pulsing ache of his injury, stitches tugging as it heightened his senses. He had something to prove to himself and all those who sought to see him fall. Together with his team, they fought on.

The third period was winding down, and the score tied. Luka wove and spun across the ice, dodging opponents as his teammates Pavel and Caleb flanked him. They had been playing together for years; no words were needed as they anticipated each other's movements and passes.

Luka feinted left, then shot the puck at Pavel. In a blink, Pavel sent it back to him - Jude snagged it out of the air and slid it over to Luka and he slammed it straight into the back of the net with seconds to spare.

The buzzer sounded as the crowd leaped to their feet, roaring.

His gaze immediately sought out Ana in the stands. She was on her feet, shouting and cheering with the rest of the crowd - but when their eyes met, her delight seemed to intensify tenfold. Pride and affection flooded through him at the sight of her enthusiasm and support. She was stunning in that moment, joy written across her face, and his heart swelled with mingled victory and love.

Overcome with emotion, Luka blew Ana a kiss without thinking. Her eyes widened in recognition, a coy smile spreading across her lips. She 'caught' his kiss in her hand, slipping her hand into her pocket with a playful grin.

His teammates were too caught up in celebration to notice the exchange. But in that fleeting moment, all else fell away. He lived, fought, and conquered for her.

•.¸♡ . ♡¸.•

In the locker room, Pavel nudged him with a grin. "Was I crazy, or did I see Ana in the stands tonight?"

Luka couldn't help but smile. "Yeah, I invited her."

He raised an eyebrow suggestively. "Celebrating the win with your girl, huh?"

"Hmm.. guys about," Luka said hastily. "The photo with her and David... you understand how crazy social media can be."

Caleb shook his head. "We know, man. We trust her. Social media rumors are insane."

Jude chimed in, "They see one thing and say something totally left field."

"Yeah, remember that one time, there was a rumor that I have hockey bunnies in every city." Pavel said with a chuckle.

"That's not a rumor." Caleb stated.

Pavel stated. "That— that is a gross misunderstanding."

Relief flooded through Luka. At least his teammates were on their side. One less thing to worry about. Still, the troubles faced remained - and there was only one person with power enough to remedy the damage done. As much as Luka despised asking his brother for favors, Vlad was Ana's only hope of restoring her job.

On his way out, Luka was stopped by a sports reporter eager to discuss their victory.

He answered questions with forced enthusiasm, anxious to escape the spotlight's glare.

The reporter leaned in, eyes glinting with curiosity. "There have been quite a few rumors circulating about the team physiotherapist as being a spy for the Seattle Seal. What are your thoughts?"

"I wish everyone would focus on hockey and not some silly rumors...but for clarity I need to say this." Luka tensed, his guard rising - but found himself unable to disguise the affection in his tone as he spoke of Ana.

"Ana Sheen is no spy or anything like that. She has been and will always be a part of the Crestmont Giants. It's a shame she can't be here doing what she loves doing. She's the most dedicated and caring doctor our team ever had. And... she's the one person who's been by my side through all of this, who I know I can count on."

His expression softened as the memories played across his mind, joy and longing mingled in his gaze. "She deserves so much more than rumors and gossip; she's the real thing, and I plan on doing whatever it takes to make things right."

The reporter's eyebrows rose, a knowing look in her eyes. Luka cleared his throat, his smile fading as he realized he had revealed more than intended in his praise.

"Wow, someone would say something is going on between you two?" The reporter chuckled like a joke.

Luka didn't laugh. "Yes. I am utterly undeniably and completely in love with Ana Sheen and I don't appreciate the death threats and rumors circulating right now."

CHAPTER 43

Ana knocked on the hotel room door, nerves fluttered in her stomach. She hadn't seen Luka since they took him off the ice after that nasty injury and during the emotional post-game interview.

His confession of love and praise of her in front of cameras and fans alike had taken her by surprise - leaving her touched and anxious in equal measure.

The door opened to reveal Luka, his brow stitched but a smile crossing his face at the sight of her. "Come to kiss it better?" he teased, tapping the small bandage on his forehead.

Ana swatted his arm, frowning. "Don't joke, you scared me half to death out there." Her hands hovered anxiously, wanting to embrace him but afraid of aggravating his injury.

His smile faded as he reached out to grasp her fidgeting hands, bringing them to his chest. "I'm okay, really. I've had much worse. Don't I get a '*glad you're not dead*' hug?"

She sighed, melting into him - though still careful not to squeeze too tightly. Her fingers traced gently around the edges of his stitches as she gazed up at him. "When I saw you lying there, I thought..." Her voice trailed off, words failing her.

"Shh, I know." Luka cupped her face in his hands. "But I'm here now. No need to worry about your pretty little head." He planted a soft kiss on the tip of her nose, hoping to coax out the smile he loved so well.

She shook her head at his playfulness, though unable to hide her smile of relief. Her hands slid down, wrapping around his waist to avoid causing him pain. "Then stop scaring me like that. I plan on keeping you around for a long time, you know."

"Oh you have to, I have announced it to the world." Luka's eyes glinted mischievously as he leaned in close. Ana's laugh was muffled by his insistent kiss.

"Well your announcement can't possibly make it worse with what I am going through now."

She leaned back to meet his gaze, "I never realized how dangerous this game can be. Maybe your father was right in telling you to quit."

Her hand came up to brush tenderly against the fresh cut on his brow.

Luka winced, though his eyes remained soft.

"My father wanted to control me. He doesn't care about anyone. So the game can be dangerous, what sports isn't? My love for hockey is something I got from my mother."

"Tell me about your mother?"

Luka took Ana's hand and led her towards the bed. He sat down, feeling the mattress sink beneath him, and gently pulled her onto his lap.

"She would have loved you. My mom... was the bravest and softest person ever. She had this warmth, how she ended up with my father is beyond me."

As Ana settled against him, he felt the heat of her body and the softness of her curves. He wrapped his arms around her, pulled her close, and breathed in the scent of her skin.

"I was very close to her and my brother was close to my father. They were alike, so it works."

With a delicate stroke, she caressed his hair as he continued. "When she left, I was all alone. I kept trying to prove myself to my dad because the seven-year-old in me believed if he was proud of me, he too wouldn't leave."

"That must have been tough."

"He didn't care. Instead, he pinned Vlad and I against each other."

"But at the party, it would seem Vlad wants to make things up with you."

Luka scoffed. "He probably needs a kidney or something."

She burst out laughing. "Well, you have to reconcile with your brother sooner or later."

"He... My brother once told me, I was the reason why my mother was gone. Yeah, we were kids, but somehow it just stuck."

She held him tighter. "You are not the reason."

"It's fine. What about you? I know about your dad, but what about your mom?"

"I was twelve when my mother fell ill and passed away. Danny was barely a month old. You can imagine a child who had to raise another child with very little help from their father."

Luka frowned, looking at her as she spoke.

"I was always something to someone else, never really knowing who I was. I had no identity outside of being a young mother, and I resented my life. I resented my mother for dying because I believed she had escaped this terrible life." A tear slipped from one eye and she swiped it as quickly as it came.

Chuckling, she said, "I'm not sure why I'm crying. I haven't even gotten to the sad part yet." She chuckled despite herself.

"Ana..."

She pushed herself off his lap and turned away from him. "No really, I even hated the fact I survived my suicide attempt. Like why? What do I have to live for? Why do I keep surviving? I'm tired of surviving... I just want to live."

"You tried to..."

She glanced down at her fingers, "Yeah a few years ago", looking up at Luka, "Drug overdose."

Luka's eyes bulged like overfilled balloons, ready to burst at the seams when he realized why she had walked out angry when he accused her back in his house.

"*Do you do drugs?*" He had asked her that question after seeing her house in shambles for the first time because somehow that was the only logical reason she didn't spend the money.

"Shit. I'm such an asshole."

"You didn't know... but yeah, you kinda were."

He reached for her hand and pulled her closer to him as his face was buried against her breasts.

He could hear her heart beating. It sounded like a drum. If he was to die now, he'd go willingly.

"I didn't mean to pour this baggage on you."

Luka's expression softened as he looked up at her. His eyes remained pained. "No. no. you have nothing to be sorry for. Tell me everything. You don't have to hide or seek comfort from another."

"I mean, I'm a doctor and if people find out about my past. It could mean a lot of damage to *your* career especially now you practically proclaim your feelings to the public. I don't want to be the reason you lost that."

"What are you talking about?" Luka pulled her to sit on his lap again, staring at her, making sure every word was understood. "You... Ana Sheen is my life. I don't care about your past or what anyone else says. I'm not letting you go anywhere."

Her breath caught at his tender reassurance. She wrapped her arms around him, holding him tight, and felt the tension leave his embrace.

Ana's phone began buzzing in the back pocket of her jeans, interrupting their quiet moment. She glanced at the screen, her brow furrowing. It was Danny's school. Her heart dropped into her stomach as she answered.

"Mrs. Harper? How is Danny?"

Luka's brows creased as he took in the panicked look on her face.

"What, what do you mean you can't find Danny. My father what—" Her pulse raced as a thousand terrifying possibilities flooded her mind.

CHAPTER 44

Ana's knuckles were white as she gripped the armrests of her seat. Her gaze remained fixed on the window, but her mind was far away, consumed by the haunting possibility that her brother might be missing. The world outside the plane seemed to blur as a whirlwind of emotions and thoughts swirled within her.

Barely an hour had passed since receiving that fateful call, and now they were in the air - the quickest flight Luka managed to book, carrying them across vast skies stretching end to end. But her thoughts remained trapped in cruel imaginings of all that might befall her brother, now lost.

Luka reached over to clasp her hand, giving a gentle, reassuring squeeze. She turned to him at last, eyes rimmed in red from silent tears.

"I should never have left him. This is all my fault."

"You had no clue this would happen. We'll find him, Ana. I promise." Luka held her gaze, conveying confidence and comfort as best he could through the gnawing fear inside. "Danny is strong and smart. He'll be okay."

They arrived in the gray light of early dawn, rushing straight to Danny's school from the airport. Police cruisers were parked outside, officers interviewing the staff who'd called Ana in a panic hours before. At the sight of the police, hope flared in her chest - only to flicker out as they explained the situation.

"We can't conduct a search or issue an Amber Alert at this time, I'm afraid. According to the information we got, your father currently shares legal custody of Daniel. Unless we receive evidence, he intends to harm the child, we have to consider this a legal parental custody dispute."

Ana stared at them in disbelief.

"My father is dangerous and unpredictable. I've been Danny's legal guardian for years. My father never cared for us... for him."

The officers remained unmoved, hands in pocket, straight faced they repeated their words. "I'm sorry, but all we can see is a father taking his kid out of school."

The last remnants of hope crumbled within her as she turned into Luka's embrace, sobs choking back in her throat. They were powerless, relying on a broken system, unable to protect those most vulnerable.

•.¸♡ . ♡¸.•

Ana's hands trembled as she entered the familiar space of Luka's penthouse. She curled up on the plush couch, her legs drawn close to her torso, as if seeking the comfort of a protective shield. Her shoulders slumped, burdened by the heaviness of her emotions.

"I should have known he was up to no good. He called me a couple of days ago. My dad. It's just—"

Luka followed close behind, pressing a glass of water into her hands - though she couldn't bring herself to drink, numbness pervading all senses.

"He'll call," Luka said with conviction. "We just have to wait. He has to call." His reassurances sounded hollow to her ears. All hope had fled since the encounter with police refusing aid.

Despite the difficult circumstances, his presence gave her strength and together they would face the challenges ahead, no matter the cost.

At that moment, her phone began buzzing on the counter, an unknown number flashing on the screen. Her pulse leaped as she answered, putting it on speaker so Luka could hear.

"Hello, my dear, Ana." Her father's derisive tone sent ice flooding through her veins.

"Where's Danny?" she sniffed, wiping off the tears. "Is he safe?"

A derisive laugh. "He's with his dear old father, where he belongs. You left him at that stupid school. Some sister you are."

"I had to work because you refused to take responsibility as his parent!" Ana shot back.

"What kind of work? You spread your legs and get some cash. Whatever. I need money, girl. I'm sure that a rich boyfriend of yours can spare it. Send me $100k. No funny business. You will hear from me soon." The line went dead without another word.

Ana stared at the phone in disbelief. She turned to Luka, anguish and fear mingling with relief that at least now they knew - Danny was alive, a captive to her father's manipulations and greed. Rage simmered beneath the shock, hands clenched into fists.

"Don't worry, baby. We will get him back."

•.¸♡ . ♡¸.•

Caleb, Jude, and Pavel stepped out of the elevator and into Luka's penthouse. Grim determination was etched into every line of their faces.

"Thank you for coming."

"So, who are we knocking the fuck out?" Pavel waved his hockey stick in the air.

"Why did you bring that?" Caleb asked.

"We came straight from the airport. Sorry, I didn't have time to keep my favorite stick." He tossed the stick around.

They strode into the living room, where Ana rose to greet them, fresh tears shining in her eyes. "What are you guys doing here?" she said, voice trembling, small laughter coming through.

Caleb clasped his hands. "You're family. We protect our own." The others nodded, echoing his sentiment.

"Family?"

Ana's heart soared, and a rush of relief washed over her as she took in these four rugged hockey players who stood before her. The weight on her shoulders seemed to lighten as she realized that she was not alone in her struggle.

Pavel turned to Luka as they moved over the kitchen area. "What's the latest?"

Luka told them about the threatening call and the failed attempts to report Danny as missing, and the police's failure to take action.

Anger flashed across their expressions.

"So we're on our own," Caleb said. "Once we start pulling strings. We'll find them."

Ana's gaze traveled their faces, these steadfast friends who stood with them through triumph and now this darkness.

"What do we know about this guy– your father?" Jude asked.

"He is a gambling addict, and he is trying to extort money from us. We don't actually think he might hurt his son but–

"He is capable... he has been before." Ana's small voice cut through Luka's words.

There was a brief moment of pause from the boys and it didn't look like she was going to explain further.

Caleb was the first to break the silence. "Who does he owe money to?"

"Some gangsters, I believe..."

Jude paced as he spoke. "Okay, so there is a chance your father is working alone to kidnap his son to extort money from his daughter. My head hurts just thinking about it."

The landline phone, perched atop a vintage table, came alive with a distinctive timbre. Its metallic tone reverberated through the room. Luka walked over answering the phone. His jaw clenched, muscles visibly tensing at the words of the caller.

"Who's that?"

A deep sigh escaped his lips, laden with exasperation. "Tell me why, there is someone named fucking David in the lobby asking for an access code. Which of you spilled?"

"Shit."

All eyes darted to Pavel.

"What do you mean, shit?"

"Don't hate me for this." Pavel held his hands up as he surrendered. "After that one game, we exchanged numbers. I don't know, I thought he was cool. He texted me asking about Ana asking about the rumors and if she was okay. Then I wrote back, Oh we're headed to Luka's house right now, Ana needs our help. That's it. You know what? It might not even be him downstairs. Do you know another David?"

CHAPTER 45

David ascended to Luka's penthouse via a sleek, private elevator. The soft chime of the elevator's arrival signaled his entrance.

Luka blocked the entrance as the doors slid open, revealing David standing at the threshold. An expression of anxiety was etched across David's face.

Luka's jaw tensed at the sight of David, who had caused such turmoil, yet now dared intrude upon their anguish.

"I came as soon as I heard about Danny." He said, glancing past Luka to where Ana sat on the couch, gazing out the window like in some kind of trance. "I want to help in any way I can."

Luka began to refuse him, but paused as Pavel approached, clapping a hand on David's shoulder. "We need all the help we can get."

Against his misgivings, Luka scoffed and stepped aside to let David enter.

He walked over to kneel before Ana, hesitating before speaking in a low, urgent tone. "I am so sorry. For everything. Please believe I never meant any of this - losing your job, the hate comments, and now Danny..." His voice cracked. "You have to realize, I would do anything to make this right. To find him."

Ana blinked slowly, as if just now noticing David was there. "Thank you."

Somewhere across the room, Jude spoke, "I can't believe you brought in your rival and isn't he also her ex?"

"I am willing to make a deal with the devil if it means bringing back the smile on her face." Luka turned to see Jude munching on chips from a bag, crumbs littered on the counter. Raising his brows, "Make yourself at home, why don't you?"

Jude froze with a half-finished handful of chips in midair between his mouth and the bag. He cleared his throat before replying.

"Hey, I'm just keeping my energy up. We've got a long night ahead of us." He popped another handful into his mouth.

Luka shook his head.

Jude's nonchalance and appetite seemed undiminished by the gravity of their situation.

David rose, walking over to confer with Pavel and Luka as they stood in the kitchen area.

"Tell us what you know and I won't kick you out of my house."

"What is Kuznetsov? feeling insecure, having me here, near Ana?"

Luka snickered, stepping closer to him. "As if. You might be her first kiss, her first boyfriend's congratulation, but I am the man that gets to wake her up every morning, the one she begs to fuck her and the one she would marry. We are not the same."

Caleb stepped between them with a subtle but authoritative gesture, his palms outstretched to keep them apart. "Okay boys, save it for the ice." Then he turned to David. "We are running out of time. Pavel said you could help."

David's response was laced with a tense stillness, his arms folded tightly across his chest as he spoke. "I grew up in the same neighborhood as Mr. Sheen. I have seen these gangsters before. They work for a guy called Angel."

"What do you know about this Angel guy?"

"Angel is the owner of a gambling house just outside of town. No one has seen him or knows what he looks like, and yet he controls half the business in this city."

Luka turned away from David. "Why haven't I heard of him?" Luka asked, not directing his question at anyone in particular.

"I grew up in the streets. We hear things, see things. You grew up with a golden spoon shoved up your–"

"Hey!" Caleb's voice cut through the tension. He pointed a finger at David, his stance stern and assertive. "Not here. Not right now."

David took a step back, showing defiance but ultimately yielding to Caleb's authority.

David muttered, his arms still crossed, his eyes narrowed in skepticism."I don't think this Angel guy is involved. At least we should hope so."

"Fine. Do you know what Casino Mr. Sheen frequents? Maybe we can find him there."

"Yep. It's just outside of town."

Jude had been munching on chips in the corner, and suddenly chimed in. "Oh shit. Guys. I might have a plan."

Luka, Caleb, and Pavel swiveled their heads, and in unison, they all said, "No."

"What–why? I haven't even said anything yet."

"Yeah, at least we should hear the kid out." David said, mildly confused.

Pavel put an arm around David's shoulder and said, "The last time this kid said he had a plan, I lost my wallet. Caleb lost his eyebrows. And... Luka.. busted his shoulder."

"And yet you wonder why I don't hang out with you guys," Luka murmured.

Jude spoke like he was animated. "All I'm hearing is that I make things adventurous. I mean, you got your wallet back, Caleb's eyebrows grew back and Luka..." he paused. "You should be thanking me because if not for your shoulder you would not have found Ana. But I promise you this time," he continued with a sly grin, "it's a good plan."

•.¸♡ . ♡¸.•

Luka shifted uncomfortably in the backseat of David's sedan, his tone filled with disdain. "Why couldn't we take one of my jeeps? We'd at least have more room."

David glanced at him in the rearview mirror. "We don't want to draw attention to flashy cars. Subtlety is key here."

Caleb snorted. "Where did you get all this 'spy shit' anyway?" He gestured to the binoculars Luka had brought along.

"It's just binoculars and a tracker. There isn't much," Luka replied.

They parked down the street from the small casino for over an hour, waiting to spot any sign of Ana's father.

With each minute ticking by, Luka's agitation grew - until at last he spotted two familiar figures approaching the entrance.

"There's Pavel and Jude," he said, sitting up straight. The others followed his gaze.

Caleb passed Luka the binoculars. Through them, Luka watched Pavel and Jude slip into the gambling house with forced casualness. His knuckles turned white from gripping the binoculars tight, praying his friends would emerge soon with news of the target being inside.

Minutes dragged by like hours. At last, Jude stepped out again, glancing in their direction. Luka caught a subtle nod; the message was clear. They had found him.

•.¸♡ . ♡¸.•

Pavel and Jude slipped into the backseat of the car, squeezing in next to Luka.

"Took you long enough."

"Sorry, the place was packed, and we had to be careful not to attract attention. Luckily, nobody was a hockey fan, which, to be honest, I find a little insulting," Jude replied. He shifted, trying to find a comfortable position in the limited space. "Just as planned, we suggested a game of poker and made sure to let the old man believe we had never played before."

"It was the truth, though. We don't know shit about–" Pavel grunted and shoved at his leg, glaring. "That's my foot you're crushing."

"Well, I can't exactly fold myself in half, now can I?" Jude shot back.

Caleb sighed, glancing back at them. "Would you two stop bickering like children? We have bigger concerns here."

"He started it," Jude muttered.

"We would not have this issue if someone didn't think a Honda Civic would contain five tall hockey players." Luka knocked on the driver's seat, where David sat.

"Luka Kuznetsov." Caleb glared.

"Sorry. Sorry." He drew in a breath. "I may be a little stressed and antsy about this."

"I don't get why can't we follow him? Why plant a tracker on him and make us lose 10 grand?" Pavel asked.

"Because, if he senses something is up, it's game over, and besides, this gives us an advantage," Caleb answered.

Luka's eyes peeled at the tablet screen, waiting for movement. "This guy hasn't left the gambling house. What the hell?" His eyes shot up to Jude. "You guys made sure you lost, and he won right?"

David said, "I guess he thought he was on a roll or something and wanted to keep winning."

Another hour passed.

Luka stared at the screen. "He is on the move." He slapped David awake. "Let's go."

David groaned, remained quiet, and drove off.

Luka stared intently at the screen of the tablet in his hands, tracking the signal from the device Jude had planted on Ana's father at the bar. "Take a left up here, then go straight for half a mile," he directed.

David followed his instructions, pulling onto a winding dirt road lined by dense forest. In the distance, the glint of moonlight upon still waters could be glimpsed through the trees.

"There, that house over there - pull over," Luka said urgently. David stopped the car, and they surveyed the isolated little lake house with bated breath.

The house was a two-story behemoth, its wooden siding faded and peeling, revealing the gray wood beneath.

Shattered windows gaped like empty eye sockets, their jagged edges creating a haunting visage against the night.

Two lights shone from within, illuminating the figure of a man walking past the windows. Their target was inside, unsuspecting.

"One of those rooms should have Danny."

Luka turned to the others. His eyes widened with an eager glint, yet his jaw clenched, revealing the knot of tension building within him.

"We go in quietly. Our goal is to get the kid out safely; dealing with his father comes second." His gaze came to rest on Jude and Pavel. "You two find a way into the house and locate Danny. Caleb, you're with me - we'll confront him directly while they search."

"Kuznetsov, check this out." David handed over the binoculars.

"What?" He took it and held it over his eyes. "Shit. I know that guy. He is the guy I fought in Ana's house."

"The gangsters?" Caleb asked.

David probed further, "What does this mean, Mr. Sheen is actually working with these men to kidnap his son?"

"I think we need to call the cops and let them know what we found–" Caleb said before the sound of a door clicked open and Luka stepped out of the car.

"What are you doing? You are going to get yourself killed."

Seconds later the others followed.

"Am I the only reasonable one here?" Caleb let out an exhausting sigh before joining them.

CHAPTER 46

Luka crouched in the shadows, his breaths visible in the cold air as he surveyed his surroundings. Muffled voices were heard from within. He paused, straining to listen - through the window, the silhouette of a man with a gun slung over his shoulder could be seen patrolling outside.

He mentally counted, one guard outside, the guy upstairs and Mr. Sheen against 4 hockey players and one David. They could take them. He thought.

Luka peered into the window to get a view of the room beyond. Ana's father stood with another man in hushed discussion.

Okay two armed men, Mr sheen against four hockey players and one David. The odds were still on their side.

"Where the fuck did you go?" came a throaty voice, dripping of anger and desperation.

"Out," Mr. Sheen replied tersely, his voice laced with weariness.

"This isn't a game. You can't go out while this is going on? You still fucking owe me," the other voice retorted, its bitterness cutting through the air like a serrated blade.

"I won 10 grand tonight," Mr. Sheen offered weakly, as if the sum of money could somehow absolve him of his guilt and debts.

"You owe me a lot more, you know that," the second man hissed.

Mr. Sheen's voice trembled as he continued, "My daughter will send the money. Once you get it, you can leave me for real this time."

The other man leaned forward, his eyes gleaming with malicious intent, "you better hope that your plan works and she does bring the money."

Rage and revulsion simmered in Luka's veins, his knuckles white as he clenched his fists. What kind of father did this to their own child?

Turning his head, Luka was startled to find Caleb crunched up beside him, the expression on his face mirroring the same mix of horror and disbelief that coursed through Luka's own being.

David came towards them, crunched down. "So there is a guard outside with a gun, but i think–"

"A gun?!" Caleb's eyes widened then added, "Guys, we have practice tomorrow."

It seemed like Caleb's worries fell on deaf ears.

Luka stated, still determined to carry out the mission. "We just have to stop them before it's too late and, most importantly, keep it quiet."

"The kid is probably locked upstairs. How do you suppose we get inside when there is a guard outside?" Pavel asked.

Jude crawled over to where the boys crouched, eyes gleaming. "Guard down."

"How?"

"I distracted him."

With no further questions asked. “Fine. Let's go,” Luka said.

Caleb groaned in exhaustion. “We are going to get killed or worse, get seriously injured.”

“I love the priorities, man,” Pavel replied sarcastically.

They moved cautiously, crawling towards the entrance of the building. They spotted the guard lying motionless on the ground, blood oozing from a wound on his head, a discarded rock beside him.

A collective gasp escaped their lips as they all turned toward Jude, their eyes wide and unblinking.

“You distracted him?”

“Yeah.” His voice sounded low with slight panic. “I didn’t mean to... distract him so hard.”

On the grassy ground lay the seemingly lifeless body. A dark, ominous pool of blood seeped from the back of the head, forming a chilling halo around it. The crimson liquid trickled slowly through the blades of grass, staining the earth beneath.

Caleb clutched his stomach as nausea welled up inside him. “I think I'm going to puke,” Without another word, he turned and hurried away from the gruesome sight, desperately seeking a spot where he could unleash the contents of his stomach in private. Then he returned to the group, his hand swiping his mouth.

Pavel tried to reassure them, speaking in a hushed tone, “You know he’s a bad guy, so maybe you did the right thing.”

“You think?” Jude’s panic remained evident in his strained voice.

"Yeah. You probably saved a lot of people." Pavel said, this time a little more convincing.

David, growing impatient, reached for the gun on the ground. "Okay, if we're done trying to excuse your friend for committing murder, we need to go."

Caleb intervened, raising his voice softly. "Stop. No fingerprints."

David hesitated, but retracted his hand from the gun. "How do you expect us to save Danny if we aren't armed?"

Pavel handed him his hockey stick.

"Seriously?"

The bloody supposedly dead man let out a low groan, barely moving.

Almost in unison, everyone breathed out.

"Thank goodness. He is alive." Caleb said. "I don't think I would be able to handle this on my conscience."

"Okay, you guys deal with this. Tie him up or something. I'm going inside." Luka went ahead, entering into the building and David trailed behind him.

"Why are you coming, anyway?"

"In case you've forgotten, I have known Danny since he was born, so I should be here."

Luka rolled his eyes. "I get it. You don't have to remind me you knew Ana long before."

"What is your plan here? Go inside with nothing but a hockey stick."

"Fine. Tell me what's your idea."

David explained how they could make some noise to cause a distraction. Hopefully, creating a small chance for them to rescue Danny.

They created a controlled ruckus by knocking over a pile of debris, their boots scuffling loudly across the floor.

"Shh, someone is coming."

Luka and David quickly sought cover behind a broken wall, holding their breath as the boss strode past, his fingers twitching near the holster of his gun.

"You're welcome," David muttered under his breath.

"Fuck you." Luka mouthed.

The room that was cloaked in darkness. The peeling wallpaper was illuminated by a single, flickering overhead light, which created an unsettling shadow, giving the impression the walls themselves were hiding something sinister.

Luka stormed in, his commanding presence filling the space.

"Where is the boy?" Although calm, his voice held a weight of will that forbade any opportunity for compromise.

Mr. Sheen, Danny's father, sat in a rickety wooden chair. His eyes widened with both surprise and fear as Luka confronted him. His appearance was a disheveled mess, his clothes wrinkled and his hair was past due for a cut.

Beads of sweat clung to his furrowed brow as he realized the gravity of the situation.

"You! This has nothing to do with you," Mr. Sheen stammered, his voice quivering as he attempted to assert control over the situation.

But Luka was having none of it. His fingers, calloused from years of gripping a hockey stick, tightened around the man's neck, and his eyes bore into Mr. Sheen's with an intensity that sent shivers down his spine.

"You are the lowest of low, the slimmest piece of shit." Luka hissed, his voice dripping with menace. "Where is Danny?"

Mr. Sheen hesitated, his eyes flying in all directions as if trying to find an escape, but the intensity in Luka's voice and the firm grip on his neck forced him to croak out an answer.

He gestured towards the narrow staircase that led to the upper floors of the decrepit building.

Danny sat in the dimly lit room, his small form pressed against the peeling wallpaper, his eyes fixed on the TV screen where an old sitcom played in the background. He didn't look like he *knew* he was kidnapped.

The laugh track from the show echoed faintly, creating an eerie juxtaposition to the dire circumstances that had kept him captive.

Luka's eyes scanned the room, taking in the stark surroundings, before his gaze settled on the young boy.

Danny looked up, his eyes widening with both recognition and hope. A radiant smile spread across his face.

With relief, Luka dashed over to him, "We're getting out of here," he reassured him, his voice warm and filled with promise.

Danny clung to Luka desperately, his tiny hands gripping onto the fabric of Luka's shirt as if he feared that this moment might vanish like a dream.

"We can't go back there," David whispered. "What if we meet that other big guy?"

They looked around for a way to get Danny out safely.

Then, an idea struck. Luka saw the window, a potential escape route, and the only way to get Danny to safety. They grabbed some sheets they found nearby and quickly fashioned them into a makeshift rope.

As they tied the last knot, they heard heavy, thunderous footsteps ascending the stairs.

Luka watched as Danny descended, his small form dangling from the makeshift rope. His arms and shoulders strained under the weight of his body, a visible testament to the physical toll this daring escape was exacting on him.

His escape was agonizingly slow as Caleb and Jude were waiting anxiously below, ready to receive Danny.

Back in the room, the boss burst in, his eyes filled with fury as he spotted the rope dangling from the window. Luka, thinking fast, used his back to shield the window, concealing their escape route.

"I knew we would meet again." The boss, enraged, drew his gun out.

Before he could aim right, David swung the hockey stick, knocking the gun from the man's hand.

The stick snapped in two. In the next second, the two men grappled, their bodies crashing against the dilapidated walls.

However, David's bravery had a purpose. He fought to buy time, to keep the man occupied for just a few more moments, as Danny's safety was their top priority.

Just as the man was gaining the upper hand, Danny, having successfully descended the rope, landed safely on the ground outside where Caleb and Jude grabbed him and rushed him away.

With Danny's escape secured, Luka seized the opportunity. He made a daring lunge for the gun, but the man was quicker as he kicked David in the stomach, sending him sprawling to the floor. The boss snatched the gun, his face twisted with menace, and aimed it directly at Luka.

Luka knew this was it.

For a moment, the room fell into an eerie silence as Luka found himself standing before a deadly weapon, its barrel pointed directly at him. Time seemed to slow to a crawl, and a chilling fear gripped his heart, paralyzing him in place.

The feeling was far too familiar and it took him back to a moment he had long forgotten.

Beads of sweat formed on his forehead as a flood of memories surged within him. Images from his past swirled in his mind, memories he had suppressed resurfaced, vivid and haunting.

He was seven years old, a carefree child, oblivious to the dangers of the world. He stood on a lonely street, innocent and unaware. When in the blink of an eye, his world shattered.

David had grabbed a wooden chair and swung it against the man.

The gun cluttered to the floor and, as the impact, connected painfully with the man's jaw.

"Guy! Get out of your head." David shook Luka.

It took almost a minute for Luka to bring himself back to the present. By then, the man had gotten to his feet, but a floorboard gave way beneath the man's massive frame. It snapped with a loud, ominous crack. With a jolt of panic, his boot got ensnared in the splintered wreckage, immobilizing him for a crucial moment. His eyes widened with shock and his face contorted with pain as he desperately tried to free his trapped foot.

In that precarious instant, Luka kicked him hard against his chest. He stumbled backward, his arms flailing wildly as his massive form teetered perilously close to the jagged window frame. Shards of broken glass rained down around him like crystalline confetti.

The room fell into an eerie stillness, broken only by the shattered glass and the distant echo of his fading cries.

Luka's heart still pounding, peered out of the window as the man's figure grew smaller and smaller until it was swallowed by the unforgiving darkness of the night.

"Is he dead?" David asked.

"I think so."

Luka stumbled to where David sat, chest heaving, stretching out his hand and helped lift him to his feet.

"You fight as much as you play hockey, shitty."

David chuckled, shaking his head. "It's been a while, but I'd say we make a good team."

Luka grumbled before answering. "I guess so. At least we didn't punch each other."

"True. That would have been really awkward."

"David... I still don't fucking like you."

"Likewise. Kuznetsov."

CHAPTER 47

Luka stepped out of the run-down house, his shoulders slightly slouched from the physical and emotional toll of their ordeal, and took measured steps. His gait, though marked by a lingering fatigue, held a quiet strength.

Beside him, David walked with a slightly more upright posture, his body still bearing the marks of their fight. The morning sun pierced their tired eyes as he blinked away the pain from his pounding head.

Luka touched his forehead and his fingers came away stained with fresh blood - his stitches had torn open.

Their Honda Civic sat in the driveway as the three friends waited.

A surge of elation coursed through Pavel's being as he yelled. "Luka Kuznetsov! You're alive, you son of a bitch!"

In the front seat sat a little boy, scared and hopeful-Danny.

Luka ruffled his hair. "Your sister will be so glad to see you." He grinned, then turned to his teammates, "where is Mr sheen?" He whispered not wanting Danny to hear.

Jude knocked against the truck of the car. "Saw him trying to run."

•.¸♡.♡¸.•

As they drove, Luka's long legs bumped uncomfortably against the back of the seat. He grumbled, "I feel like a pretzel in this thing!"

"Why don't you sit in the front?" Caleb suggested, "you can carry the kid."

"Hell no." Luka leaned forward in his seat. "Not because of you, kiddo. I just can't stand seeing this guy's face in my peripheral vision." He nudged David.

Danny smiled. Luka was glad he seemed alright. This could have a traumatic effect on anybody.

"So what do we do with..." Caleb gestured vaguely to the trunk. It was obvious he didn't know how to handle a situation where a father kidnapped his own son.

Jude interjected, "We can drop him off at the police station, what do you think?" He turned to Luka.

Luka's eyes appeared to be distant as he fidgeted with his fingers, folding and unfolding them in a nervous manner. He was lost in thought.

He always had the memory of watching his mother walk away. Now he knew. There was more. He ran after her that day. He crossed the street without looking. The sounds of the car's tires screeching, metal crushing metal in a symphony of impending doom echoed in his ears. It was supposed to be him, but the car was meant to hit him, not his mother.

She had pushed him out of harm's way, sacrificing herself to protect him. The scene played out like a surreal tableau in his memory.

For years, Luka had suppressed the trauma of that day, burying the memory deep within his psyche. The incident had become a distant echo in the recesses of his mind. He had been looking for her, blaming his father for her disappearance, but all his father and brother did was hide the truth from him.

Just minutes ago, the gun pointed at him became a symbolic embodiment of the danger he had once escaped, a chilling reminder of the fragility of life.

Pavel tugged him, pulling him out of the trance. "Earth to Luka. We are talking to you."

"What happened there?" Caleb asked, staring at him through the rearview mirror.

"Nothing." He finally said. "I'm fine. I'm good."

CHAPTER 48

Luka had texted Ana that they had found her brother.

The car pulled up in front of the building in the early hours of the morning, and Ana was already waiting outside.

"Is he okay? Are you okay?" she asked anxiously. The boys carefully helped Danny out of the car. She wrapped her hands around him. "I was so worried about you."

She had a wheelchair ready.

"I'm fine. Really, I am." Danny eased into the wheelchair. "Your boyfriend is freaking cool," and added, "all of them."

Jude leaned over to Pavel and made a side comment. "The way he said it seemed like..."

"Don't."

Ana pulled her gaze off her brother and settled on Luka, Caleb, Pavel, and Jude before her eyes stopped on David as he emerged from the vehicle. "I can't thank you enough."

She stepped forward, burying herself in Luka's arms.

"I can think of a few ways," he whispered into her ears.

With a subtle shake of her head, Ana couldn't help but release a quiet chuckle.

"We're just glad everything worked out." David commented.

But before And could respond. There was a knock from the truck.

"What was that?"

"The police will handle that."

•.¸♡.♡¸.•

Luka stood on the balcony of his penthouse, the bustling city below bathed in the soft glow of the evening. The echoes of the rescue mission to save Danny still reverberated in his mind, but his thoughts kept drifting back to a heavy, unresolved burden from his past.

With a deep breath, he took out his phone and dialed his brother Vlad's number. The voice on the other end answered with a casual, "Sure, what's up?"

Luka hesitated, knowing that the question he was about to ask would unveil long-buried pain. "Mom is dead, right?" his voice trembling with emotion.

There was a drawn-out silence, and in that emptiness. Luka's heart clenched in anticipation.

Vlad's voice broke through. "You remembered."

"Why didn't anyone tell me, damn it." He yelled, anguish in his tone.

"I'm sorry, you somehow blacked it out of your memory and the doctors said it might be because of the guilt you felt. No one knew you had run after her, and no one saw the car coming, but mom... it has not been easy for any of us. We were all trying to protect you."

Luka closed his eyes briefly, his fingers gripping the railing of the balcony. "So you were right when you said it was my fault," he confessed, the words heavy with guilt.

Vlad's response was gentle, as if he had been waiting years to say it. "No. I was angry, and I might have resented you, but it was not right for me to blame you."

"But it's true," Luka insisted, his voice barely above a whisper. "If I hadn't—"

Vlad interrupted him, his voice firm. "You were a kid. We were all children. I'm sorry; I know I have been a terrible brother. I want us to try to be better brothers. Mom would have wanted that."

Luka nodded, his vision blurred with unshed tears.

"Hello? Luka? Are you there?"

He hung up the phone. The burden from the "disappearance of his mother" he had carried for a long time seemed to be replaced by the guilt of her death.

Leaning against the metal railing, his gaze fixed on the horizon, where the setting sun painted the sky with warm hues.

Ana approached him from behind, her arms wrapped around him in a warm, comforting embrace, understanding the emotional turmoil within him.

Luka asked. "How is Danny doing?"

"A bit shaken up, but he is good. All he is talking about is how you threw someone out the window." She chuckled.

He shrugged. "It sort of happened. Is he sleeping?"

"Went to sleep the second his head hit the bed."

"That's good." Luka murmured, staring at the faraway city skyline where it touched the twilight sky.

The bustling sounds of the city faded into the background as Luka sought solace in this quiet retreat.

"I didn't mean to but I heard your call." Ana came around, one hand tilting his face to her. "Do you want to talk about it... about her?"

"You know, I'm not really much of a talker."

"It doesn't have to be with me, maybe a therapist, perhaps?"

Luka leaned to press his forehead against hers. *"so mnoy vse budet v poryadke, poka ya s toboy."*

"Christ. What does that mean?"

"That I will be fine." He wrapped his arm around her.

"I don't think that's what it meant."

•., ♡ . ♡ ,.•

A week Later

It was the deciding game 7 of the Stanley Cup finals between the Crestmont Giants and the Seattle Seals. The winner of this game would hoist the Stanley Cup trophy.

The Giants struck the first goal by Caleb. As Pavel and Jude celebrated on the bench, Luka scanned the sold-out crowd. That's when he spotted Ana and Danny, wearing Crestmont jerseys and cheering wildly for the Giants.

Luka was filled with determination, wanting to win this game for his team, but also Ana. He dished out a few big hits and set up the Giants' second goal with a textbook pass to set up a one-timer.

The game remained tight as both teams battled ferociously. With under a minute left and the score still 2-1, Luka picked up the puck on a turnover and decked around David. He fired a wrist shot that beat the Seattle goalie, giving the Giants a crucial two-goal lead.

As time expired and the arena erupted in celebration, Luka glided passed David, giving him the finger and sticking out his tongue.

David rolled his eyes.

His teammates surrounded him as they cheered in their happiness at helping bring the Stanley Cup back to Crestmont City.

He looked up into the stands where Ana and Danny had their arms around each other, beaming with joy. He skated over to them.

Ana smiled. "I'm so proud of you."

Danny congratulated Luka and hugged him.

"Thanks, bud," then he returned his sights to Ana. "Perhaps a congratulatory kiss is in order."

He wrapped his other arm around Ana's waist and pulled her in close.

Grinning triumphantly, Luka pressed his lips to Ana in a fierce kiss. His lips met her warm mouth and his enthusiasm seemed to melt the ice from his veins.

She slid her hands into Luka's sweat-damp hair and kissed him back passionately. The roar of the cheering crowd faded into the background as the kiss deepened.

For a blissful moment, it was as if they were the only two people in the arena. All of Luka's hard work, perseverance, and determination over the long season had culminated in this crowning achievement.

EPILOGUE

It was a hive of bustle and celebration in Luka's penthouse apartment.

A crowd which was mostly the Crestmont Giant hockey players crossed from the kitchen to the living room and out onto the spacious balcony, while others chatted animatedly.

The air buzzed with laughter and the aroma of delectable food wafted through the rooms, enticing everyone to indulge in the culinary delights prepared for the occasion.

Jude was the center of attention as he made drinks in the kitchen. Pavel sat at the dining table admiring a colorful painting on an easel Danny proudly showed him.

"You make a lot of money if you turn this into NFT."

Luka yelled out, making his way to the door. "Don't introduce him to those silly get-rich-quick schemes."

"They are not schemes." Pavel called out, before whispering to Danny. "I will teach you."

Luka answered the door to find Caleb and Lily.

He grabbed Luka's hand before giving him a bro-hug. Lily too came in for the hug. "Thanks for inviting me."

Luka replied. "You are part of the team, so..."

Caleb leaned over to Lily. "There she is. You can go talk to her."

Luka looked confused. "Problem?" He asked as he watched Lily gingerly approach Ana.

Ana was handing a cup of what she presumed to be the only non-alcoholic drink at that party to her brother.

"Lily, it's been a while. Glad you are here." Ana's arms opened wide for a warm, enthusiastic hug, pulling Lily into a tight hug. "Want a drink? I think Jude can fix something for you."

"Yeah, maybe later. Can we talk... privately?" Lily's voice wavered slightly, her words punctuated by brief pauses and a hint of hesitance.

Ana's eyes softened, and she reached to grasp Lily's trembling hands. "Let's go upstairs."

Lily's eyes fixated on the modified steps, designed for Ana's brother's wheelchair. It was a subtle detail, but one that speaks volumes about Luka's love for Ana.

A knot tightened in Lily's stomach, guilt devouring her core.

Ana motioned for Lily to take a seat on the plush beanbag chair positioned near the window. The gentle rustle of the curtains, swaying in the breeze, adds a tranquil touch to the room.

The distant echoes of laughter and music wafted up from the party below, creating a vibrant backdrop to the somber tension that hung in the air.

But Lily could not sit, as restlessness seized her, compelling her to pace back and forth across the room, her steps echoed with each word she spoke.

"Ana, I... it was me. I leaked the photo of you and the other guy. I sent it to my friend in journalism class. I'm so sorry... I didn't mean for it to blow up like that. I was jealous and God, I hate the feeling of being jealous. I mean, Luka loves you and you love him. There is nothing I can do about that. I am so fucking sorry." Her words tumbled forth. "I couldn't sleep knowing what I did after seeing those hate comments. I had to come clean to Caleb and--honestly, I just felt bitter because I have never been anyone's first choice. I have never had anyone look at me, at least not the way Luka does to you, but it doesn't matter, anyway."

Without hesitation, Ana stepped forward and enveloped Lily in a comforting hug, offering solace and forgiveness.

Lily's trembling shoulders relaxed, the burden of guilt slowly dissipating like dissipating fog.

"You don't hate me?"

"Oh, you are young and you are going to make mistakes. I get it. And besides, I can't hate you. You are the only female friend I have in the training center after being surrounded by rowdy hockey players, and your presence is like a breath of fresh air."

Despite the tear that rolled down Lily's cheek, her lips curved upward in a trembling smile. "Really? Because I wouldn't mind having you as an older sister."

"I won't mind that either. As your older sister, here is an idea. Why don't we get reasonably drunk and dance till our feet hurt?"

Lily nodded. "That sounds like a good idea, but not too much or Caleb would freak out."

Meanwhile, the party continued in the living room and outdoor balcony.

Pavel had challenged Jude to a beer-Pong rematch while Luka watched them alongside the other teammates. Caleb barely paid any attention as his eyes peeled on his phone screen.

Danny had suddenly taken an interest in music as he joined the DJ and they blasted music. Everyone was dancing and having fun.

Ana was pouring herself a glass when she looked up and noticed Jude celebrating his second win, but Pavel didn't seem too bothered about his loss.

He shifted back against the wall, staring across the room. Following his gaze, she saw the familiar blond girl dancing to the music, her ponytail swaying to the beat. Lily's motions were light as she swayed to the music.

Ana looked back at Pavel, who still hadn't taken his eyes off Lily. It was obvious that day. How had she not seen it, the teasing, the silly insults and pranks.

Moving through the crowd, Ana slipped beside him. "Why haven't you asked her out?"

"She would say no," Pavel answered before he realized, "What? Who? Did you say something?"

Ana arched her brow.

"Fine." He shook his cup before taking a sip, "I don't know if there is a worse version of being Friendzone. Maybe brother-zoned? Because that's where I am. I mean, she calls me by my last name like everyone else, so yeah. Not sure she even knows my first name. There is also the little piece of information that she is Caleb, my captain's younger sister. She is kinda off limits."

Ana wasn't familiar with bro code and silent rules between teammates, but she didn't see anything wrong with dating your friend's sister. "Just ask her, what is the worst that could happen?"

"Let me paint you a scenario. She says yes, we date then break up and Caleb hunts me down and breaks my legs. Or this one is my favorite. She says no, and things become weird with us. Then Caleb finds out why things became weird and breaks my leg."

"Why your leg?"

"Oh, I was thinking thing something else but–

"Pavel... stop thinking so much and be serious, tell me. What really is stopping you from asking her out?"

He didn't respond with words, but the look in his eyes told Ana that something significant was holding him back. It was as if a storm raged behind those dark, contemplative eyes, an inner turmoil he hadn't shared with anyone.

"I could talk to Caleb if that's–

He cut her off. "Thanks, but nah. I much rather annoy her till she gives me that adorable frown that definitely *does not* make my heart melt and make my dick hard all at the same time than risk losing her completely," and walked away, joining the party before she even finished her words.

Luka joined Ana, putting an arm around her. He asked if everything was alright.

"It's all good now." She kissed his cheek, smiling broadly and filled with the joy of being surrounded by friends both old and new on this celebration night.

"So I got some news for you. As a way to rekindle our relationship, my brother is offering your job back. Hmm? What do you think?"

Ana paused a minute, then shook her head. Her voice barely audible over the music. "Would it be so bad if I didn't want to work? Maybe I could pick up a hobby or something. I want to take time off and find out what I want to do. I don't know. I just don't want to care about making money as much."

Luka leaned in closer, his warm breath tickling her ear as he whispered, "A stay-at-home girlfriend?"

"Is that what they call it? Then yeah. That. I want to be that."

"No. I won't allow that."

Her face fell, and her shoulders slumped, but before disappointment could fully take hold of her, he continued with a mischievous smile, "Except on three conditions."

She tilted her head slightly, a curious glint in her eyes. "Just Three?"

Luka leaned even closer, their breaths mingling as he spoke in a low, husky tone, "Love me, kiss me, and never leave me."

A radiant smile spread across Ana's face, and her eyes sparkled with delight. She couldn't resist the irresistible charm of Luka. "Is that all?" She teased, her voice soft and sultry. "I bet I can make that work."

Luka cupped Ana's face. His touch was both tender and possessive. His thumb traced the curve of her cheek, sending shivers down her spine.

Their eyes locked, the world around them fading into the background. The music continued to play, and the party carried on around them. Luka and Ana leaned in for a slow soft kiss—a kiss that spoke of promises kept and dreams fulfilled. Even as their lips slowly parted, they remained locked in an embrace, their foreheads resting against each other, their breaths mingling.

Luka's gaze flickered down to Ana's lips one more time before going for another kiss. Deeper this time. Luka's kiss was filled with a hunger that could not be quelled, while Ana followed his lead, which told volumes about her trust in him.

Luka's other hand found its place at the small of Ana's back, gently pulling her closer. He held her as though she were the most precious thing in the world, cherishing every moment, every sensation.

They pulled away, breathless and flushed. Their eyes remained locked, speaking volumes of the connection they had forged. A wave of sheer delight and happiness poured over them as a soft chuckle escaped Ana's lips, followed by a deep, resonant laugh from Luka.

The weight of the world seemed to lighten at that moment, and Luka and Ana realized that their love was a power that could weather any storm, a flame that would burn forever.

THE END

Want more of Luka and Ana... Interested in Knowing how they spend their summer. I have a bonus Novella as well as some deleted scenes with NSFW/SFW arts.

Join me over on REAMSTORIES [1]

1. https://reamstories.com/julesrae

THANK YOU FOR READING. IF YOU LIKED IT, PLEASE DROP A REVIEW AS AN INDIE AUTHOR, EVERY REVIEW COUNTS.

HIS SECRET PUCK BUNNY: A brother bestfriend hockey romance (THE CRESTMONT PLAYERS BOOK2)

Lily Vega yearned to break free from the gilded cage of expectations and obligations that had long trapped her. Her journey of liberation and sexual awakening led her to surrender herself to the whims of a masked stranger. Their encounters ignited a fire within her, propelling her to unimaginable heights of pleasure, far removed from the innocence that had defined her.

Meanwhile, Mason Pavel had been obsessed with Lily for years. Though tempted, he buried his illicit desires out of respect for his friend and to protect Lily's reputation. Loving his best friend's sister might not be forbidden, but acting on his dark twisted desires should be.

Seeking distraction, he found himself entangled with a mysterious vixen at a BDSM club only to discover that she was none other than his best friend's sister.

Mason and Lily are forced to confront the undeniable truth that what they share goes beyond lust.

HIS PUCK PRINCESS: A mafia/ hockey romance (THE CRESTMONT PLAYERS BOOK 3)

Caleb doesn't do violence, but Yuri is violence personified.

Caleb Vega, the captain of the Crestmont Giants hockey team, main focus has always been on training and leading his team to victory. He has never been interested in romance nor had a girlfriend. However, being forced by his friends, he goes on a blind date and unexpectedly meets Yuri

Yurieva Vaenga is a woman with a haunted past and a connection to the city's dark underbelly. Her path crosses with the soft-hearted hockey player after he mistakes her for his blind date. Bored with her life and seeking an escape while hiding her true identity Yuri makes a bold proposition—she wants Caleb for a night, a reason she keeps to herself.

As their relationship develops, Caleb becomes increasingly aware of the risks associated with being involved with a mafia princess, especially as the Crestmont Giants face their toughest challenge on the ice.

Can love survive when one plays by the rules and the other rewrites them in blood?

ACKNOWLEDGMENT

Writing "His GoodPuck Charm" has been a labor of love, and I couldn't have brought this story to life without the support and inspiration of many incredible people, like my alpha reader, Lucia and editors.

I got inspired to write an atlete being superstitious after reading his egotistical puckboy by eden fidley, Iced out by Ricci then soon after I picked up a manhwa with the same premise. I was hooked.

These characters have been swimming in my head and I needed to get them out so I am thankful that I was able to tell their story.

I want to thank my readers most especially my subscribers. You are the best. Thank you, everyone, for being a part of this adventure. This book is as much yours as it is mine.

With love and gratitude, Jules.

ABOUT THE AUTHOR

Jules Rae is a Nigerian author who rarely sees herself in romance novels, so she decided to take it upon herself to write one. When she is not writing possessive fictional men, she is tackling her tedious 9-5 corporate work. She is currently living in Nigeria with her husband.

Don't forget to sign up for her mailing list and be the first to get an update and free preview of her next book.

Find the Author.
Instagram: @jules.rae.author
Email: officialjulesrae@gmail.com

Facebook page: @JulesRaeAuthor

MORE BOOKS BY THE AUTHOR

A GIRL CALLED OMOYE

She carries the Scars....He carries the Guilt.

Let me tell you a story about a girl called Omoye.

We were just kids when I met her for the first time, I was drawn to her like we were meant to be in each other's life somehow.

I believed that was when I fell in love with her.

All we did was play as kids do. I chased her around the street, it's not my fault that we were not alone. It's not my fault that he took her with him. It is not my fault I couldn't stop him. It's not my fault that he stole her innocence, I was only a boy.

Yet, as I look into her eyes right now I can't help but be ridden with guilt. I did this to her. I hurt her. I am determined to protect her, I am no longer a child. I want to make things right. I can't make the same mistake twice. (Check TW)

CALL ME AARINOLA: A multicultural office romance

A taste of her, made him realize he had been starving.

- **Aarinola Kehinde**, a quick-witted and intelligent student from Nigeria, is challenged to maintain her visa status. Fortunately, she lands an internship, and all is well until her boss says, "I want you to quit."

• **Ivan Gates** has one goal, to make sure FutureTech remains number one. The last thing he wishes to think about is his new intern. She is everything he hates but still, he can't stop thinking about her.

After what was supposed to be a one-night stand but Ivan shifts from the calculated grumpy boss to an infatuated teenager, he wants to be with her, but... it may cost him everything, including the secrets he has managed to keep buried.

CALL ME AARINOLA is an office, grumpy x sunshine romance with a hint of drama and lots of spice. It's part of the Skyline Novels and can be read as a standalone.

WARNING: This book contains sensitive topics like physical abuse, and explicit sexual content.

Made in the USA
Middletown, DE
02 January 2025

68629388R00230